To
Bob an Charlotte
Happy Holidays and
best wishes
Jack Summers '98

THE DEADLY PRACTICE

THE DEADLY PRACTICE

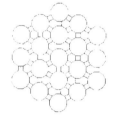

JACK SUMMERS

Pittsburgh, PA

ISBN 1-56315-087-5

Hardcover Fiction
© Copyright 1999 Jack Summers
All rights reserved
First Printing—1999
Library of Congress #98-85363

Request for information should be addressed to:

SterlingHouse Publisher, Inc.
The Sterling Building
440 Friday Road
Department T-101
Pittsburgh, PA 15209

Cover design & typesetting: Drawing Board Studios

Printed in the United States

*Dedicated with love
to Scott and Marcia, two great kids
who make their father proud
and to my beloved editor,
without whom nothing is possible.*

HENRY VI

BY

WILLIAM SHAKESPEARE

PART II, ACT IV SCENE II, LINE 86
DICK TO CADE:

*"THE FIRST THING WE DO,
LET'S KILL ALL THE LAWYERS."*

CHAPTER
1

bolt of lightning that illuminated the room like day and a sharp crack of thunder that shook the wall of the apartment pulled Detective Sergeant Marty Cox from the horrors of the nightmare into a stormy, Monday morning. He was fully awake now, and shaking. The bed was damp with perspiration. It took him nearly a full minute to separate the vivid dream from the reality of his bedroom. How many times had he had that same dream? At least it was becoming less frequent.

Marty listened to the wind drive raindrops against his bedroom window. Had his subconscious mind heard the storm and culled the nightmare from the hidden recesses of his memory? When he was troubled, the dream was more likely to recur.

Glancing at the digital clock's red numbers, he turned off the alarm whose Banshee shriek would have ended his sleep in another ten minutes. Marty pushed back the covers and slowly put his bare feet onto the carpeted floor. Standing, he yawned and slipped into the three-quarter length, silk kimono that was draped across the foot of the bed. Feeling as gloomy as the gray sky outside, he retrieved a can of Pepsi from the edge of the dresser and fought to keep the depressive dream from overwhelming him.

The spring wind whipped the slender saplings across the street and bent them nearly double as it drove the chilling raindrops against the sliding-glass, patio doors. Fishing a package of cigarettes from the pocket of the kimono, Marty struck a farmer's match with his thumb and held it under his first Camel of the day. Inhaling deeply provoked a sonorous cough; smoking was a stupid habit, and, one of these days, he would quit, if he ever had a good reason to do it.

Blowing a cloud of blue smoke toward his reflection in the glass, he took a look at himself. Since his fortieth birthday last month, Marty was convinced that his waistline had perceptibly inched forward. It was certainly bigger today than it was yesterday. At this pace, he would look like Humpty Dumpty by the end of the month. A trip to the gym was definitely in order.

A sustained rumble of thunder caused the pane of glass in the door to vibrate, disturbing the raindrops that trickled down the door. Scratching himself, he took a large pull from the can of Pepsi. Marty liked the feeling of the warm, flat liquid stinging his throat.

"Shit," he muttered out loud. "Why in hell did I ever come back to Akron? All the while I was growing up here, he thought, "I was either shoveling snow, raking leaves, or dodging rain drops." That was the charm of the northeast corner of Ohio. Something was always falling from the sky. The thought did nothing to improve his mood.

Chicago hadn't been much better. The winters were more harsh; the summers as muggy, but, at least, he didn't have to tend the concrete parking space that comprised his front yard. Draining the Pepsi, he finished the Camel and made his way to the shower.

Lathering his hair, he tried to shake off the blue funk that the gloomy morning had wrapped around him like a shroud. Most of all, Marty tried to push the real reason for his somber mood back into the closeted reaches, of his mind. Janet had died twelve years ago, on a rainy spring Monday, like this one, and it still hurt.

Sticking his head under the shower, he rinsed his hair. They had showered together almost every morning. It was a sensual, loving way to start their day. Tears stung his eyes as he remembered.

Janet, five-feet-three inches of nervous energy, had been an Akron University cheerleader. The star quarterback, he had literally fallen over her one August afternoon when the cheerleaders were drilling too close to the practice field.

Theirs was the all-American love story. Since he was a foot taller than she was, their classmates called them Mutt and Jeff. She stood on the couch in the dorm to kiss him goodnight. From their first date, there had never been room for anyone else in either of their lives. They were married the summer after their junior year.

As he toweled himself off, Marty looked into the reflection of his pale green eyes in the mirror. The pain there was visible as the hurt flooded out again.

There were no pro contract offers, and he never expected any. The scholarship had been a means to an end, and he obtained a degree in criminal justice. He left the university with an arthritic knee, a varsity jacket, and the most wonderful woman on the planet.

The job with the Chicago police department had been both exciting and exhilarating. After a minimal stint in uniform, he quickly made detective and was assigned to the homicide squad. Maybe if he hadn't been so ambitious, if he hadn't taken the job, Janet would still be alive. Despite the irrationality of it, he could never rid himself of that stubborn remnant of guilt.

For five deliriously happy years, Chicago had been a daily adventure. Near thirty, with their biological clocks ticking, they had decided it was time to start a family. He remembered the look on her face when she told him the rabbit had died. They'd danced around the kitchen like a pair of excited teenagers. Janet had been on her way to the obstetrician when it happened.

Selecting his clothes from the walk-in closet in the bedroom, Marty tried to break the rehash of those troubled weeks, but he couldn't. Each time the nightmare came, he punished himself with this litany of self-incrimination. It seemed as if he went over them like a mantra. If he could chant it often enough, then he might somehow change the way it ended.

Providence? Divine intervention? Divine punishment? Why did God do this to me? Hell, why would God do it to *her?* She had never harmed anyone. Janet was a kind, loving, considerate human being. When he had run out of cliches, got tired of condemning God, and spent his anger at the innocent salesman who had been driving the gray Buick that started the chain reaction, he came to the inescapable conclusion that there would be no answers to his *why.*

Her loss hadn't stopped his life that June morning, but its crushing weight kept him from living to the fullest. At first, grief and pain were his only companions. Withdrawing into a shell, he pushed the shell into a well of self-pity, and turned to the bottle for the solace he couldn't find anywhere else.

Marty and Janet had spent most of their time with each other, and the few real friends they had he'd pushed away. He still carried remnants of the bitterness and heartache.

In the months after the accident, he drank constantly, and his performance on the job had deteriorated accordingly. That last day, he had come to work directly from the bar. Counseling had been repeatedly offered, and he had repeatedly refused it. When his best friend on the force came to talk to him, he had driven him away in a drunken rage. He should have apologized to his friend, and he made a mental note to do it, but knew he never would.

His boss, Captain Marquardt, had realized what he was going through. There had been pity and compassion on Marquardt's heavily lined face as he allowed Marty to resign, rather than firing him. Now, Marty was grateful for that, but, the day it happened, he hadn't been grateful.

A flash of lightning accompanied by a nearly instantaneous rumble of thunder shook the entire house. His father always said that thunder was the sound of God bowling. Was it God who came to him that day in Chicago, or was it really Janet?

Exactly two months after Janet had died, he had awakened in his apartment covered with dried vomit and with no recollection of where he had been the night before. After a fruitless search for a clean shirt, Marty had sat down on the floor and cried. For the first time in his life, he couldn't think of a single reason to go on living. He still had his back-up service revolver, and all he needed to do was suck on the barrel and pull the trigger.

He remembered the acrid taste of the oiled metal when he had placed the barrel of the revolver in his mouth. Ludicrously, he had been worried about chipping his teeth. Slipping his finger onto the trigger, Marty was mustering courage to pull it when an inner voice told him to stop and call his father.

Karl Martin Cox had no place in his life for the supernatural. Although he had been raised as a Methodist, Janet's death had caused him to doubt the existence of God. The experience that morning hadn't resolved his quandary. Did the voice belong to Janet, God or something supernatural? In the end, he determined that it had come from his own inner strength that he had been unable to tap until he bottomed out.

Twenty-four hours later, he had arrived at his boyhood home in a rural suburb of Akron. His father, Martin Senior, was a second-generation, German farmer with little formal education and more common sense than a room full of professors. An only child, Marty had been the sole beneficiary of that wisdom as long as he could remember.

The elder Cox's one passion was nickel and dime poker that he played once a month with five of his cronies. He had used that analogy as he talked to Marty. "Son, you've been dealt a bad hand. You can keep on playin' it and end up busted, or you can fold, reshuffle, and play a better one. Nobody else can make that decision for you. It's yours to make. Did you love, Janet? Were you happy?"

Stung by the question, Marty had replied, "Of course I did. Two people couldn't have been any happier than we were."

"Would Janet be proud of the way you're acting?" Marty had hung his head. "Janet would have wanted you to be happy. She wouldn't want you to spend the rest of your life stuck in a bottle and mopin' around like some monk in a monastery. She would have kicked your butt and said get on with your life. Don't spoil the memory of what you had. That's what she'd say if she were here."

Then, his father had made a simple statement that had become Marty's salvation. "Remember, as long as someone lives who loves you, then you can never die. That's immortality son . . . love."

It was hard, but with his father's help, he'd managed to straighten out his life. A year later he was whole again.

When Captain Marquardt, had found out that Marty had things back together, he had written him a letter of reference. That, and Marty's experience, helped him land a job with the Akron police department, and after two years in a patrol car, he was now back on the familiar turf of homicide. It wasn't Chicago, but he liked his work. More importantly, he liked himself, and he could smile again.

As he knotted his tie, his father's face blinked across his consciousness like a flickering image on a television screen. A warm glow permeated him, as it often did when he thought about his dad. It was as if his dad were there, looking over his shoulder. He wished he could talk to him again. But wishing would never make it so.

Two years ago his father had died, but he had found it easier to accept that providence. The sudden heart attack was not totally unexpected, since the elder Cox had survived two others. It was quick, and he hadn't suffered. And, as long as Marty lived, his father would never die.

Surveying his appearance in the mirror, Marty inspected his sideburns for strands of gray. They were nearly invisible among the sandy, healthy strands, but he had found one or two. Finding no new ones, Marty went to the door and retrieved the *Beacon Journal.*

He carried the paper into his spartan kitchen that sported a single luxury, an automatic coffee maker. It ground fresh coffee beans and then brewed the coffee at a specified preset time, so that every morning when he finished his shower, he was greeted with the delightful aroma of freshly brewed coffee. Pouring a mug of his favorite French roast, he wished he were back at the cabin.

The past weekend had been a rare weekend off, and he had spent it on his own fifty acres of wilderness. He had built the primitive cabin himself, and it had no TV, telephone, or radio. There was no contact with civilization. When things weighed him down, he could go there and sort them out. It had been a delightful weekend, and he was recharged.

Marty finished buttering his toast and poured his second cup of coffee. Sitting down he turned his attention to the front page of the paper. The glaring headline of the *Beacon* caused him to freeze with the coffee cup inches from his lip.

Third Murder Victim Found

He cursed himself for not owning an answering machine. Making a mental note to get one when he had time, he rapidly read the article as he finished the coffee. Turning off the coffee maker, he slipped his arms through the straps of his shoulder holster and adjusted it under his arm. Removing the pistol, he flipped out the cylinder and confirmed that it was loaded. Replacing the weapon, he donned his jacket, and adjusted it until the weapon was less obvious.

Marty pulled the two-year-old Chevy Lumina onto the wet streets. The rain had abated for the moment, but the sky looked like a sponge that was waiting for the perfect time to wring out. Reaching for the car phone, he punched in the office number.

"Homicide, Sergeant King," said the gravelly voice of the day shift desk sergeant. Andrew King was a sixty-year-old veteran of the force with thirty-five years of experience on the street. His grandfatherly appearance belied the sandpaper personality beneath it.

"Andy, Marty. Just read the paper. Is it the same M.O.?"

"Seems to be. We tried to get you yesterday."

"Sorry. I was at the cabin. Autopsy done yet?"

"Are you ever going to get a phone in that damned place? If Ma Bell won't cooperate, you should at least take a cell phone with you. Take the one out of the car for Christ's sake. Coroner has the body. Hot-foot it over there, and you might catch the autopsy.

"Is his majesty in town?"

"If you mean our esteemed coroner, Doctor Peters, no. He's off traipsing around Africa or someplace. Doctor Daniels has the con," King said, using the naval term for the duty officer on a ship.

Marty felt a pleasant tingle as Dr. Daniels' name was mentioned. "Cellular phones don't work at the cabin. Transmission towers aren't close enough. I'll talk to the folks at the telephone company again, I promise."

"How about a C.B. radio?" King persisted. "Then we could do that breaker one-nine crap."

Marty chuckled. "That's a ten-four good buddy. Over and out." Hanging up the phone in time to miss King's caustic sign off, he worked on lighting another Camel. Punching a button, Marty activated the tape player, and Buddy Holly and the Crickets filled the cab with strains of "Peggy Sue." Marty loved music, but couldn't stand anything written after 1980.

They had found three derelicts in the past six months. The first two had been shot in the back of the head at close range with a forty- four magnum, making them difficult to identify, but, with a little luck, he had succeeded. Both were out of state drifters with no one who cared, and he had been unable to come up with anything connecting them to each other.

The murders appeared to be the random acts of a serial killer, but something about that bothered him. In Chicago, one of his best tools had been his gut instinct . . . that disquieting hunch that said something didn't fit. It would come. He wanted this bastard! They were derelicts, but they were still human beings, and nobody had the right to slaughter them.

With that rationalization firmly in mind, Marty turned onto the crosstown Martin Luther King Jr. Freeway. Exiting the freeway as it ended on Perkins Street, he drove the short distance up the hill to the new coroner's office. It was an improvement over the out-of-date, Gothic monstrosity that had served as the coroner's office and morgue when he first joined the force. Pulling into the parking lot, and turning off the engine, Marty sat for a moment in front of the glass and sandstone building drumming his fingers on the dashboard. He finished the Camel and ground the butt into the overflowing ashtray.

Maybe there would be something new this time. There was a lunatic out there that he had to stop. As he opened the door, he admitted to himself that he had another reason for wanting to attend this autopsy.

After Janet died, Marty had lots of offers to help him through his emotional trauma. Some were legitimate sentiments backed by offers to help with the cooking or to do his laundry. Others were thinly veiled offers for gratuitous sex. He turned them all down. In the past twelve years, he had dated just two women . . . with disastrous results, and he had decided it was his fate to live alone. Then, he met Doctor Nora Daniels.

Doctor Daniels was a pathologist at Summa Health Systems City Campus and an assistant coroner. Wilfred Peters, the elected coroner, was usually too busy to do his own autopsies, since he was running around the country testifying as an expert witness in other jurisdictions. So, he recruited help from the local pathology departments at Summa and Akron General Medical Center. Peters had the autopsies on the first two victims, but Nora had come in to ask a question and Peters had introduced them.

Daniels was bright, personable, seemed to have a good sense of humor and was the consummate professional. As if that wasn't enough, you could consider her cover-girl, good looks and figure. She was drop-dead-beautiful. Marty doubted she would ever find anything about him remotely appealing, but he had allowed himself to dream.

Maybe today he would muster up enough courage to ask her to meet him for a drink. Unlike most reformed alcoholics, if indeed he ever was one, once his emotional life was under control, he had had no problems with a glass of wine or a drink or two. The problem hadn't been the alcohol, it had been him. He always faced his demons, and most of the time, he won. Doctor Nora was certainly not a demon, but the thought of asking her out made him more than a little anxious.

Whistling an off-key melody, he locked the car and dashed across the parking lot as God found him a suitable target and wrung out the sponge, drenching the already soaked parking lot with torrents of stinging raindrops.

CHAPTER
2

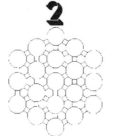

topping in the scrub area, Marty exchanged his sport coat for a surgical cap, gown and mask. Despite the mask, he could still smell the pungent odor of formaldehyde in the autopsy room. Combined with the sweet smell that emanated from the corpse on the table, the mixture made his stomach churn. This was his fifth autopsy, and he decided he would never get used to it.

Nora Sue Daniels, M.D., adjusted the surgical mask beneath her half-glasses and was looking up at the ceiling-mounted microphone that hung a foot above her head. Glancing at him, she reached up and pulled the microphone toward her.

"Jon Silver used this last night. He's six-feet-five," she said, pulling it down in front of her with a rubber-gloved hand. "Are you sure you're ready for this, Detective?" Was she smiling behind the blue mask?

"I'm as ready as I'll ever be," Marty said with a nervous chuckle.

Turning her attention to the prone figure on the stainless steel table, she said, "This is number three. How many do we need before we start calling them serial killings?"

"Two we call copy-cat, but three makes it serial."

"I might be more help if I had done the autopsies on the first two. Dr. Peters did those himself, just before he left for somewhere or other . . . England I think. It's Africa this time."

"I was there for the first two. That's the first time we met." Blushing, he hurried on in an attempt not to compound his embarrassment. "I heard that Doctor Peters . . . travels a lot," Marty said, his tone playful.

"When there's a chance for publicity, Peters makes certain that he gets his share. Then it's off to somewhere else," Nora replied. "I've known Pete a long time, so I'm not talking behind his back. I tell him to his face, too. Some people say I'm blunt. I prefer to think I'm honest."

"That's good," Marty said, feeling more courageous. He hadn't flirted in a long time, and he hoped he wouldn't be to rusty. "I like honest women."

The wheels turned behind her eyes, but she didn't say anything. His little burst of courage wilted.

"This guy's face must be a real mess," she said, surveying the carnage made by the bullet as it entered the back of the man's skull.

Marty looked at the naked body on the stainless steel table for the first time. Unlike the other autopsies he had seen, where the corpse was on its back, this one was face down.

"Uh . . . I haven't seen many autopsies, but the others all started with the body face up," he began, wrinkling his forehead as he attempted to think of a tactful way to continue. That was one of his bad habits, and he knew it. Sometime, he opened his mouth before he put his brain in gear and ended up seeming heavy-handed or confused.

She saved him with a laugh and an explanation. "Sometimes it's easy to get hung up on the obvious things and you miss something really important. That's why I start my posts with the patient face down. I call it orderly. My friends call it anal." She laughed again.

"The subject is a middle-aged, white male," Nora began, stepping on a foot pedal that activated the microphone in front of her.

"Subject has a large caliber entrance wound in the right occipital area." Picking a flexible steel tape from the array of instruments on a metal table at her elbow, she measured the hole. "The wound is seven centimeters from the midline and four from the mid-point of the right ear. There is charring and deep powder burns around the wound suggesting close range discharge."

Placing a latex-gloved finger into the hole in the skull, she probed with her finger. Fixing his attention on a cracked tile on the wall on the opposite side of the room, Marty looked away until he was sure his breakfast was going to stay down.

"The wound is smooth and clean with minimal metallic debris. The missile penetrates all layers of the cranial cavity. There are no other visible wounds. I like to be certain I don't miss anything hidden among the hair strands. In one case that he'd like to forget, Doctor Peters ruled death from natural causes. Couple of years later, the guy's brother gives a death-bed confession to murder. They exhumed the body, and it had two bullet wounds in the hairline."

"Whoops," Marty said. "How did he explain that one?"

"It was a small caliber pistol," Nora replied as she continued her meticulous survey of the naked form. Marty added her sense of humor to the plus column in his evaluation of her.

"There is considerable ecchymosis at the base of the neck, and a pettichial rash over the back. What's this?" Attracted to bruises on the backs of the elbows and knees, she carefully probed them with her fingers. "No masses beneath the skin surface. The skin is just discolored. Must be capillary level hemorrhage," she said.

The significance of the findings escaped him, but he liked the way she looked at him. And she talked to him, not at him. She looked toward the door.

As if on cue, a huge man in surgical greens, gowned, gloved and wearing a plastic bib-apron matching Nora's, lumbered through the door. "Clarence, this is Detective Martin Cox. Detective, my prosection assistant, Clarence Mackey."

"I'm pleased to meet ya, sir," the giant said in a voice that was childish in its meter, but formidable in its timber.

"I'm happy to meet you too, Mr. Mackey."

He looked quizzically at Marty. "I ain't no mister. I'm just Clarence," he said, his tone more serious than the situation required. Clarence was evidently slightly retarded.

"My name is Marty, Clarence." Marty smiled at him, and the man returned a lopsided grin.

"Help me turn him, Clarence," Nora said.

They rolled the body over. Marty had been unfortunate enough to witness some sickening sights, but this one was gruesome. The entire right lower jaw, mouth and part of the nose had been blown away. It looked as if the face had been bi-valved by an ax, and the right half ripped apart by a giant hand. The left eye hung grotesquely from its socket, and what was left of the mouth twisted into a macabre grin. Gritting his teeth, Marty searched for the cracked tile.

"Really a mess," Nora said, suggesting it repulsed her as well. Returning to her professional tone, she described the carnage.

"My pathology professor always reminded me to see what I look at. 'Students look right at a lesion and never see it. They look but they don't see,' he'd say repeatedly." She deepened her voice accordingly.

"See this fine rash over the anterior chest wall and the subtle bruises at the elbows, fingers and knees?" She pointed to minute red dots that Marty hadn't noticed before. "Pettichial hemorrhage. It would have been easy to miss."

"Okay, Clarence, let's go in."

Clarence handed her a surgical scalpel, and Marty returned to the cracked tile. When he looked back, she had finished the Y-shaped incision that Marty had seen on other postmortem examinations. Each limb of the upper portion of the Y started just below the point of the shoulder and joined in the region of the upper abdomen. The tail of the Y continued down across the abdomen to the base of the penis.

"The incision gives great exposure, but we can't use it on live patients," Nora commented.

Skillfully mobilizing the upper triangular flap she finished the entry incision. Nora was right about the incision. In a matter of minutes, the entire internal contents of both the chest and the abdomen were visible, much to Marty's consternation. If he saw a thousand autopsies, he'd still need cracked tiles.

Nora continued to describe the general appearance of the cavity noting the tiny punctate hemorrhages that peppered the root of the intestines. "These could be agonal," she said, "but it's strange for a gunshot wound."

"What's strange about it?" Since he was here, he might as well learn as much about forensic pathology as he could.

"The bowels are mushy and filled with liquid. This lacy stuff is mesentary," she said running the length of both the large and small bowel between her fingers. "It's the framework that carries nutrient blood vessels to the bowel. See, it's studded with tiny hemorrhages, too," she added, pointing to the tiny blotches.

"Strange," she muttered, as much to herself as to him. "These are chronic changes, and we shouldn't see them in acute injuries." Cutting the attachments that held them in place, Nora removed the intestines.

Clarence scooped out the abdominal contents and transferred the dripping mass to a hanging metal scale, recorded the weight, then lay the bowels in the sink. Opening the large bowel along its length with a pair of scissors, Nora unleashed a smell that made Marty gag and nearly throw up.

"Look at this," Nora said. He complied with difficulty. "The entire large intestine has sloughed its lining. The mucosa, that covers the inner muscular layer of the bowel, has detached secondary to large amounts of underlying hemorrhage. The bowel was trying to turn itself inside-out."

Forcing back the nausea he asked, "Is that unusual?"

"We sometimes find this in bodies that are several days old, but it doesn't fit with this one, especially when the small bowel and stomach look the same," she said, pointing to the angry bleeding ulcers that lined the stomach.

Removing the heart and lungs as a unit, she skillfully severed the vascular attachments, pulled the organs from the chest cavity, and transferred them to the scales. The chest cavity contained a pint of soupy fluid that she cultured while doing a running commentary into the microphone.

Weighing the internal organs, she continued, "The kidneys and spleen are similarly congested. The spleen is unusually swollen and leathery. The surface sheen has been replaced by a grayish exterior, giving the organ the appearance of a salami."

Clarence gave her a bewildered look. When he realized she was joking, an uneasy smile glinted in his eyes. "That's good, Doctor Nora," he said nervously.

"The liver is mottled and hemorrhagic," Nora continued, selecting a knife from the tray and cutting the liver in half.

"This doesn't fit either," she said, her voice tipped with a hint of anxiety. "The entire center of this liver is liquid. The tissue is usually pretty pulpy, but this looks like Jello."

"I wonder if there's fluid here?" she asked, making an incision into the knee joint. "Culture," she said to Clarence as dark brown fluid oozed out.

"The goo in the bottom of the culture tube is nutrient broth," Nora amplified, pointing to a substance in the bottom of the tube that reminded Marty of Vaseline. "Each tube contains a different kind of nutrient. This one, for example will only support the growth of tuberculine strains."

"I see," Marty replied pinching his upper lip between his thumb and the side of his index finger. "Do you think this is an infection?"

Nora shrugged her shoulders, and for a moment Marty was sure she was going to wipe her forehead with her bloody glove, but she didn't. "Could be. The generalized inflammation is extensive."

"I'm going to take some extra tissue from the suspect areas and imbed them in resin. I may want to do electron microscopy on them later. If this is an infection, it will be important to look at the cells under the electron scope's magnification"

Nora frowned. "This is the part of the post I like least—the brain. In this case, it's worse, due to the extent of the injury."

Beginning over the right ear, and staying just inside the hair-line, she made an incision down the hairline, across the back of the neck from side burn to sideburn to the mid portion of the left ear. Developing the flap of tissue under the incision down to the bone, she scalped the corpse. Marty closed his eyes as his head started to swim. The procedure reminded him of a scene from a grade-B Western.

By the time he opened his eyes again, she had pushed the scalped tissue forward over the brow like a bizarre wig. When she picked up a reciprocal, electric saw to remove the top of the skull and expose the brain, Marty resumed his examination of the wall tile. As the whirling blade bit into the skull, the air was filled with the smell of hot bone-another smell Marty didn't like.

The contents of the cranial cavity had been devastated by the blast turning the entire right frontal region of the brain into a gelatinous mass of ruined tissue. The path of the bullet seared across the brain like a comet, plowing from entry site to exit wound in an expanding cone of destruction.

"Brains have to be cured before they can be examined. It's too soupy to work on now," she said, placing the brain into a plastic bucket. Soup wasn't something he ate much of, but Marty felt certain he would never order soup again.

Pouring a diluted formaldehyde solution into the bucket, Clarence covered the brain with the pungent liquid and snapped on a plastic cover. Nora poked long, cue-tips into the fluid inside the cranial cavity and then into fresh culture tubes. After replacing the bone, she pulled the scalp back into position and stitched it down with transparent sutures. "Close him up, Clarence."

Laboriously, Clarence closed the wound in a single layer with heavy embalming suture and a large, straight needle. It was a crude but effective closure, and Clarence did it reverently. The job required all his concentration, and Clarence was proud of the way he closed.

When Clarence was finished, he transferred the body to the cold storage drawer and took the soiled instruments to the sink to clean them.

Pulling off her stained gloves, Nora loosened her surgical mask, pulled the cap from her head, and shook her short brown hair into place. "We can go upstairs if you have time for a cup of coffee." she said. "They keep a pot for the duty crew. It's not bad if you're into motor oil."

"Ow! Ow! Ow!"

Turning toward the sound of the cries, they saw Clarence standing by the sink holding his bleeding index finger as tears filled his child-like eyes. The cut was a small slice from the scalpel blade.

"Nothing serious, Clarence. How many times must I tell you to use a hemostate to remove the blade from the end of the knife handle? You know that little catch sticks sometime. If you use your fingers you can cut yourself. That's what happened, isn't it, Clarence?"

"I'm sorry, Doctor Nora," the man-child sniffled. "I won't do it no more."

"That's what you told me the last time." Drying his finger, Nora taped a band-aid over the wound. "You have to be very careful, Clarence. There are a lot of germs in here. You could get a bad infection and get real sick." Clarence's expression suggested that her scolding was worse than any lethal infection might be.

"Then who would I get to help me? You know how much I depend on you," she said with a reassuring smile.

Clarence grinned sheepishly. "Thank you, Doctor Nora. I'll try real hard to remember. I just don't remember too good sometimes."

"I'll need to fingerprint the body when it's okay with you. Maybe it will help us get a line on who he is," Marty said.

"You can do it now. I'm going to the office. When your finished come on up. I'm buying."

"Thanks," he said. He always made eye contact when he talked. So did she. Her brown eyes were expressive and danced as she talked.

When he came upstairs, she handed him a chipped, china mug filled with black coffee, and Marty blew across the rim before tentatively taking a sip.

"Thank you, Doctor. Is this as hot as McDonald's? Maybe if I spill some in my lap we could sue the county and both retire," Marty joked.

"That's the trouble with this world, too many attorneys. Besides, we don't have enough money for pencils, so go ahead, sue, Detective."

"Please call me, Marty."

She nodded. "Did you see the other two victims, Marty?"

"Actually," he looked embarrassedly down at his well-shined loafers, "I was there, but I didn't do as well as I did today. I'm afraid I can't be much help."

"I thought you did great. If autopsies cause you so much grief, why do you go?"

"I have to. You know, duty, stuff like that." He flashed her a quick smile to mask his embarrassment at being caught caring too much. "I've gone to a couple more since then, to toughen myself up. I did do pretty good today, didn't I?"

"Yes, you did." The smile brightened her radiant face even more.

"What can cause the kind of inflammation we saw in the body?" Fishing inside his jacket, he produced a spiral note pad with a pen.

"Any number of things. Allergies, bacteria, viruses, industrial toxins. We may never find the cause. In this case, I have to believe it was a systemic problem. Your boy had to be a sick cookie when he died. The killer may have done him a favor."

"Was he sick enough to go to the free clinic or to an emergency room somewhere?" Marty asked. "If he did, there would be records, and we might find out who he was. His family, if there is any, has a right to know what's happened to him"

"If I were as sick as the findings say he should have been, I'd see someone."

"Do you think what he had might be contagious?" he asked.

"If it is, we'll know in forty-eight hours when the cultures finish cooking. We culture the crap out of every body we post. Contagion is always possible. Most infections show up in two days, except the slow growers like tuberculosis. Some of them could take up to two weeks."

Marty thought about Clarence and prayed that it wasn't contagious. "Is crap a medical term, Doctor, like goo?" he asked.

"You bet," she chuckled. "And I'm an expert on the subject. In this job, I spend at least half my time up to the knees in it."

"At the station house it gets deeper than that," Marty shot back and they laughed again. Marty hadn't felt much like laughing in the past few years, and he liked the way they sounded when they laughed together. Doctor Daniels made him think about a normal life again.

"My name is, Nora. Doctor sounds awfully stuffy when you say it. I'd vote for a virus. It might even be something like Legionnaire's."

"Most bacterial infections are sensitive to antibiotics, but lately we're getting some super bugs that nothing will touch. Then, there's the new monsters that are resistant to everything to start with. Do you remember if there were any similar findings on the other victims?"

"As I said, I don't remember." He rubbed his upper lip pensively between his thumb and index finger. "I think Doctor Peters said something about the internal organs being swollen on the first case. I don't remember any rashes."

"The internal organs were swollen here, too. They might be connected. I'll check the other reports later today," Nora said, glancing at her watch and frowning at the time.

Taking the cue, Marty stood to leave. "Thanks for the coffee and the help. Anything will be appreciated. We don't have a thing. We don't have a time cycle. We don't know how he chooses his victims. There isn't a hint of a physical description. He has to be looney, and I want him off the streets."

"I'll do my best." She extended her hand. "You don't strike me as the sexist type, Marty. How can you be so sure it's a he?"

"Statistics. In the years they've tracked serial killers, there has only been one female."

He had lingered on the handshake as he answered her question. It was a pleasant feeling. Her grip was gentle but strong. At the door he turned back.

"I don't suppose you'd consider joining me at Georgie's later for a drink? Just to discuss autopsy reports." He felt like a condemned man who was waiting to find out if his sentence had been commuted.

"Sure. Why not? Seven be okay?" she answered.

"Yeah...I mean, yes. Great. Great. See you there." He escaped the office before she could change her mind.

CHAPTER 3

y the time Marty checked in at the station it was nearly noon. The department kept a membership at the Downtown Athletic Club to encourage fitness. A few die-hards used it regularly, while many officers considered the one-handed doughnut dunk a better form of exercise. Since Marty was scheduled to testify in court later in the afternoon, he decided to start his new exercise routine today.

It was still pouring, so Marty drove the four blocks to the club in the renovated Y.M.C.A. building and parked across the street. As he got out of the car, Marty nodded to a man sitting in the nondescript pickup parked next to him. The man looked edgy and avoided eye contact so Marty made a mental note of the license number.

Rain hammered the roof of the car as Marty searched the back seat for his umbrella.

A patrol car rolled by, and Marty waved to the two uniformed officers. The man in the pickup was looking away from the street and frowning. Raising his umbrella, Marty dashed for the front door of the building.

Spending the better part of an hour working out on various strength machines he took his second shower of the day. In the lobby, a tall man, who Marty recognized as Judge Aaron Spellman, was standing in front of the mirror between two elevators adjusting the knot in his regimental, striped, silk tie. The judge smoothed the collar on his custom-made shirt and picked a piece of lint from the sleeve of his Brooks Brothers blazer. Impatiently, the Judge looked at his watch.

Doctor Roy Stark came out of the elevator. Marty had seen Stark a couple of times for routine eye care. The doctor was also quite a squash player. Stark nodded to Marty, who said, "Good morning."

Reaching into his pocket Stark withdrew his wallet. "Here's your twenty, judge. Did you have a bad weekend? You haven't been that aggressive in weeks."

The expression on Spellman's face was smug satisfaction. "Since I'm a judge, I can't sue you. I've got to get into your pocket somehow."

He laughed. Stark didn't. As they walked out, Spellman handed the twenty to an ancient black man at the registration desk.

"How old do you think Junias is?" Spellman casually asked Marty as they walked toward the front door.

"No one has any idea. He's been around as long as the club. When Junias dies, the club will too. The members believe that, and Junias does all he can to perpetuate the myth," Marty said with a smile. It was the first time the judge had ever condescended to speak to him.

"Damn, I just had the Mercedes washed," Spellman grumbled. "Every time I get that stupid pile of junk washed it rains. I could open a side business as a rainmaker. Just drive into the middle of the blighted area, turn on the c.d. player, pop in some native-American chants, and wash the son-of-a-bitch. I know it would rain."

"Bad idea, Judge."

"Why?" Spellman asked, a tinge of irritation in his voice.

"Who's going to hire a rainmaker named Spellman?" Stark chided. "See you Aaron, I'm going to make a dash for it."

"I left a perfectly good umbrella on the front seat of the car. Why the hell didn't I bring it with me?" Spellman said, and the two men dashed down the steps into the downpour. Neither noticed Marty's umbrella.

"Some things have to go wrong in that perfect little world of yours or you'd get more insufferable than you already are," Stark said sarcastically.

Dashing across the parking lot, Spellman punched the key-less entry, opened the door and leaped in, dragging a sheet of rain across the front seat with him. Marty could see Spellman's lips moving, and he knew what the judge was saying.

Walking to his car, Marty saw Spellman wiping rain from his sun-tanned face with a silk, pocket handkerchief. The Mercedes diesel rattled to life, and Spellman whipped out of the parking lot in a rooster-tail of spray.

Marty sat in his car thinking about Spellman. Before his elevation to the bench last year, Spellman had been a highly successful plaintiff's attorney and president-elect of their association when he was appointed to the bench. Spellman had tendered his resignation as president, but his fellow trial lawyers refused to accept it. He would preside over their annual meeting in Akron this year. The judge would have been furious if his cronies had accepted the resignation. Spellman's reputation as ruthless and vindictive was widespread.

A joke they told about judges fit Spellman. Question: Define a federal judge. Answer: A dumb lawyer who knows the governor. Although he wasn't a federal judge, Spellman was indebted to Governor George Canopolis, now Senator Canopolis, for nominating him to fill the unexpired term of Judge Arnie Azure, whose heart vapor locked in the middle of a murder trial.

Pulling into traffic, Marty glanced at his watch. He still had time before he was due in court. As he turned down High Street, the Knight Center loomed in front of him. The modernistic, brick and glass structure was the perfect size for the Trial Lawyer's Association convention, the first major convention to be held in the center. The administration was bending over backwards to make things fly.

A sign out front caught his eye. The National Rifle Association was hosting an antique weapons show. Marty had never been a fan of the N.R.A., but the show sounded interesting. In the parking lot at the side of the building, he noticed Spellman getting out of the Mercedes.

Spellman had the umbrella this time and tilted it against a whipping wind that threatened to turn the struts inside out as he hurried toward the side entrance. In his haste, Spellman misjudged the size of a large puddle and soaked his shoes and the legs of his pants in a spray of water that reminded Marty of a first grader leaping into a spring puddle. The judge's mouth moved furiously.

The pickup Marty had seen earlier was parked across the lot. The driver was sitting inside, looking toward the Mercedes. When he noticed that Marty was observing him, the man in the truck bent to fiddle with something in the glove compartment.

The Cox gut got one of those feelings, and Marty turned on the police radio between the front seats of his car. A computer screen winked green, and he tapped in the access code connecting him with the Department of Motor Vehicles central computer. Entering the pickup's license number Marty drummed his fingers on the steering wheel as he waited impatiently for a reply. Ordinarily patient, Marty drew the line at waiting for mindless machines to chatter back.

The screen filled with information. The 1985 G.M.C. was registered to Ezra Troyer, Post Office Box 12, Sugar Creek, Ohio. He was fifty years old, and he was listed as a farmer. Troyer had never had a ticket of any kind dating back to the original registry of the truck and the issue of his driver's license which carried the same date. The photo showed an unremarkable man with long hair and unkempt beard typical of the Mennonites who lived in the Sugar Creek area.

Switching off the radio, Marty decided to go inside. Troyer got out of his truck, too. He was five-feet-ten with a stocky build and wore dark blue trousers with suspenders, a blue, cotton shirt with no collar and the broad brimmed hat favored by the Mennonite farmers. Marty scratched his chin pensively. Why would a Mennonite farmer be interested in an antique weapons show?

Paying his admission, Marty entered the exhibit hall. Keith Darlington, the pudgy executive director of the Knight Center was fussing along side Spellman like a greasy version of the Pillsbury dough boy. Darlington waddled rather than walked, and swung his arms in an effeminate way. At the grand opening of the center, Marty had volunteered for the security force and had met Darlington.

Spellman was a reputed homophobe, and according to one of Marty's fellow officers who was going to Akron University's law school at night, the judge had written a prejudicial article in a legal journal concerning a malpractice suit against a gay physician.

Marty had met Darlington's wife at the opening and realized that the man was effeminate, not gay. Regardless, Darlington's swishy behavior had to unnerve Spellman.

"Frightful weather, isn't it, Judge?" Marty heard Darlington ask in a girlish voice as Marty walked toward a display of Civil War cap and ball pistols.

If you took away the weather as a topic of conversation, Marty thought, half the city would be speechless. Standing a discreet distance away, looking absently at a crossbow display, was the Mennonite farmer. What was there about him that wasn't right?

"Let's get on with this, shall we? I have to be in court in an hour," he heard Spellman say as he frowned and looked at his watch for emphasis. The two men walked down the hall and up a staircase to the second level.

Although he didn't follow them, Marty could hear their conversation easily. There was little ambient noise and the second level was open.

"Medical malpractice is always a hot topic, and Everett Goldman, my partner from San Francisco, is giving that session as the keynote address."

"Is that the same Goldman I saw on television last summer when that movie star's wife died after surgery?"

"The same. Lady went in for a routine laproscopic gallbladder. The surgeon poked a hole in the woman's bowel and didn't recognize it. She developed an overwhelming infection and died in a couple of days."

"He got a lot of money for the husband, didn't he?" asked Darlington.

Marty couldn't hear the answer as the duo disappeared into the conference room, but he didn't have too. Yes, Goldman got a lot of money for the actor who was so grief stricken that he married a young chippy with big tits two weeks after the settlement. And, Goldman got a lot of money for himself, too.

Goldman's association with Spellman had been part of a lengthy article when Spellman was appointed to the bench. Spellman had joined Goldman's firm fresh from Harvard Law School and practiced with him for eight years. Despite a national reputation, and a plethora of business, Goldman chose his partners with care. They had to be cold, ruthless and as unscrupulous as he was. The two were a perfect match.

Why had he abandoned such a lucrative business and come to Akron,

Ohio? The reason was Shelia Kauffman, heiress to one of the larger fortunes in the Midwest. After a whirlwind courtship, they were married and moved to Akron. Spellman handled the family's legal affairs, managed Kauffman Enterprises, and still found time to accept selected malpractice suits if the paycheck was big enough. Rumor said that Spellman also found time for his attractive mistress, Sylvia Cohen. Before they met, she was the most popular barmaid on the west side of town.

Marty strolled among the exhibits for the better part of an hour. There were outstanding displays of everything from flint axes to Gattling Guns. The weapons were a chilling reminder of how eager mankind is to find ways to kill more efficiently.

When Marty came outside, the parking lot held a few scattered vehicles, and the rain had slowed to a drizzle. He was almost to his car when he noticed the Mennonite again, hurrying toward his truck from the direction of Spellman's Mercedes. Marty started to call out to him, then thought better of it.

Troyer left the parking lot without looking in Marty's direction. When Marty reached the Mercedes, he inspected it carefully. Looking at the tires, he then felt under the fenders and checked the hood and trunk seams for tampering. Finding nothing, Marty went back to his car feeling foolish and drove out of the lot.

As Marty drove by the rear door to the building, Darlington walked into the parking lot with Spellman. The pig-faced little man looked like a funeral director who had just found a coffin tipped over during a service. Wringing his hands nervously, Darlington appeared to be trying to appease the scowling Spellman. "You love this you bastard. You love to make other people grovel," Marty thought.

By the time Marty turned up High Street toward the courthouse, the rain had stopped completely. The gun-metal sky began to crack, and the sun seeped through the openings, sending slivers of light toward the ground.

Turning off the street, he drove into the underground garage across from the ancient courthouse. Driving onto the second level, Marty turned the corner. The scene that greeted him caused him to dart into one of the many empty parking slots and switch off the engine.

Spellman stood beside the open door of the Mercedes in the middle of the parking ramp. His face was flushed, and he pounded the palm of his left hand with the fist of his right. "God damn it!" Spellman shouted loud enough for Marty to hear over the click of the idling Mercedes diesel. "God damn it! God damn it!"

Jerking a pen and pad from the breast pocket of his coat, Spellman scribbled something on one of the pages. Storming back into the Mercedes Spellman slammed the door. With a squeal of tires, he backed into the empty space across the aisle. Slamming the door again, he stormed towards the stair well like a dirt devil across a desert landscape.

Getting out of his car, Marty walked toward the stairwell that had swallowed up Spellman. The object of Spellman's outburst was a battered, 1980 Oldsmobile parked in the space reserved for Judge Aaron Spellman. The fenders were shredded with rust, and the body appeared to be held together by an ancient layer of dirt.

The owner of the decaying vehicle had committed the unpardonable sin of treading on his majesty's turf. It didn't matter that the garage wasn't a quarter full. Spellman would likely have the car towed, and heaven help the owner if his path ever crossed Spellman's.

There was a line at the metal detector that guarded the ground floor entrance to the courthouse. To his surprise, Marty saw Troyer going through the detector. When Troyer spoke to the guard, Marty heard the distinct phrasing and accent of the Amish.

The magnificent courthouse was a tribute to a past age when buildings were designed to endure. The marble floors and walls, cornices and polished wooden railings were weathered but noble. The tread of countless feet had worn a path in the marble stairwell.

Marty slipped into the back row of the gallery of Judge Spellman's courtroom. It was still early, and he wanted to watch the judge in action. Looking slowly around the room he spotted Troyer, who blended in with the dozen other Amish men already seated in the pew-like seats on the other side of the courtroom.

The cases for the morning were bail hearings for grand jury felons. One of the Amish was on the docket. A young Amish farmer had gone berserk and had beaten his next door neighbor to death with a shovel. The brethren were not here to provide support but to be certain that he received proper punishment.

The bailiff's door opened, and a striking blond, with long legs, walked into the room. "All rise," she commanded, and the spectators stood as Spellman entered the courtroom like a Roman emperor.

Spellman was as cruel and arrogant from behind the bench as he had been with the helpless Darlington. Feeding on the fear and misery of the refuse of humanity that paraded before him, he carried out the hearings without a trace of compassion or mercy.

The case following the helpless Amish boy was that of Cedric Willis, Junior. Spellman seemed to sit a little straighter in his seat when the case was called, and a malevolent smile turned the corners of his lips.

Marty knew the case and felt sorry for the boy. The ascetic, bookish teenager, dressed in an ill-fitting prison jumpsuit, slouched into the courtroom like a man on his way to the gallows. He took his seat dejectedly at the defendants table and looked around the courtroom like a rabbit at bay before a pack of hounds.

The defendant's attorney helped the frightened teen to his feet and steadied him as the leggy bailiff read the charges. "The People versus Cedric Willis, Jr. on charges of grand theft auto and assault."

Spellman acknowledged the court-appointed defense attorney. "How does your client plead, Mr. Hollister?"

Hollister, a disheveled, nervous looking man responded, "Not guilty, Your Honor. And, we request bail pending the grand jury hearing."

"Grand theft auto is a serious charge, Mr. Hollister. Make your bail motion." The judge's voice was cold.

"My client is a Buchtel High School honors student. He has never been in trouble. His mother died when he was five, and he has been raised by his father, Cedric Willis, Senior." He nodded toward a withered, shabbily-dressed black man sitting in the front row.

The look on Spellman's face said, "Got you, you son-of-a-bitch." Marty was fascinated. What was going on?

"The senior Mr. Willis is a custodian at K-Mart, and the family resources are limited," the attorney continued. "Due to the defendant's exemplary record, we ask that Mr. Willis be remanded to the custody of his father on his own recognizance. We do not feel it would be in the best interest of the defendant, or the People, for Cedric to be incarcerated with hardened criminals."

Removing his half-glasses Spellman rubbed his eyes in feigned weariness. Putting the glasses back on, he fixed the defense attorney with a gaze that held him like a pithed frog. "Mr. Hollister, are you aware of the rise in violent crime in Summit County area these past two months?"

"Yes, sir, but...."

Spellman cut him off before he could finish. "Are you aware that the owner of the automobile was sitting at a traffic light when he was pulled from the car and beaten senseless before the vehicle was stolen?"

"Yes, sir, but my client wasn't there. You know that charge is against the Dewar brothers who . . ."

Again Spellman knifed in, severing Hollister's rebuttal. "Mr. Hollister, it is the job of this bench to be certain that justice is done. A vicious crime was committed that sent an elderly man to the hospital in serious condition. I plan to make certain that hoodlums think twice before they come before my bench."

The judge's comments were nowhere near the truth. A cursory look at the story that appeared in the newspaper would convince most readers that the attack had not been as vicious as the Judge described. Two boys had roughed up an old man in a car-jacking, but it was nothing like the judge described.

The boy at the defendant's table looked ridiculously like a cartoon character. All Marty could see through the horn-rimmed glasses that had slipped down on Willis' sweaty nose were the whites of his eyes and his pearly teeth as he grimaced in anguish. Spellman evidently enjoyed the misery of the Willis family.

"Bail is set at two-hundred thousand dollars."

A faint cry, like the sound an injured bird might make, escaped the senior Willis's lips. The younger Willis fainted. The bailiff rushed to the defense table with smelling salts while Hollister lifted the boy's head and kept him from sliding onto the floor. In a few moments, the younger Willis blinked and sat up. Bewildered at first, when he realized where he was, he looked at Spellman and leaped to his feet. The front of his prison jump suit was stained with urine.

"No!", he shouted, the terror in his voice audible. "Please, don't put me back in there. I didn't sleep a wink. I can't take it for a whole month. If you put me back in there, I'll die. I didn't do nothing wrong," Willis pleaded over a supportive murmur from the gallery.

Pounding his gavel sharply on the bench, Spellman turned a withering gaze on the assembly. The murmurs died immediately, as if they had been sucked from the air by a giant vacuum. Sweeping the gallery with an icy look in his eyes he waited until he was certain that he had everyone's attention. "You will remain orderly, or I will instruct the bailiff to clear the court-room."

"I'm sorry our jail offends your sensibilities, Mr. Willis, but you should have considered that before you got into that car. Post bail or be the guest of the county." He rapped the gavel down again. "Next case."

Willis was led away, crying. Spellman watched the senior Willis leave the courtroom, and he relished the scene. The old man was crying, too. His shoulders sagged and shook as he sobbed. The dejected, beaten man shuffled slowly down the aisle.

The next case was the first of the Dewar brothers. These young felons, cousins of Cedric Willis Jr., already had enviable criminal records. They had confessed to beating the old man in the Cadillac, and said that Willis wasn't there. The second Dewar brother said that they lied to Cedric. Willis didn't know that the car was stolen. Spellman glared and gave the Dewar boys both judicial barrels.

After his testimony, Marty exited the stairwell in the parking garage and walked toward his car. Cedric's father was wandering up and down the aisle. His eyes rimmed with tears, and he seemed to be dazed.

As Marty walked by, the old man said, "They took my boy, now they took my car. We didn't do them no harm."

"Why they doin' this to us?"

Marty didn't answer, since Willis was talking to himself. Cedric Willis Junior's father was the unfortunate owner of the rusted Olds. Marty balled his hands into fists. A sensitive teenager, guilty of nothing more than gullibility, was in a jail filled with hardened criminals because his father had made the mistake of taking Spellman's parking place, and his father was wandering around the parking lot with a broken heart.

Getting into his car, Marty slammed the door. Why didn't the God that took Janet take Aaron Spellman?

CHAPTER
4

The onion-skin dome of Tangiers Restaurant loomed ahead on Market Street. The marquee announced the Scintas performance tonight and that Fats Domino was coming in two weeks. Decades of international entertainers had played the Sultan's Cabaret, the nightclub portion of the complex.

Marty walked down the hall lined with autographed photographs of the entertainers, politicians and celebrities who had patronized the Akron institution.

It was 6:45. Not bad. He often got so engrossed in what he was doing that he lost track of time, yet, he hated people who were constantly late. Half an hour later, Marty waved from a table by the window in the far corner of the room and stood to greet her.

"Sorry, I got so engrossed in what I was doing that I lost track of time. Thank God my foot fell asleep, or I might have gone on for another hour," Nora said apologetically.

He accepted the apology with a shrug. "No problem, I just got here myself," Marty replied, hoping the two cigarette stubs in the ashtray and a nearly empty cocktail glass wouldn't degrade the gentlemanly gesture.

"Getting engrossed is something I understand. Do it myself on occasion, but I'm not sure about the foot part." Marty felt a little awkward as he stumbled over the small talk. He hadn't done this for a long time, and he had forgotten how difficult it could be.

"I talk in circles sometimes, another habit that drives my friends crazy," she said, her eyes twinkling. "When I do something that takes lots of concentration, I take off my shoes and tuck my leg up under me. I did that today, and my foot fell asleep. When I got up to stamp some circulation back into it, I realized I was late."

"I'd wait longer than 15 minutes for you," he thought, and the simple revelation of that kind of feeling toward a woman made him uncomfortable. "What would you like?"

"Beefeaters and soda with a twist of lime. I prefer Boodles, but you can't get it in this country very often."

"Do you happen to have Boodles Gin?" he asked the waitress that he summoned to the table. She shook her head. "Okay. Beefeaters and soda with a lime, and I'll take a Chivas on the rocks." Noticing the question on her face he added, "I'm off duty."

Chatting aimlessly for a few minutes relieved the tension Marty sensed between them. When the waitress returned with the drinks he said, "Let's get the business out of the way first. Then, if you'd like, we could get a bite to eat. What did you find?"

Sipping the gin, Nora made a face, stirred the drink and tested again. "Don't they teach them to stir in bartender's school?"

"They don't mix drinks anymore," Marty replied. "They just push a button on this gizmo that looks like a TV remote, and the fizzies come out. Pre-measured, computerized, brainless."

"To business," she began. "The other autopsies were as incomplete as I expected them to be, but Peters left me enough for some assumptions. "The first victim . . . ."

"His name was Joseph Dinker," Marty interrupted. He conjured up a picture of the dead man's face. Marty wanted to tell her how he felt so it wouldn't sound corny. Arranging his thoughts, he continued.

"When I can, I use their name, try to get to know something about them. These are real people with lives that someone has taken. I don't want to detach myself from them. Dinker had a typical street history. Got a little deranged from the pressures in his life; had a breakdown and wandered away from the family. They were embarrassed. I think they were relieved when I told them he was gone—Sorry, didn't mean to deliver a sermon," he finished apologetically. Marty noticed that his hand was shaking slightly as he sipped the Chivas.

Nora sensed his discomfort and looked away. "That's opposite of the way I do it," she told him. "I purposefully try not to think of them as people with a name. I treat them reverently, but I depersonalize them to lessen the reality of what I have to do to them. It's only the remains of a person, but that's hard to separate if you get too close. I hate to work on hands. Hands are so—human."

Grateful that she understood and had shared her own defenses with him, Marty said, "What did you find out about Joe Dinker?"

"Peters' notes had a lot of gaps in them, most of which I can fill in with solid guesses after the post today. I didn't have time to pull the micros out to check. I'll do that tomorrow."

"Micros?"

"Sorry. If I throw too much medical jargon at you, stop me. It's a bad habit doctors get into. If you went to a pathology convention you'd think we were on Vulcan talking to Spock's relatives."

"A closet Trekkie?" he asked.

"Guilty," she replied. "We take pieces of tissue from everywhere as you saw today, paying particular attention to anything grossly abnormal. These are sliced thin, mounted on glass slides and treated with stains and dyes that show us different things."

"How many micros on the average case?"

"It depends. Anywhere from twenty to a hundred, depending on what we're doing . . . lots on the one today, for example."

Marty whistled. "That's a lot of samples."

"And, we keep the abnormal ones for at least as long as it takes pluto-nium to decay, just in case the family ever decides to sue."

"You must have rooms full of slides."

"Not really. We keep the blocks for a year or so after the case has been signed out. In murders, the samples are kept until after the trial and the appeals, if there are any. Unsolved cases are stored in the basement of the county morgue forever."

"New York City must have warehouses full." Marty mused. "I'm glad they kept these samples. Maybe we can get a better handle on what hap-pened to these men. I'm sorry to keep sidetracking you. Please go on." Marty felt comfortable with the way she explained things to him. She didn't talk down to him, and she was easy to follow.

"The first thing I looked for was the rash. As I said this morning, the boss is less than complete when it comes to the superficial findings. He didn't disappoint me. A big fat zero there."

"The good news is that all three of the head wounds are nearly identi-cal. I'd swear in court that they were all done by the same person. And, your shooter is left-handed."

Marty took a pull of Scotch and frowned. "The men were shot from behind the right ear. What makes you say he was left handed?"

"The angle of the bullet wound. It's inside out. A probe through the path of the bullet suggests the shooter was left-handed or trying to make us believe he was."

"Great. That's our first, solid clue. What's the bad news?"

"Peters didn't culture anything. He did pick up the joint hemorrhag-es. Both of the other victims had them."

"Interesting." Marty scratched his chin and produced a package of Camels from his jacket pocket. "Do you mind?" When he inclined the pack in her direction, she closed her eyes and took a deep breath. The look on her face was one of delicious confusion.

"Go ahead, but you may have to give me one. I've quit, let me see," she paused and counted on her fingers, "seven times. I can resist the urge,

unless I'm drinking and other people are smoking. The two go together."
The consternation on her face was evident. Marty pocketed the pack.

"No, please, go ahead," she said, flushing with embarrassment.

"I won't tempt you. I tried to quit once or twice. I couldn't resist when other people were smoking. You'll find I have a great deal of will power . . . about some things. If I wanted to tempt you, I'd try to think of something a lot more interesting than a Camel."

Marty flushed at his own boldness. Nora's brown eyes reflected pinpoints of light from the candle on the table. There was a lovely softness in them that was distracting. She had high cheek bones and a turned up nose that bordered on haughty. "So, what's next?" he asked.

"The fluid in the joint spaces was blood mixed with inflammatory fluid. When joints get inflamed, they produce clear fluid as a defense mechanism. The fluid in these men's joints wasn't clear. It had a lot of blood in it. You might see something like that in a football player with a knee injury."

"That's an analogy I can understand. I have a pre-arthroscopic scar on my knee, compliments of Akron U football."

"Then, you know what I'm talking about. But, I don't think our boys ran too many fly-patterns. I was a Browns fan," she answered before he could ask the question.

"Any woman who likes football can't be all bad," he said, and thought he saw a twinkle in her brown eyes.

"All three men had involvement in the hands, wrists, elbows and knees. You don't get identical involvement in three different people from trauma. No two people fall from a five-story building and end up with the same injuries. This has to be a disease."

"What about Kevin Steel? That's victim number two. Did he have it too?"

"Yes, the findings in Dinker, Steel and John Doe are identical."

"I'll be damned," he said, reaching for his notebook.

"It gets better. John Doe had changes in the internal organs as well. There was excess fluid in most of his internal organs. His lungs were so saturated with blood and fluid that he would have been painfully short of breath. I'd bet he couldn't walk without stopping every step or two to catch his breath. The other two major collections were in the spleen and liver."

"The liver was the kicker. All three livers were the same." She was talking rapidly, and consciously forced herself to slow down. She was a strong-willed woman. Janet was always the arbiter, the peacemaker. Could he handle a strong-willed woman?

"Livers were necrotic in the center," she said sipping the gin.

"Necrotic means dead on Vulcan, doesn't it?"

"Necrosis is cellular death. Whenever a cell dies, it swells, bursts its membrane and disintegrates. The resultant destruction is called necrosis. In this case, the center of the liver looked like yesterday's pudding."

"That's a scrumptious analogy. Is there any way to tell what causes it?"

"That's like looking at the ashes and asking where the fire started. The end result looks the same regardless of the cause."

"So, they all had the same disease when they died. At least we've found something that connects them.

Plus, we're looking for a left-handed man. That's more than I've been able to come up with since this thing started."

"I wish Peters had been more complete with his description of the intestinal pathology. Those changes that you saw in the lab this morning should have been there on the earlier victims. I only hope he took good sections of the gut. Maybe the micros will help."

Leaning back in his chair Marty clasped his hands behind his head. "How will the intestinal findings help?"

"Remember how John Doe's gut lining had separated itself from the underlying muscle? I called it sloughing off. Either he was going to pass his own guts in a bowel movement, if had lived a few hours longer, or he was dead a lot longer than we think he was."

"Anything in the other posts to suggest what might do that?.

"I double checked the textbooks to validate my memory. There are two things that fit. With decomposition, the gut lining comes off. The other is associated with rare diseases that aren't endemic here."

"Like?" he asked.

"Yellow Fever or Dengue Fever can cause the liver changes, but not all the other findings. The closest thing to what these men had would be one of the viral hemorrhagic fevers that are endemic to Africa."

"I read about those in *Newsweek.* Pretty nasty critters."

"You bet. The only problem with my brilliant diagnosis is that we have to postulate that three Akron street people all went to Africa together in the past three months or lived in the same doorway and shared toothbrushes."

"Does paint an interesting mental picture. Who runs the vagrant's travel agency?" Marty seldom poked fun at the less fortunate, but he wanted to lighten the tone of the conversation.

"None of the diseases are common, even in jet-setters. There are vaccinations and preventative medications for the common ones. You have to venture into the rain forests, or come in direct contact with the excretions of an infected person to catch the nasty ones. The only tropical disease I ever saw in Akron was a Goodyear International executive who forgot to take his quinine while working at their rubber farm in Africa. He got a rip-roaring case of malaria."

"Could malaria do this? Suppose someone like your executive brought a super strain of it back from vacation."

"Doesn't work that way. Malaria isn't contagious, without a vector. The mosquito bites someone who has malaria and takes up the germ that's in the victim's blood. Inside the mosquito, the germ changes and becomes infectious to the next person the mosquito bites. It injects living germs, ready to go to work."

"Malaria can kill. Even with modern therapy, twenty percent of patients develop fatal complications. If they do, the liver lesions they develop are very similar to what we've seen in these three men. It also causes a distinctive symptom."

"What's that?" He motioned for the waitress and ordered fresh drinks. When the waitress was gone, he urged her to continue.

"They urinate black urine."

"They what?"

"The liver necrosis causes them to dump large amounts of bile into the urine, and it turns black. It's really dark green, but it looks black. They call it blackwater fever."

"I've heard that term before. Could our men have done that, even if they didn't have malaria?" Marty felt nervous talking about urination. Why? She was a doctor. It shouldn't bother her if he used a slang word when he didn't know the right medical term. Was it that important for him to make a good impression on her?

Shrugging her shoulders, she said, "That's a possibility. The puzzling thing is the lack of jaundice. When the liver is that badly damaged, they should get yellow tinges to the skin and the whites of the eyes, like people do with hepatitis. These fellows didn't have that. The other possibility would be *vomitos negros.*"

"Black vomit?" Marty said.

"Very good, Marty."

He inclined his head. "College Spanish. What does that mean from the medical standpoint?"

"In some of the hemorrhagic fevers, the virus burrows into the stomach lining and the patient develops King-Kong-sized ulcers that bleed into the stomach. The blood clots, are partly digested until they look like old coffee grounds. When the stomach is full of clotted blood, the patient vomits The result is emesis that looks like coffee grounds, so it's called *vomitos negros.*"

Marty felt a surge of adrenaline. At last he had something to work with. "That's something I can use! If our boys spent any time at our local roach motels, someone would remember black urine or a bowl full of disgusting black coffee grounds. Anything else to look for?"

"I don't know. I'm only speculating about those findings. There's a professor at the medical school, Doctor Alex Bell, who could be of real help to us. He's a virologist and runs the biocontainment facility there. Has quite an international reputation in exotic infections. Used to work for USAMRIID."

"I bet he gets lots of grief with that name," said Marty, "and lots of phone jokes."

"He's very sensitive about the name and tolerates nothing but Alex. But, he'll ring your bell if you make any phone jokes."

"Grim!" Marty exclaimed, squinting as if he had just bitten into something sour. "Two more questions. What's a biocontainment facility, and what's USAMRIID?" he asked.

"The top floor of the research building at the medical college is a secure area where they are allowed to work with lethal viruses, bacteria or toxic chemicals. There are special containment hoods, secure storage facilities and special handling areas with negative air pressure rooms."

"USAMRIID is The United States Army Research Institute for Infectious Disease Center at Fort Detrick, Maryland. It's the main biological research facility dealing with level four infectious agents. Every new infectious agent ends up in their biocontainment facility. For perspective, AIDS is a level two agent. The levels designate the type of containment area that's needed to work with them. Level-one is just a shower. Level-four requires full space suits."

"Holy shit!" he exclaimed. "Sorry Nora. That just slipped out."

She smiled and put her hand on top of his. The sensation was electric, and he shivered. "It's really unholy shit," she said putting him at ease. "That's why Bell left. He didn't like the military ramifications of the work. Before they even get the damned things classified, some general is turning the organism into a weapon."

When she took her hand off his, he wished she hadn't. "I guess I should go see the doctor. Do you think you'd have time to go with me? I'd appreciate it. He won't intimidate me, but if you were there, you could be sure I ask the right questions and translate the scientific jargon. You explain things nicely. Even a dummy like me can follow."

"I'd be glad to. "And, if you're a dummy, I'm Joan of Arc."

"Okay, St. Joan, tell me when you're available," he said. "Your day is more hectic than mine. I can go anytime."

"We'll have to wait till next week. I called his office after I read the autopsy report. I wanted to ask him some questions about the results, but he's on vacation and won't be back till the end of the week. My secretary will set something up for us then."

"It's really nice of you to do this for me."

"Don't be silly," she replied with a wave of her hand and a smile that told him she didn't mind. I've gotten as interested in this thing as you have. There's a lethal disease to track down. I have as much at stake in this as you do." Then, with a pink tinge coloring her face she added, "Besides, it'll give me a chance to get to know you better."

"That's enough work for tonight," he said while signalling the waitress for their check. "Let's eat. I'm starved."

CHAPTER
5

The humid air struck Marty like a punch. Even at the early hour, heat radiated from the pavement in front of his apartment in shimmering waves. A hint of August in the spring. A rumble of distant thunder confirmed that the inevitable storm accompanying the front was not far away. Turning to retrieve his umbrella from the rack by the door, his thoughts were interrupted by the ring of the telephone.

"Morning, Marty," King greeted him. Marty felt his pulse quicken.

"Hi, Andy, what's up?" he asked, keeping his anxiety hidden.

"A lot more than my pecker, that's for sure. His majesty, Aaron Spellman called. Wants someone at his office, *post haste.* Went to the trouble to call us himself. From the sound of his voice on the phone, I'd say something has his knickers in a knot. You're the chosen one. Must be your charm. The judge awaits you in his chambers." King added.

"Any idea what it's about?" Marty asked, relieved that it wasn't another killing.

"Nope. He just wants you there yesterday."

"Aye-aye, mate."

Twenty minutes later, Marty was ushered into the Spellman's private chambers by the singularly attractive bailiff he had seen in court. When she moved, it was with a whisper of silk against silk, and he wondered if the above-the-knee length of the tight-fitting skirt met with the decorum of the court. He thought about Nora and was struck with an unreasonable guilt feeling.

Spellman sat in the large, comfortable chamber behind a polished, mahogany desk that was free of clutter. The side walls were lined by floor-to-ceiling bookshelves, laden with matching, green legal volumes. A door in the corner of the left wall was covered with a full-length mirror. The wall behind the desk contained a large window that looked out on the park at the side of the courthouse. The rest of the wall was filled with diplomas and photographs. One of the pictures was a smiling George Bush and the inscription read, 'To Aaron Spellman. Thanks for everything.'

Without getting up Spellman motioned Marty toward an uncomfortable wing-back chair across the desk from him. "This is Detective Sergeant Martin Cox, Your Honor," the blond said, in a voice that dripped over her generous lips like honey from a comb.

"Thank you, Janell," Spellman grunted. "Hold my calls."

"Yes, sir." Spellman waited until she undulated from the room.

"I believe a man should surround himself with only the best things life has to offer. Do you agree, Detective?"

Marty nodded.

Marty knew that Spellman was fifty-five years old, but he didn't look it. Tan and trim, with broad shoulders and a narrow waist, Spellman's ruggedly handsome face was dominated by penetrating eyes and a nose that bordered on ample. A fresh scratch was visible across his left cheek, though it was mostly hidden beneath carefully applied makeup. A square chin jutting defiantly forward completed the picture. His barbered black hair was neatly combed, and probably dyed. It was a touch too black to be natural. The sleeves of his tailor-made shirt were rolled up displaying a Rolex watch. His judicial robe hung on a hall tree in the corner of the room.

"This conversation is confidential, Detective. I have a problem that I expect to be handled with complete discretion. Is that understood?" Spellman's tone said he was man used to being obeyed, and that this was not a request.

"I will be as discreet as circumstances allow, Your Honor. Please start at the beginning, sir, and tell me what's going on," Marty said with more respect than he felt.

"I was a plaintiff's attorney for medical malpractice in a prominent San Francisco law firm before I came to Akron. When I met my wife, Shelia, I came here to be council for her family business, and to manage the Kauffman family holdings."

The smug look on Spellman's face suggested that Marty should be impressed by this revelation. He wasn't. Spellman was an opportunist, and the opportunity had been named Shelia Kauffman. Her father had left his only daughter a rumored one hundred million dollar empire.

"Two weeks ago, each of the five members of my old firm received an unusual piece of mail. The letters consisted of the same message, and were composed of letters or words clipped from newspapers. I got one too."

"Here in Akron?"

"No, it was mailed to my old office address there."

"What did it say?" Marty asked, reaching for his note book.

"Let's kill all the lawyers."

"Let's kill all the lawyers?" Marty drummed his fingers on the notebook. "Sounds familiar."

"Shakespeare. From Henry the something-or-other."

"I assume they gave the letters to the forensic people out there?"

"Yes, and they found nothing, except the prints of the recipients, the postman, the usual."

"Do you believe this is a legitimate threat?"

"I didn't, until something caused me to consider it. One of the partners in the firm died. The firm is taking the threats seriously, to the point of acquiring personal security. I poo-pooed the idea until I found this in my mail." He shoved a folded scrap of paper across the desk. "My prints are on there, as are Janell's.

Using the tip of his pen and the back of his notebook so he wouldn't add a third set of extraneous prints, Marty opened the note. It read, YOU CAN'T GET AWAY. YOU'RE STILL GOING TO DIE.

"Did the others in the firm get this note?"

"No. I'm the only one who received this one."

"Do you think the notes are connected to the death of your former associate in San Francisco?"

"God damn it, something is going on!" Spellman leaped to his feet nearly knocking over his desk chair. Turning to the window and stuffing his hands into his pockets, Spellman stared out at the brooding sky for a moment, then turned back to Marty.

"I'm not sure what I'm saying Detective. I don't believe this is coincidence. Hayden was as healthy as a horse, and in forty-eight hours he's puking blood and on his way to the morgue."

"What were his symptoms?" Marty asked, sitting forward.

"Rosewood went to San Diego to play in a tennis tournament with another of the firm's partners. He developed a high fever, chills, jaundice, started throwing up blood and passing bloody stools."

Scribbling furiously in his notebook, Marty asked "Is there anything else? It's vitally important." Marty asked. "It may be connected to the derelict murders we're working on here."

"Come, Detective," Spellman snapped. "How could my law firm have anything in common with murdered street bums?"

"I didn't mean to imply that there was a connection between the men themselves. The victims here were ill and might have had symptoms like those you ascribed to Mr. Rosewood," Marty said.

Opening his desk drawer, Spellman withdrew a large Manila envelope. "Joe Worthy, the partner with Rosewood, faxed these to me this morning. It's the complete autopsy report on Rosewood."

"Do know the name of the officer in charge of the investigation?"

"No, but it's in the folder with the autopsy material."

"Thank you, Your Honor. The coroner will need to see these right away."

"Just keep my name out of it," Spellman commanded with agitation.

"Yes, sir." Marty tried to disguise his sarcasm. Here was a man who believed himself to be in mortal danger, and the only thing that really bothered him was keeping his name out of the newspaper.

The bailiff stopped Marty as he was leaving the office. "A Sergeant King from the station called. Please return his call as soon as you can." She flashed him a smile that would have melted butter.

"Hello, Andy. What is it now?" Marty asked with mock exasperation.

"It's just your lucky day, me bucco. We had a phone call from a Ms. Sylvia Cohen. Seems she wants to register a complaint against her boyfriend who knocked her around last night."

"Since when is a domestic my problem?"

"When the alleged perp is Judge Aaron Spellman."

Marty nearly dropped the telephone. "Are you serious?"

"Yep. Since you and the judge are old friends, you should be the one to handle it."

Ms. Cohen lived in a condominium complex called Eagles Chase. On the front porch of number two twenty-five, Marty waited for a response to his knock. The wood on the frame was splintered around the latch.

"Who is it?" asked a female voice from the other side of the door.

"Sergeant Cox, Akron, P.D. You called the station." Marty held his I.D. up to the peephole in the door. A bolt slipped back, and the door opened slowly.

A striking blonde opened the door. Unlike the bailiff, who oozed voluptuousness, it flowed from Ms. Sylvia Cohen. Five-feet-five, her honey-colored hair was professionally highlighted. Large breasts, a narrow waist and the figure showing through the expensive dressing gown made her a woman who turned heads.

Her face disrupted the illusion of perfection. Red eyes and smeared eye shadow suggested that she had been crying. She attempted a weak smile through a puffy lower lip, and a small bruise was evident at the corner of her well-formed mouth.

"Come in, Sergeant," she said in a rusty whisper that reminded him of dry leaves on an autumn sidewalk.

Inside, she ushered him into a comfortable chair in the living room, and she sat down opposite him on the couch. When she crossed her legs, Sylvia revealed more thigh than Marty was comfortable with.

"You told Sergeant King that you wished to file a complaint. Tell me what happened?" Opening his notebook, he waited, pen poised.

"I . . . I'm not sure if I want to file a complaint. Can you just . . . talk to him? You know, scare him a little."

"Judge Spellman is not the type of man to be intimidated. I couldn't confront him without an official complaint."

Anger flushed her face. "Then get the hell out of here. He can do whatever he God damn pleases and get away with it."

"He wouldn't if you sign a complaint," Marty replied quietly.

"If I sign it, will you assign someone to keep him away from me?"

"No, but you could get a restraining order from the court."

"Sure. One of his cronies is going to do that for me, right? Excuse me, Judge, but would you slap one of your buddies on the wrist?" Her laugh was bitter. "I don't think so. If I sign a complaint he'll come over here and beat the shit out of me again. He already said that he'd punish me, and that he could kill me get away with it."

"I'm sorry Ms. Cohen. But, unless you file a complaint, I can't do anything at all." Marty shrugged his shoulders helplessly.

Marching to the door, she held it open for him. Pausing as he came alongside her, Marty tucked his card into the pocket of her robe. "If you change your mind, you can reach me at this number anytime."

Tearing a breath from the humid air, Marty stuffed it into his lungs. It was getting easier to dislike Spellman all the time. Could Sylvia Cohen have written the letters? An angry woman was a formidable force, but Marty was sure that Sylvia could never kill anyone.

Pulling away from the curb, he dialed in the coroner's office on the car phone. Doctor Daniels was teaching at the medical school this afternoon and wasn't expected back until tomorrow, Nora's secretary told him and offered to take a message. No, he'd call later. He'd give her the folder tomorrow, but he still had wanted to see her.

Back in his office, he opened the manila folder and removed the autopsy report. There were a number of black and white photographs organized with a paper clip. Since Rosewood died in a hospital, the police report was routine. It was signed by Sergeant Patrick Riley.

Since he was unfamiliar with the medical terms, most of the autopsy report made no sense to him. Unclipping the stack of pictures, he leafed slowly through them. They were grizzly shots of a middle-aged male with a bloated face and blotchy skin. There were several photos of the back of the man's knees and his elbows.

There was a knock on his door. "It's open," he said.

His partner, Elliott Dorsey, came in to the office and tossed a folder onto the desk. "We got lucky. "We have a name for John Doe number three," he said with a hint of a southern drawl and shifted the toothpick he was chewing to the other side of his mouth.

"Our boy was fingerprinted by the F.B.I. when he worked in a chemical plant that made some nasty stuff for Uncle Sam. If it hadn't been for that, it might have taken months like it did for the others."

Opening the file, Marty stared at the FAX photo of a middle-aged man with a bow tie and sports jacket. The eyes in the photograph looked through Marty toward some barren landscape beyond.

Seth Mancuso was fifty-nine when he walked away from his North Beach neighborhood six months ago. His wife of thirty-two years had died after a tragic bout with cancer. After a year of trying to deal with it, and drinking too much, he had simply walked away.

I could have been a blank face on a missing person's sheet or a body in a doorway somewhere, the back of my head blown away, Marty said and gave a prayer of thanks. In his heart he knew his dad heard it.

E.L., as Dorsey was called, was thirty, stood an eyelash over six feet tall and possessed the physique of a rugged, number two pencil. He looked at the world down a patrician nose through dark brown eyes that seldom revealed the thoughts in the active brain behind. Dorsey's aristocratic Virginia background hadn't instilled sympathy for derelicts in him, and his distaste was evident by the sarcastic expression on his narrow, mustached face.

"Thanks, E.L.. Where the hell is North Beach?"

"San Francisco," Dorsey replied, as if he everyone in the universe should know where North Beach was.

Marty sat in stunned silence for a moment. "San Francisco?"

"Yes."

"California?"

"Are you a bubble off plumb today, partner? It's like the song, San Francisco, Cal-ifornia, U-S-A," Dorsey crooned, terribly off key.

"I've got to talk to someone with San Francisco P.D., homicide, " Marty said, reaching for the phone.

"Do you know what time it is there, Marty," asked Nancy Claridge, the switchboard operator. "They're probably in the middle of roll call, but . . .." She let the implied question die.

"Uh . . . good point. I'll try later. Time difference," he said sheepishly glancing at his watch and mentally subtracting three hours. Marty shrugged his shoulders and E. L. grinned at him.

"Why makes you want to talk to homicide, partner? This is missing persons to them. This isn't murder from their perspective, just ours."

"I know, but Doctor Daniels thinks Mancuso may have had an unusual infection when he died. A lawyer who worked with Spellman when he lived in California just died of something similar to what our victims had when they died. I wanted to talk with the officer in charge of the case out there."

"So check, but remember the time zones. Don't want the big city hot shots to think we're a bunch of midwestern schlemiels." Dorsey waved a manicured hand and ambled in the direction of the coffee pot.

Marty spent the next three hours going over the files of the three victims in laborious detail. Neither of the first two had had any connection to California or with each other, either. The only common bonds were the Furnace Street Mission, where they slept on cold nights, and The Salvation Army soup kitchen, where they dined occasionally.

As he was lifting the telephone receiver to call San Francisco again, Dorsey stuck his head in the office. "Shooting victim in the shrubbery under the All American Bridge near Howard Street. Gunshot wound to the head. Let's roll."

Grabbing his jacket, Marty followed E.L. to the car. Perfect timing. He'd have fresh tissue for Nora to study.

It was impossible to hide his disappointment when the victim turned out to be a known drug dealer. The boy's short life had ended with an ounce of lead between the eyes and a second through the heart. They finished at the scene by three-thirty and headed back for the office. There were three suspects and one petrified eye witness. If they could convince the woman to talk, the case was open and shut.

There was a message on his desk to call his boss, Captain Trowbridge. "Marty, Chief. What's up?"

"I want you to go to San Francisco tomorrow night. Judge Spellman and his wife are going there for a funeral, and I want you to go along as personal security. See what the bay area boys are thinking, too."

Frowning, Marty rubbed his upper lip between his index finger and thumb. "Isn't that jumping the gun a little, Captain we . . .."

"It doesn't matter what it is, Marty, the judge is concerned, the mayor is concerned, the keeper of the Kauffman trust that donates to the mayor's campaign funds is concerned, so you're going. Pick up your tickets, some traveling cash and your itinerary from my secretary."

Marty collected the tickets. He wouldn't be going until late tomorrow night. There would be plenty of time to talk to Bell and bring Nora up to speed on what was happening.

The operator connected him with the San Francisco P.D. homicide. "Homicide, Sergeant Riley speaking," said a rich, tenor voice.

"Sergeant Riley, this is Detective Sergeant Marty Cox from Akron, Ohio. I understand you're in charge of the Rosewood case?"

"That's right. What can I do for you?"

"Believe it or not, we have a serial killer here in mid-America. Three of our local street residents have had their heads taken off with a forty-four magnum. Only problem is, our boys may also have had an unusual infection. Our last man was from your neck of the woods, North Beach. Wandered out here sometime in the last six months."

"What's all that got to do with the Rosewood case?" Riley asked.

"The symptoms for Rosewood are the same as our guys had when they died. Thought I'd check it out."

"The Rosewood case isn't an official homicide. The only reason I picked it up was because of some notes a crackpot sent to the members of the firm, and that firm has a lot of political muscle downtown. It looks like Rosewood died of natural causes."

"A local judge here got one of those notes. He used to be with the firm out there, and he's coming to Rosewood's memorial service. We know political muscle here, too. I'll be baby-sitting the judge. Would it be possible for us to get together while I'm out there?"

"Sure. I'll give you a couple of numbers."

Marty liked the sound of Riley's voice and looked forward to meeting him.

"Line one, Cox," someone yelled.

"Marty, it's Nora." Her voice was as excited as a teenager who had just received her first prom invitation. "Can you come over to my office at the hospital? I've got something to show you."

CHAPTER
6

ifteen minutes later, Marty walked into Nora's office. Smiling, she extended her hand. When he took it, she didn't let go of it right away. An excited flush tinged Marty's cheeks, and he squeezed her hand gently. "I've been as busy as a one-legged paper hanger today," she said, her eyes dancing with excitement. Despite being sparsely furnished with an over-stuffed couch and a highly polished maple desk, it had a comfortable aura. The piles of paper on the corners of the desk were neat and square. Spring flowers in the ornate Chinese vase on the edge of the massive desk desperately needed water. The surprise was the autographed poster of Helen Reddy on the wall, with the word *ROAR* in block letters beneath.

"You a fan?" He pointed to the picture.

"Closet feminist. Have a look at this." She was obviously more intent on what she had found than small talk. Nora was keeping him at arms length. The syndrome was familiar.

Walking to the microscope, she steered him to the adjoining stool. The scope had a second eyepiece in tandem with the one Nora used, so he could see what she was seeing. Sitting down on the stool, he peered in. It reminded him of the weather radar on the evening news, and it was going to snow in Cleveland.

"You're looking at a white blood cell that's magnified one hundred times normal size."

Moving the pointer to the blue circle in the center of the round field, she said, "Here's the nucleus." She outlined the darker circle inside the cell. "See how the edges of the cell are uneven, crinkled up?"

"Okay, Doctor Genius, why are you so excited about this."

Smiling triumphantly, she gave him an impromptu hug that excited him more than it should have. "You are the world's best straight man. These are the same findings that we saw in victim number three. These are better than the ones I had planned to show Alex tomorrow. That's not the good news." Pausing, she looked at him expectantly.

"What's the good news, asked Mr. Straightman," he said smiling.

"This is victim number one. At least Peters froze some blood. I lost some cells in thawing, but I recovered enough for my analysis."

"How about number two?

"The blood was the same on all three."

"Damn," Marty exclaimed.

"Look at this." Adroitly, she moved the pointer across the slide. "Here." The arrow came to rest beside a straight, black line in the middle of the cell. "I found these on all three samples. It's a viral particle. I'm sure of it." She moved the pointer to one end of the little line. "Look at this."

Marty rubbed his chin. "At what?"

"Don't you see it?"

"I see the same line you showed me before; you're at one end now."

"Maybe it is hard for you to see. I know what I'm looking for, and I can barely see it. The end of the line is thicker than the rest. It's an inclusion body or part of the virus itself. See how the edges of the cell bulge like an overloaded grocery bag."

The new slide she placed on the stage showed homogeneously stained pink cells in lines radiating from the center to the edges of the slide. "This is the liver," she said zooming in on an individual cell at higher power. "See, the same changes are present in these cells."

"You mean here?" Marty guided the pointer this time.

"That's it." Her eyes shimmered with an excitement that Marty usually associated with sex. She was as passionate about her work as he was his, and he resisted the temptation to think about her other passions.

"I've asked Jacque St. Jean, our electron microscopist, to scan it for me. His scope will make this line six inches thick."

"How long will that take?"

"He can have it tomorrow afternoon."

He told her about Rosewood, Spellman and San Francisco. "Here's the folder with the autopsy report on Rosewood. Maybe you can make something of it."

"Great," Nora said pulling three sheets of paper from the folder on the table, each containing a graph. "These are the flow cytometry studies on each of our boys," she said as she spread them out on the table.

"What's flow cytometry?" Marty asked.

"It's a fast way to look at large numbers of cells in a short time. First, you treat the cell with something that will make it fluoresce when light strikes it. In this case, we used an antibody called CD-3. It binds itself to the T-cells. Then we force the treated cell suspension through progressively smaller glass tubing until the cells are lined up single file. At the most narrow part of the tube, we bombard the cell with a laser, and the treated cells give off a flash of reflected light that is recorded by a sensor. It counts the number of cells that flash, and measures the intensity. A computer puts the data together in a graph like this one."

"Don't the other cells flash with the laser?" asked Marty.

"Yes, but not with the same intensity. Look at the graphs. The peaks here, and here," she pointed to sections of the graph where spikes raised from the horizontal axis and dropped down again, "are the normal background of the other cells. These are the T-cell peaks." She pointed to a nearly-identical peak on each of the three graphs." All three of our guys were making T-cells out the wazoo."

"If they were making T-cells that fast, the immune system isn't suppressed, it's working like gang-busters. That makes it viral, and it's unlike anything we've ever seen before. Follow me."

"I do and I will. I do follow what you're saying, and I will follow you anywhere." Marty tried to grab the words and pull them back before she heard them, but it was too late. A confused look crossed her face. Was she angry, hurt, or something else?

Resolving some internal conflict, her eyes softened and she said, "Would you like to come over to my place for dinner? I'm a gourmet cook, and I haven't had a man over for dinner in a long, long time."

"I'd love to," Marty managed to answer.

"The other thing I want to show you is the lung," Nora said, selecting another slide from the wooden box on the table." I assumed that the fluid in the lungs was from heart failure. When the heart loses its ability to pump effectively, fluid backs up into the lungs."

"Remember how you spell that word," Marty cautioned.

"I know, and the assumption was wrong, but I have time to retract the assumption before I have to suffer the consequences."

Spinning the pointer to the lower portion of the field of view, Nora continued, "See this mass of tiny blue cells that seem to be sticking to the lining of the lung?

"Uh-huh," he grunted.

"That's major league inflammation; lots of it. It's all over the lung tissue. Something was attacking these lungs. On high power, you can see the lung cells bulging. I'll bet your sport coat they're viral particles."

"I wish you were sure enough to bet something of your own."

"After Jacque does the EM on the liver cells, I'll be sure."

She made another slide change. "Here's the bone marrow. It's hypercellular. This body is working like hell to protect itself from something."

She guided the pointer over a pale blue background, then popped a different slide under the scope.

"This is the bruised area on the back of our latest man's leg." Changing slides again, she readjusted the pointer. "There's hemorrhage in this tissue. See these little dish-shaped pink staining cells? They're red blood cells . . . and look at these veins. These dark blue blobs in the center of these rings are blood clots. The rings are the walls of the vein. They were bleeding and clotting *at the same time!*"

"Please tell this dumb homicide dick what that means?"

"It means this is a totally new viral disease process. That's what it has to be. I've got to show this to Bell. It's brand new. It looks like a tropical hemorrhagic fever. It produces bleeding, jaundice, liver necrosis and the whole nine yards."

"On the other hand, there's the blood clots in the legs and the fluid in the lungs. We see these lung changes with Hanta virus. Hemorrhagic viruses don't do this. It's like the two had combined, or at least two separate species of Ebola, have combined."

"Sounds like the Frankenstein of the virus world. Is it possible that those two viruses *could* have merged to form one monster germ?"

"I don't see how that's possible. Ebola and Hanta occur in different parts of the world. Two species of Ebola might get together, but Hanta and Ebola, highly unlikely. Let's wait and see if Jacque confirms my suspicions."

Frowning, he pondered if he should share the crazy idea that was pinging his brain like a sonar beam against a submarine hull. "Nora, could someone be infecting these guys on purpose?"

Nora looked at him as if he had just told her there was a little green Martian coming across the hospital lawn toward the office. "I can't imagine that. First, an agent capable of this degree of infection would be enormously dangerous to handle. Second, the list of people with the knowledge to pull it off would consist of two or three Nobel Prize laureates. Third, why street people? And finally, you shouldn't repeat that in front of anyone who thinks you're sane."

"Yeah, it was a crazy idea," he admitted, somewhat embarrassed. Marty rubbed his eyes. "I don't know how you can stand to look through these things all day. I'd have perpetual migraines."

"That's not all I do. Her brow wrinkled into a frown. "I started off the day with an autopsy on a 17-year-old kid from the county jail. He hung himself with a rope made from torn sheets and a makeshift gallows. He was an honor student, a good kid caught in the wrong place at the wrong time. Spellman set his bail so high that his dad couldn't raise it, and they threw the kid into the general population. He had multiple facial fractures, ribs broken, and lungs contused.

She shrugged her shoulders. "The boy was violated, likely raped. They jammed something into him. His anus was scratched and dilated, and he had a rectal tear with a laceration into his belly. He had such peritonitis that the slightest movement must have been agony. He would have been dead in a few hours without treatment. The noose killed him, but the reason was on the autopsy table."

"That's a terrible way to die. What a waste." Marty remembered the

CHAPTER
7

Clarence Mackey finished cleaning the instruments they had used on the autopsy of the young, black man from the jail. Carefully, he removed the surgical blade from the knife handle with a hemostat. His finger still hurt from the last time he cut himself, and he had promised Doctor Nora that he'd be careful. He loved Doctor Nora like he loved his mother.

He was clumsy and couldn't hold things well. Even his mother called him Clumsy Clarence, because he was always breaking something. One day, when he was playing cowboys and Indians, he knocked her favorite tea cup onto the floor. If only she were still alive, he wouldn't even mind her being cross with him. Now, he had to do everything for himself. Sometimes he forgot to do things. He hated that, but he was never going to forget to use the clamp on the blade.

Peeling off the rubber gloves, he gingerly removed the Band Aid from the laceration on his left index finger. *It was such a little cut,* thought Clarence. Why is it so sore? The edges of the cut still didn't touch, and angry, red streaks ran down his finger onto the palm of his hand like lines on a road map. His mother told him that the lines were roads. Maybe these streaks were roads, and they would take him some place fun, like Disney World.

Tentatively, Clarence poured peroxide over the cut and danced around from one foot to the other as it frothed over his hand. He wasn't sure why Doctor Nora wanted him to do this, but she was the smartest doctor in the whole world, and if she said to do it, he would. The peroxide stung, but those bubbles were fun to watch. The finger hurt lots more than it did yesterday.

His shirt was soaked. If it was so hot in here, why didn't he feel hot? Feeling cold, he started to shiver. He'd better change shirts before he caught pneumonia. He wasn't quite sure what pneumonia was, but he knew it was a bad thing to catch. Some of the dead people they worked on had it.

In the men's locker room, he toweled himself dry and changed into a fresh scrub shirt. He sat down on the bench by the locker for a few minutes, and when he stood up, he got dizzy and grabbed the edge of the locker to keep from falling.

The dizziness passed, and he moved back to the sink to finish the instruments. There was pressure behind his eyes, and his head was hurting. Maybe he was getting a headache. Had he ever had a headache before?

When it was time to go home, he was sure he had a headache. His head throbbed, and it made him feel sick at his stomach. Changing into his street clothes, he took his lunch pail from the top shelf of his locker and walked to the bus stop. Each step made his head hurt worse.

Clarence was glad that the Sheltered Workshop had helped him find an apartment on the number five bus line when his mother died. At least he didn't have to worry about getting home. Walking down the block to Market Street, he stopped at the corner. He didn't have to cross the street until he got home. When he came to work he did everything backwards, and now he never got lost anymore. Feeling queasy, he threw up a mouthful of bitter tasting bile. Although he was alone on the sidewalk, he was so embarrassed that he wanted to cry.

"Clarence, you okay?" Sammy asked, as Clarence climbed onto the bus and dropped his fare into the box. Sammy, the tiny, black man who drove the number five bus looked out for Clarence.

"You don't never get sick, big buddy. You sit down right behind me here, and rest. If you fall asleep, old Sammy'll wake ya."

Clarence was glad when Sammy woke him up. He was having a terrible nightmare. Bad germs as big as a house were eating his fingers and hands and telling him they were going to eat him all up. His head still hurt, and his stomach was still sour and upset.

Looking both ways twice after the light turned red to be sure all the cars were stopped, he crossed the street and made his way painfully up the stairs to his tiny efficiency apartment and lay down on the bed without taking off his cloths.

In a matter of minutes, he felt the contents of his stomach coming up. Dashing to the bathroom, he threw up funny stuff that looked like the grounds in the bottom of the coffee pot when he cleaned it out. He made his way back to bed, took off his shoes, crawled under the covers and started to shake, partly from fear and partly because he was so cold.

When Clarence woke again, he was wet with sweat and ached all over. He was afraid he might be dying. It was dark outside, and he knew it was late. When he turned on the bedside lamp, the light hurt his eyes. He found Doctor Nora's phone number and laboriously dialed it. Nora's answering machine cut in on the third ring.

"I'm not in right now. If you want to leave a message, wait for the tone." Even her recorded voice sounded like heaven to him. He dutifully waited for the beep.

"Doctor Nora, this is Clarence . . . Clarence Mackey. I'm bad sick. I think maybe I got an infection in my cut, or maybe pneumonia. Please call when you can. Thank you. Your friend, Clarence."

Snapping off the light, Clarence cowered under the covers like a frightened child trying to ward off the closet monster.

CHAPTER
8

Nora lived on the west side of Akron in a development called the Rectory. Comfortable mirror-image townhouses constructed of brick, sandstone and oak beams surrounded a modest spring-fed lake. A number of young professionals lived in the high priced condominiums. Marty was impressed by the immaculate streets and manicured grounds.

On the way, they stopped by the West Point Market. There were things in bins he had never seen before, and cheeses whose names were totally foreign to him. They spent a playful hour settling on a menu.

Marty carried the groceries into the kitchen from the two-car garage, half of which was cluttered with boxes, skis, a mountain bike and assorted gardening tools. Depositing the packages on the island work space, he followed her into the main entry way.

A two-story foyer rose to a tinted skylight and a lofted second level. The great room was dominated by a sandstone fireplace flanked by a bay window on one side that looked out onto the lake, and a sliding glass door that led to a wooden deck on the other. A sectional sofa made a conversation pit in front of the fireplace and earth-tone rugs underscored the casual motif.

"Loosen your tie and unpack the goodies while I slip into something more comfortable." Winking conspiratorially, she disappeared into the master bedroom to the right.

Hanging his jacket on the peg of a hall tree, Marty removed his tie and draped it over the coat. Loosening the shoulder holster, he put it under the jacket.

Next the handcuffs went into the jacket pocket. He felt like Leslie Neilson in *Naked Gun,* and expected a half ton of Police paraphenalia to tumble onto the floor.

In the kitchen, he looked around as he rolled up his sleeves. White tile counter tops trimmed in yellow coordinated with muted yellow floor tiles. Fashionable watercolors of vegetables hung above the built-in microwave oven. On the opposite wall, in front of a full, bay window whose draperies were adorned with bold, yellow sunflowers, was a cheery breakfast nook with a chrome and glass table.

Unpacking the groceries on the butcher-block island, the simple action brought unexpected tears to his eyes. He hadn't realized how much he missed having someone to share things with. Quickly blotting his eyes with the back of his hand, he felt a rush of relief.

"The hootch is in the cabinet by the stove," Nora called from the bedroom. "Mix us one, will you? There's Brie on the top shelf of the fridge and the crackers are on the end of the counter."

"Nag, nag, nag," he called back playfully. A muffled chuckle drifted through the closed door. Locating the liquor, he was pleased to find an unopened bottle of Chivas beside half a bottle of Beefeaters. Selecting two squat tumblers with the Chicago skyline etched in gold on the sides he poured the drinks over ice.

The cheese was on the top shelf of the refrigerator, and there was a bottle of tonic and twists of lemon on a plate under plastic wrap. Nora had apparently planned this rendezvous long before she told him about it. He set the cheese out to warm, finished the drinks and opened the box of stoned wheat crackers. Carrying his drink and a cracker to the bay window, he was looking over the yard when he heard her come into the room and turned to face her.

"Looks like you found everything," she said

She was wearing a pair of faded jeans as tight as a second skin and an oversized Cleveland Browns uniform shirt with Jimmy Brown's number thirty-two on the back. She was barefoot, and her freshly scrubbed face seemed to shine. Then, he realized that he was staring at her open mouthed.

"Uh . . . yeah . . . no problem." He walked to the counter and fetched her drink.

Nora took a long drink of the clear liquid. "Marty, I like you a lot, and I want to get to know more about you. I haven't had a man in my life for a long time, and I'm not even sure if I'm ready for it now. It's easy to lose myself in my work, trying to find an answer to a question, cement a diagnosis, uncover a cause of death in a patient, and I can usually convince myself it's enough."

Pausing to take another drink, her expression was strained and sad. "Then, I meet you; someone I could care for, and the fear starts. What if he doesn't like me? What if it doesn't work out? So, I push the person away and retreat into my shell. I was married once, and I did everything I could, but it wasn't enough."

Tears formed in her eyes, and she angrily wiped at them with her hand. "Damn, here I go rambling like the village idiot!"

Marty took her gently in his arms and pulled her head to his shoulder. She stiffened at first, then relaxed and leaned against him. Tilting her chin back, he kissed her lightly on the lips.

"I'm scared, too, Nora. I was married, and she died. I've been hard on myself since then. Let's just take it one step at a time. Let's be patient and see what happens. Now, feed me," he said.

"Thank you, Marty," she said and moved into the pantry returning with a 1989 Opus I Cabernet. "Corkscrew is in the top drawer." She inclined her head toward the proper drawer and handed him the bottle. "Let it breathe while we work."

Nutmeg-laced cream of carrot soup that she had made yesterday so the flavors could draw through started the meal. Endive with chopped leeks and tomatos in a Balsamic vinaigrette followed. The entree was salmon in a dill cream sauce accompanied by new potatoes in garlic butter and steamed green beans. Pears poached in port, topped with Stilton cheese and walnuts, completed the promised gourmet feast.

"It was as good as advertised," Marty said as he patted his bulging stomach, which he *knew* had inched forward this time. "How do you eat like this and stay so thin?"

"I don't eat like this often. It's no fun to cook for one," she said, a hint of wistfulness in her voice.

"I know. I've eaten a lot of lonesome TV dinners."

"I'm more the yogurt and pineapple type," Nora said, her exuberance returning like the sun from behind a cloud.

When they had finished cleaning up the kitchen, Marty carried a bottle of Cognac and two snifters onto the redwood deck. Nora brought two mugs of Colombian Blue Mountain Coffee. An enormous full moon peaked over the tops of the distant houses and infused the lake with countless sparkles of moonlight. Settling into rattan chairs, they sat silently for a while, drinking in the warmth of the night.

"I could get used to life in the 'burbs," Marty said.

"I'm glad you like it. I do. Damn, I want a cigarette!"

"So do I," Marty countered. "But, we're not smoking."

They sat and sipped. "I want you to know about Janet," he said. "We were the happiest couple in the world. She was three months pregnant when she was killed. It wasn't anyone's fault. I wasn't there, but I know the details, and my mind has created a recurrent nightmare that forces me to relive it periodically."

"It's always the same. I'm in a rain storm that's so bad that the wipers can't clear the windshield. The spray from the cars is so heavy that they look like waves pounding a rocky shore line. The wind buffets the car from the side, making it hard to steer. I'm covered with sweat, and my hands ache from gripping the wheel. When I wake up, my hands cramp so badly that they ache for hours."

"The cars are bumper-to-bumper and going much too fast. I hear a muffled thump, like a distant explosion. A gun-metal gray Buick Century, in the outer lane of traffic and slightly ahead of me, has violently blown the left front tire. The impact of the deflated wheel with the concrete spews slivers of rubber from the tire that turns into a shower of sparks from the wheel as the rim grinds itself flat against the pavement. I always see this hub cap," he said pensively. "This hub cap flies off and skitters through the traffic like a flat stone across the surface of a pond."

"I can see the driver through the window. He's a middle-aged man with silver sideburns. It's the salesman who was driving the car that hits Janet's car. I saw him at the hearing. He was devastated, but how I hated him at the time. Then, he loses control of the heavy sedan and it careens across the flood of traffic at a right angle, and slams into the side of her Ford Escort. Both vehicles ricochet back across the traffic like pool balls on a felt table."

"A Peterbuilt, loaded with dog food, locks its brakes. The damned dream is so real I can smell the plumes of blue rubber smoke that wells up from the locked wheels. The trailer jackknifes and the monster truck slams broadside into the driver's door of the Escort. I see Janet's face through the window, her mouth open in a silent scream of terror," he said, rubbing his tearing eyes.

"The Ford crumples like a tin can under a jackboot, and I can hear the scream of tires and rending metal as cars start piling up. It sounds like the end of the world. That's when I wake up." She reached across and took him by the hand.

He told her about the drinking: about his father; about his recovery. "I never thought I'd have any feelings toward another woman. If you care, you're vulnerable. I never thought I would lose Janet, but I did. I want to care, but I'm afraid. Can we heal each other, Nora?"

"I don't know, Marty. My husband's name was John. I met him when we were both interns. We were married a year later. I supported him while he did a fellowship for cardiac surgery. John was bright, charming, and I adored him. Those were the happiest two years of my life. When he finished training, his ego was bigger than he was. Five years later, he left me for a twenty-three year old nurse whose boobs were bigger than her brain." Nora paused to sip her brandy.

"My pain was a different kind than yours, I think," she continued. "Yours was from loss, mine was from failure. I can't tell you how worthless I felt. My best wasn't good enough. When I was a little girl, I tried so hard to please my father, but it was never good enough. If I made a B in history, he thought it should have been an A. When I got into medical school, he was disappointed that it wasn't Harvard. I even tried to convince myself that the failure of my crummy marriage was my fault. It's taken me years to realize that it wasn't, and I *am* a good person. It's not always my fault when something doesn't work out."

Nora looked at him across the distance between the chairs. Her eyes were misty in the moonlight. Marty stood and pulled her to her feet. Her hair smelled of scented soap, and she melted into his arms. When he kissed her tenderly on the lips, it stirred emotions that Marty hadn't felt in years. Her eyes misted over, and a single tear escaped. "Do you believe in love at first sight?" she asked.

"I do now," he answered.

"I barely know you, and you make me feel things that I haven't felt since John left. There's so much I want to tell you. I want you to know everything about me. I want to know everything about you. I want to know if you sing in the shower, what kind of razor blades you use, whether you snore or not. I want to be loved again by a solid man."

"I'll never let you down. Just give me a chance to prove it."

The phone rang. "Perfect timing," Marty grumbled.

"That's the first new thing you can learn about me," Nora said, drying the happy tears that had tracked down her cheeks as Marty spoke. "I think of everything. I signed out to one of my cronies, and the answering machine will catch the call. You can't get away that easy."

"I don't want to get away. I plan to be the only man you'll ever need."

This time, she kissed him, and they stood in the moonlight, hugging each other like two frightened children. Nora broke the spell and said, "I have an early post in the morning, and I want to get finished in time for our appointment with Bell."

Inside, he walked toward the hall tree. Nora touched him on the arm. "Marty, . . . I'm not ready for . . . for intimacy yet, but I would like for you to spend the night here."

In the illumination of a single lamp, her room appeared feminine with frills and ruffles in muted shades of blue and green. The covers on the four-poster canopy bed were turned down. "I'll put a tooth brush out for you," Nora said disappearing into the adjoining bathroom.

In a few minutes she returned dressed in a long flannel night-shirt. "I like to be warm," she said apologetically.

"You look great to me," Marty said, kissing her on the cheek.

When he came out of the bathroom, she was under the covers. She turned out the lights, and he stripped down to his shorts and crawled in beside her. They lay against each other sharing their mutual warmth as they caressed, rubbed, explored. The sensation was so wonderful that Marty felt sure that sex couldn't be much better.

Marty woke with a start, confused about where he was. The room was foreign. Waning moonlight filtered between the slats of the Venetian blinds, painting strips of light across the alien landscape until it came to rest on Nora. The sheet had slid down across her chest exposing the outline of her breasts through the flannel gown. They gently rose and fell as she breathed.

Rolling onto his back, Marty looked up toward the ceiling. Marty turned his thoughts to the killings. Somewhere out there was a cold-blooded killer who might be carrying some kind of virus. He had to be stopped now. Was he overlooking anything?

He looked across her to the digital clock on the nightstand. The red numbers told him it was five in the morning. Nora groaned, but didn't open her puffy eyes.

"Mornin', darlin'," she said.

"Hi." He kissed her gently on the nose.

She traced his face with the tips of her fingers as if she were blind and reading him by braille. He kissed her on the lips.

"Not fair," she grumbled.

"What?"

"Everyone has bad breath in the morning. You don't have bad breath. It's not fair. My mouth tastes like the Polish cavalry just marched through it, horses and all."

"Not so. You smell," he licked her cheek, " and taste wonderful."

"Your getting me ready for the big let-down. Now you're going to tell me you have to leave me," she said sheepishly.

"Don't want too. Got to get a fresh shirt, pack for my trip to the coast and go to the office. But, don't worry. I'll be back. You're not getting rid of me that easily."

"Call me later," she said through a yawn.

Marty was not sure how he got home. He remembered leaving Nora's driveway, and then he was pulling into his. The trip was a blur of mixed thoughts and emotions.

In the kitchen. The red light on his new answering machine was blinking. He pressed the rewind button and rummaged for a coffee filter while the tape rewound.

"Good evening, Detective Cox. Patrick Riley here. Sorry to bother you at home. It took me forever to pry your home phone number out of your switchboard operator. Your call got me to thinking, and I did some computer searches that I think you'll find interesting. I'd like to talk to you as soon as you have some time. Good night."

A beep, followed by two more short beeps signaled no more calls. Marty wanted to get going so he could follow up on the death of the Willis boy before he went to see Bell. He dumped the beans in the grinder, filled the tank with water and headed for the shower.

CHAPTER
9

arty arrived at the office of Buck Dumont just after seven. Buck answered his knock. "Hey, Marty. What brings homicide to the lock-up," Buck asked, extending his huge, black hand.

Buck was a shade over six-feet tall, with a barrel chest and arms like tree trunks. An upper body tapered to a narrow waist over solid, athletic legs. When he smiled his contagious smile, Buck displayed an even row of ivory teeth.

Buck had been the lock-up supervisor for twenty years, and was still one of the most respected men on the force. Buck had the innate ability to communicate with even the most hard-case inmate, and he treated all prisoners fairly and with compassion. When discipline was necessary, it was swift and contained whatever force was needed.

"This isn't an official visit, Buck. I was in Spellman's courtroom for the Willis case. Unfortunately, I was at the morgue when they did the post. I don't have much doubt it was suicide, but I promised Doctor Daniels I'd check."

Shaking his head sadly, Buck said, "That was a tragedy. That poor little bastard shouldn't have been here. I know the family peripherally. My nephew goes to Buchtal."

"Yes, I'd forgotten that Randy was your nephew. Think he'll get a scholarship next fall?" Marty asked.

"Ohio State, Notre Dame and West Virginia have all set up recruiting visits.

"The kids a great linebacker. I'm sure he'll get one. Now, what can you tell me about the Willis boy?"

"The senior Willis was a real war hero. Won the silver star in Korea. Cleaned out a North Korean machine gun nest, and saved his platoon. Got shot up pretty bad in the process. Hard worker. Good Christian family. Did right by all his kids. The other kids all have college degrees. Junior was a late in life "oops" child, and his mother died when he was ten. The other kids were all grown, and Cedric, Senior gave all his attention to the boy."

"That's the impression I got. The old man was devastated."

Buck's eyes reflected the pain he felt for the Willis family.

"Last time I saw Junior, he was sitting in his cell staring at the breakfast on the tin plate in front of him. Poor kid was twitching spasmodically, and his lips were bruised and swollen. They had broken his glasses, too. I tried to get him to talk, but he wouldn't."

"His emotional pain was far worse than his split lip. Junior's expression looked like a dentist was drilling without novocaine. I blame myself for some of it. Oh, not personally, but everybody here works for me. If something happens out in the tier, I'm to blame." Buck's expression saddened.

"When they brought Junior back from court, we put him in his own cell. The night crew decide to throw a drunk into the cell with him. Some time during the night, the man dragged Junior out of his bunk and tried to stick his half-hard dick into the boy's mouth."

"Junior kicked the son-of-a-bitch in the balls and screamed at the top of his lungs. The night shift turn-key was afraid the black prisoners would make the incidence racial, since the drunk was white, so he moved the drunk to the isolation cell."

"The next night, two black prisoners tried to rape Junior. They backed him into a corner, and he came out fighting. The pair would have beaten him to death if another inmate hadn't intervened. The good Samaritan turned out to be a friend of Cedric's father, but the guy was transferred to the state pen the next day."

"Assholes taunted the kid. Worked on his nerves. That was worse. I don't think he slept much, and he was constantly exhausted, jumping at every shadow. They eventually came back. Junior fought them like a cornered tiger, but he took a beating in the process. That's when the splinters in his spirit showed up. Sooner or later he was gonna fall apart. The staff psychologist was too busy to see him before he died."

"We moved him to the windowless isolation cell we use for violent inmates. He felt safer there, but complained he still couldn't sleep."

"There's a pair in here, a tall man called Swag who's got the worst breath and rottenest teeth you've ever come across and his sadistic little buddy, Manny. I don't have proof yet, but they did it. I'll take care of them eventually. Manny's got a voice that sounds like fingernails on a blackboard. They'd scrape the isolation door with somethin; make threats; you know the drill."

"Cedric, Senior came by that last afternoon and stopped in my office. It was pitiful." The tough jailers eyes misted. "The old man's heart was broken. He had on what must have been his only suit, a worn, double-breasted ten years out of style. His red-rimmed eyes looked worse than Junior's, and he looked a hundred years old.

"I don't know what else to do, Buck," he told me. "That's a pile of money, and there ain't no way I can get it. I tried every place I know. Just ain't no way."

Buck's voice was almost a whisper. "Then he started to cry and the anguish poured out of him like a dam bursting in his soul. Marty, it broke my heart to see the anguish on that man's face."

"Junior's attackers got to him right after his father left. They beat and raped him. We think they shoved a broom stick up his butt."

"What about the men who attacked him?" Marty asked, angrily.

"Both in isolation cells where they are going to stay until one of them talks. Then, I'm going to do everything in my power to be sure they get everything we can throw at them."

"Junior braided a cloth rope from strips of his bed sheet. There's a stool in the corner of each cell, and he stood on that. He drove a hook that he made out of a bed spring into the ceiling. From the holes in the ceiling, it took him five tries to find a stud. Then, he put his hands into his pockets and kicked the stool over."

"Damn," Marty muttered.

"The animals who raped him will get theirs, but the person responsible for the kid's death is gonna walk. He won't serve one day or feel one twinge of remorse." Buck's black eyes narrowed as he fought to control his anger.

"Spellman?" asked Marty.

"Yeah. The judge is a malicious, spiteful son-of-a-bitch, and one of these days, he'll pay. I'm not all that religious, but I do believe in God. And, if there is a God, one day God will shove a broomstick right up Aaron Spellman's arrogant ass."

Marty stood and extended his hand. "Sorry, Buck. I know this was painful for you, but I had to know. I'll pass the info to Doctor Daniels. See you soon."

Walking into the promising, spring morning, Marty stopped, took a deep breath of the clean air, and looked around. Spring was the season of rebirth that carried with it the promise of new life and new beginnings. For the Willis family, this spring would be a season of anguish and despair, and if Marty didn't get the killer off the streets soon, it might be a season of anguish and despair for the whole city.

CHAPTER 10

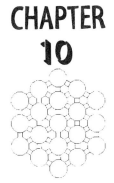

orty-five minutes later, Marty pulled the Lumina into the space marked "Doctors Only" outside the Emergency Room entrance of Summa Health System's City Hospital Campus. The space reserved for the occasional police car was occupied by a Toyota with a dented fender.

A life-flight helicopter stood silently on the pad behind him, and a hospital security guard paced back and forth in front of it to keep curiosity-seekers away. A steady stream of people marched in and out of the automatic doors like a colony of ants.

It was a glorious spring morning. The air had been scrubbed clean by an overnight shower, and the sky was a spotless, blue canopy from horizon to horizon. The sun infused the morning with shafts of sunlight, and sparrows quarreled over their places on the branches of blossoming, ornamental fruit trees. The depression he had felt after talking to Buck started to lift a little.

He was ten minutes early, but didn't mind waiting. Was the morning really that spectacular, or was it the anticipation of spending the day with Nora that improved the elements. She bounded out of the E.R. door and waved to him.

Nora had abandoned her lab coat for a smartly-tailored, brown suit. The form-fitting skirt accentuated her figure nicely and stopped just above her shapely knees. A cheery, gold blouse with a bow at the throat and a matching, gold tam gave her a cover-girl look.

As he opened the door for her, she bounced by and gave him a friendly peck on the cheek. The simple gesture made him tingle.

Driving down the Perkin's Street ramp, they took Route 8 south.

Thank you for last night, she said. I can't tell you what that meant to me. I think you're a wonderful man."

"I might be falling in love with you, too, Nora," he said quietly.

"I'm sorry that I couldn't get us an appointment with Bell yesterday," she said, changing the subject quickly. "He called in sick, and rescheduled us for today. That may be a blessing in disguise. We can catch his lecture on antibiotic resistance before we go talk to him. The guy's brilliant. They nominated him for a Nobel Prize while he was at Berkeley."

"Did the cultures of the fluid from Seth Mancuso show anything? That's John Doe's name, Seth Mancuso."

"That's wonderful, Marty." She put her hand over his. "The bacterial cultures were negative. We checked the blood smears for inclusion bodies, viral particles or any of the cellular changes we see in less common diseases. Everything was negative, but the white cells don't look totally normal to me. I want to get Bell's interpretation before I go out on a limb."

"What did you find?"

"Let's wait till Bell looks at my slides."

"Okay," Marty smiled. "I can wait."

They negotiated the central interchange and drove past the reminders of Akron's glory days as the rubber capital of the world. On both sides of the recently widened freeway, the remains of Goodyear's scaled-down operation were visible. General Tire's abandoned facilities lurked to the right of the expressway like the specter from the past. Orange barrels appeared, funnelling them into one lane and slowing traffic to a snail's pace.

"The orange barrel must be Ohio's state animal," Nora offered.

Agitatedly drumming his fingers on the steering wheel, Marty said "I lied."

"Lied about what?"

"I can't wait. What did you find?"

Chucking, she said, "I see changes in the white cells. I passed the slides around the department to get the opinion of the other staff, They split two and two. None of the residents saw anything."

"Changes must be subtle, if the residents couldn't see them. If you saw them, they're there." Marty stated it as a fact. The traffic exited the barrels and came up to speed.

Narrowing his eyes, Marty clenched his jaw. When he spoke, the disgust in his voice was evident. "I talked to Buck Dumont today."

When he finished, she said, "Spellman has to realize that he killed that boy as surely as if that broom was in his hand."

They drove silently for a few moments. The city gave way to gently rolling farm country eroded by small businesses and urban sprawl as they drove past Tallmadge, then Kent. In another five minutes they exited at Rootstown. The basic science campus of The Northeastern Ohio Universities College of Medicine lay to the right of the expressway in the center of what once was a working farm.

"Why did they put the campus so far from the hospitals?"

"This school is an experiment in medical education," she said."They admit students directly from high school and six years later graduate them with both undergraduate and medical degrees. They use three universities, Akron, Kent State and Youngstown State for the first two years. There's no formal teaching hospital. Students go to private hospitals in Akron, Canton or Youngstown. It saved a ton of money when they didn't build an expensive hospital. Rootstown is close to the geographic center of the distance between the three Universities so the basic science campus is here."

"Sounds like an inexpensive way to train medical students."

"It is, and the kids do as well on their boards as those from traditional schools. With the money crunch coming for medical education, this may be the wave of the future. Go right here, and park at the far end of the lot by the research building," Nora instructed.

"They're trying to beef up research, thus, the new building and the bucks to bring a major leaguer like Bell here. If he's not the best recombinant chemist in the world, he's on a very short list."

The research building, though made of the same brick, had a modern glass entry-way and was a story taller than the rest of the buildings on the campus. "What's recombinant chemistry?" Marty asked.

"Genetic material is constructed of blocks of amino acids held together by chemical bonds. Bell identifies the sequence of acids in a given chain of a chromosome. Then, he removes them, rearranges them, tries to understand what each combination does." Marty nodded.

"Bell's lecturing in the Olsen Auditorium. If we cut across the grounds in back of the complex, we can come in on the upper level into the back of the room."

The lecture hall was a steeply-banked affair with a chalkboard that covered the front wall of the room. Theater style seats were fitted with adjustable writing boards, and Marty took out his spiral notebook. Two men in white smocks fussed over the slide projectors in the media booth at the rear of the hall as yawning students filed in and slumped into their seats.

At precisely eight o'clock, the corridor door on the lower level exploded open, and a stocky, middle-aged man strode into the lecture hall like the lord of the manor. Thin, sandy colored hair that was graying framed a square face, and watery blue eyes were magnified by circular, bifocal glasses. His shoulders were broad, and his upper body suggested that he might lift weights.

An unlit pipe was clenched tightly in his thick lips, and as he walked to the lectern, he removed it and tucked it into the breast pocket of his starched lab coat. A stiffly starched white shirt with patterned tie contrasted with the casual dress of the students.

Bell's dress and appearance seemed to conflict. On the surface, he was the prim, starched professional, but the way he walked and moved reminded Marty of a dock worker.

Bell waited impatiently at the rostrum. When nothing happened, he cast a withering glance toward the projection booth. The lights dimmed, and a screen unrolled from the ceiling covering the chalk board. A slide, depicting a bottle of multi-colored gelatin capsules appeared on the screen.

Without preamble, Bell began to lecture. "These are miracle drugs. Since 1928, when Alexander Flemming blundered onto the penicillin growing on his molding lunch, we have been at war with bacteria. At this point, it's impossible to tell who is winning."

"Penicillin was tested during early World War II, and by 1946, staphylococcus had already developed resistance to it. Researchers found new drugs, so the bacteria regrouped and beat the new drug."

"In the 1960's a noted New York microbiologist told an assembly, 'Don't bother with a career in infectious disease. It's a declining specialty. Concentrate on the real problems of cancer and heart disease.' Was he ever mistaken. Instead of a world without infections, a combination of human nature and a gross underestimation of the power of the enemy has placed mankind on the verge of a biological Armageddon."

Bell's voice rose gradually like an evangelist in a pulpit. As he pronounced the impending fall of mankind, he banged his fist on the lectern. It had the desired effect. The last of the semiconscious medical students pulled themselves to the edge of their seats.

"The press bombards the public with promises of miracle cures," Bell continued. "Patients demand antibiotics for every cough, sneeze or unusual urination. Eighty percent of colds are viral and don't need to be treated. Spineless physicians give in to unreasonable demands for fear of loosing a patients or getting sued if they miss a strep throat. They give in to the lawyers when a twenty-four hour delay to await culture results does nothing to affect the prognosis."

"What does this type of behavior lead to in the realm of microbiology, Ms. . . . Means?"

An apple-cheeked brunette in the front row fidgeted and answered tentatively, "Resistance."

"Precisely," Bell cried, slapping his open palm on the lectern. It cracked like a thunderclap in the cavernous hall, and everyone jumped at the unexpected noise.

"Nice to know you are awake, Ms. Means," Bell added sarcastically.

Marty shook his head in awe. Bell was the puppet master, and he had the entire audience on his strings. Every student was wide-eyed.

"Man thinks of evolution in the terms described by Darwin, where plants and animals require centuries to complete adaptive behavior. The smartest rats outwit the cat and survive, while the dumb ones are dinner. Enough smart rodents survive to assure that the species will continue. Others slip up often enough for the cats to survive. That's nature's balance. It gets out of balance when man comes along to muck it up."

"Bacteria and viruses still follow Darwinian logic. The difference is that a single bacterium can produce a millennium of generations overnight. A single germ can produce 16,777,220 off-spring in twenty-four hours. Right now, your skin is swarming with bacteria. You are swimming in a sea of microscopic organisms."

The analogy caused Marty to shift and rub his hands together. He could feel them crawling on his skin.

"Think about it. A bacterial population is dosed with an antibiotic. Most of them die. What do the others do to develop resistance?" He paused and looked sadistically around the room. The students cowered, waiting for someone to be singled out. A thin smile of satisfaction creased his lips, and he continued without choosing.

"Bacteria can exude an attracting chemical, much like the perfume Ms. Means uses on Mr. Sorrenson. The students tittered at the expense of the couple on the end of the front row, who shifted uncomfortably.

"When two bacteria touch, they open pores and exchange a loop of DNA in a form of unsafe microbial sex," he paused until the laughter had died down, "and the offspring are now resistant. Cholera did this with the common *E. Coli* in our intestinal tracts and developed resistance to tetracycline."

"Equally frightening is the fact that bacteria can develop resistance to antibiotics they've never met. Doctors may be imprudent in prescribing antibiotics, but they cannot hold a candle to the farmer, who pumps beef and dairy products full of antibiotics to fatten their cattle and produce milk that will last longer on the grocer's shelf. Resistant strains of bacteria are produced and passed on to humans. Now, the FDA is considering a patent that uses gene splicing to give us a tomato that stays fresher longer, and produces resistance to the antibiotic Kanamycin. Researchers are also tinkering with the growth hormone gene in cattle. Where can it all end?" The lecture hall was silent.

He advanced the slides and a chart appeared. Forty percent of staph are resistant to every drug but one." In rapid succession, he ran through three slides depicting a boil on a child's leg. Another picture showed the leg completely covered with sores that were open and draining. In the last slide in the series, the smiling child revealed a healed scar from ankle to hip.

"This is an example of the flesh-eating staph that the British press was so fond of reporting last summer. Fortunately for the child, the infection was curable with wide drainage. Many patients aren't so lucky."

Kermit the frog, with a smiling Jim Henson appeared on the front wall. "This man wasn't so lucky. He contracted a resistant strain of pneumonia, like those in the outbreak that occurred in Kentucky two years ago. He died, despite the best medical care available."

A young woman on a respirator was the next star in the grizzly slide show. "In a middle-class suburb of Los Angeles, a sixteen year old Vietnamese student infected the local high school with a strain of tuberculosis that was resistant to standard antibiotics. Thirty percent of the school tested positive, though everyone didn't get sick. Of every seven new cases of TB world wide, one is now caused by this resistant strain, and five percent of those infected are dying."

In the new slide, a child on a respirator replaced the adult. "A pertussis outbreak gave whooping cough to over three hundred-fifty children last year, half as many as the prior 13 years combined."

Next came a cruise ship. "Four hundred people on a Baja, California cruise developed an unidentified intestinal ailment that brought the ship to port early. In a separate incident, eleven cases, twenty-four suspect, and one confirmed death from Legionnaire's disease on the cruise ship, Horizon."

A Boeing 747 filled the front wall. "Here is the real culprit. An infected individual can cause a bacterial infection to be carried around the world in six weeks by modern air travelers. We flirt on the fringes of potential self-annihilation."

An ominous silence filled the room as if the horror Bell was describing had already come to pass. "Oh my God," exclaimed, Ms. Means. A nervous titter swept the classroom breaking the tension. Marty felt relieved. If Ms. Means hadn't said it, he might have.

"My God, indeed, Ms. Means. Cancer and heart disease will always be here. If we do not win the war against the microbe, nothing else you do will make any difference at all."

"Tomorrow, we look at vaccines and their effects on bacteria and viruses. Read chapters 10 through 12 in the text and try to get some sleep for a change. I'm tired of looking at half-closed peepers. Let's go to lab." On cue, the lights came up. Removing the empty pipe from his pocket, Bell clamped it firmly between his teeth and marched from the room.

"Well, what do you think of Professor Alexander Bell?" Nora asked.

"Impressive. He's a marvelous teacher. To borrow one of your medical terms, I don't know crap about any of this stuff, but he explained it so I understood most of what he said. And, I don't mind telling you, what he said scares the hell out of me."

"Me, too. I read last week that a researcher at Yale had a sample of Brazilian Sabia virus in a high speed centrifuge when the test tube cracked and sprayed live virus all over the inside of the instrument. He was gowned, masked and gloved as he should have been, cleaned up with a bleach, and followed decontamination procedures to the letter."

"Unfortunately, he *was* infected. A week later he shows up in the E.R. with a temp of 103. An experimental drug stopped the infection. By then, he had exposed the family he visited for the weekend, five people, including two children, and some seventy-five people at the hospital after that. That's truly frightening."

"I'll tell you something even more frightening," Marty replied.

"What's that?"

"If your theory about the virus in Seth Mancuso is right, we might be on the verge of a viral outbreak here, and we have a serial killer who is contaminated with the blood and may be spreading it all over Akron. Let's go see Dr. Bell."

CHAPTER 11

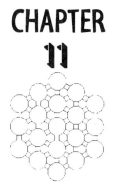

arty and Nora joined the flow of students from the back of the lecture hall and followed them outside. Bell's foreboding prophecy reverberated in Marty's head. The killer had to be contaminated with the victim's blood when he shot them. If that blood was infected, the killer would murder far more innocents than even he intended.

"Aren't we going to the lab?" he asked.

"Bell won't be in the student lab. He'll be in his office or his private research lab. The grad students who were in the audio-visual booth run the student labs. Alex has a private laboratory that takes up the entire top floor of the research building."

"Sounds like my kind of day. Jog, have a little breakfast, talk for an hour and take the rest of the day off."

Frowning, Nora said, "Some academics are that lazy. Good ones, like Bell, work fifty hours a week in their labs alone, not to mention the time they spend preparing and giving lectures. Bell earns his money. In fact, the money from his grants pays most of his salary."

"Why would someone of Bell's caliber come to a small school with no reputation for research?"

"I asked him that at the welcoming tea they had for him the first day he was here. I phrased it a little differently." She smiled mischievously, "He said he had the most important work of his career to finish, and the bigger institutions had too many distractions. He wanted privacy, and he gets it here."

Entering the glass and chrome two-story entry-way of the research building, they walked to Bell's office at the end of the hall. The front of the office was half glass, and they could see Bell hunched at his computer, intently peering at the screen.

Responding to their knock on his door without looking up from the screen, Bell called out, "Come in. It's open." Marty was surprised at the voice. It was different from the one in the lecture hall.

The office was organized clutter, and the air was filled with a cloud of blue smoke from his pipe. Bell's office was apparently immune to the signs proclaiming the building a no smoking facility. Journals and books, some open, some closed, were strewn over most of the useable space in the office. The walls were bare, save for Bell's diplomas and a stylized drawing of intertwined DNA strands. Leaping to his feet, Bell rearranged the piles from two chairs opposite his desk onto the floor and motioned for them to sit down. Bell didn't seem to realize that they were coming.

"Nora, how good to see you. It's been too long." He kissed her benevolently on the cheek.

"You too, Alex. This is Detective Sergeant Martin Cox, of the Akron homicide detail. We sneaked into the back of the auditorium to hear your lecture."

Marty was surprised at the strength of Bell's grip, and his watery, blue eyes held a strange expression.

"Have you come to arrest me?" Bell asked with mock alarm.

"Should I, Doctor?"

"I don't think so. I've not been a naughty boy at all." They laughed. "What can I do for you?"

The man in the office was nothing like the one in the lecture hall. There, Bell had been aggressive, commanding, in charge. Here, he was shy, almost reticent. He was almost a different person.

"Marty and I are working on the serial killings of the street people. Have you heard about them?" Bell nodded assent. "The posts on the victims suggest the men may have been infected. We can't be sure about the first two. No cultures were done, but the organ damage was nearly identical to the latest case. We have cultures on him."

"What did the cultures show?"

"Nothing. All aerobic and anaerobic cultures were negative." When she saw the quizzical look on Marty's face she added, "Translated, that means, some bugs grow in air, some grow without air. Both kinds of cultures were negative. Same goes for TB, although I didn't seriously consider TB as a possibility."

"Then, you're postulating a viral etiology?"

"I have some slides." She placed a heavy, cardboard folder on the desk in front of him. "I think the white cells on this peripheral smear show viral toxicity. There's disagreement at my place, so I figured we'd get the definitive opinion from you."

"Flattery will get you anywhere, my dear. What exactly did you find in the way of organ damage?"

"This is going to sound bizarre, but I found changes that suggest a hemorrhagic fever. Their livers were necrotic in the center, the lungs were congested, and there was evidence of pulmonary edema and respiratory failure."

"Didn't the paper say that these men were shot in the head?"

"Yes, sir." Marty replied. "Each of them had a large caliber wound in the back of the head."

"I have doubts there, too" Nora said. "I looked at the brains of the first two victims this morning. There are no vital reactions. Neither brain shows any evidence of traumatic hemorrhage or swelling, only the truly impressive blast injury from the large caliber weapon."

"Ballistics tells us it's probably a forty-four Magnum pistol. The most powerful hand gun in the world," Marty added, in his best Clint Eastwood. The humor was lost on Bell.

"Why would someone shoot people who were already going to die?" Bell stopped to stoke his pipe, which had gone out. "Okay, Nora, let's have a look at your slides."

Opening the cardboard container like a book, Bell took a slide to the microscope in the corner of the office. A metal tube ran from the eyepiece to a second eyepiece two feet away like the one in Nora's office. Waving Nora to the stool next to him, Bell placed a drop of oil on the first slide, added a glass coverslip and focused the scope.

"This is what I saw, Alex." Nora moved the pointer on her eyepiece. "There, by the cursor."

"I see it." He said, moving a similar knob on his scope. "They could be viral inclusion bodies. The cell membrane is crenated."

"Crenated cells are ones that have lost their integrity and are about to die," she said to Marty without taking her eye away from the scope.

"Thanks," he replied. It pleased Marty that she remembered he was there and wouldn't understand some of what they were saying.

As Bell studied several of the slides, the silence was broken only by the moisture in the stem of his pipe that crackled as he inhaled. Nora moved over and let Marty look, but he didn't have a clue as to what he was seeing. Just more snow over Cleveland.

At last, Bell looked up. "You have a strong case, Nora. There's at least a fifty-fifty chance that these are viral changes. I only have one problem with your hypothesis. If you believe that your sidewalk citizens are dying of this virus, rather than a bullet in the brain, I'd expect to see more destruction than this. These are subtle changes. We should see cells exploding, cellular debris, ghost cells everywhere. These men didn't crash and bleed out, either."

"Crash and bleed out?" Marty asked.

That peculiar expression that Marty had noticed earlier returned to Bell's eyes. "You heard my lecture on bacteria. As terrible as they are, bacteria are not the worst."

"Unlike bacteria, who possess within themselves the genetic coding, the raw material and the cellular ability to reproduce, the virus does not. They are mindless bits of DNA or RNA, covered with a protein shell. If they're DNA, they directly force the invaded host cell to reproduce the viral DNA. If they're RNA, they contain the messenger codes to force the DNA of the host cell to make more RNA virus. The virus is a cellular serial killer that can force a cell to destroy itself."

"The virus frequently invades the white blood cells, like the HIV virus does. It takes control of the host cell and sets up a cellular sweat-shop forcing production of more virus. The infected host cell slowly consume's itself, producing the organism that is killing it. The more destructive of these culprits also attack the host immune system so the body is unable to mount a defense against the organism and has no chance of stopping this insane form of cellular suicide. HIV is the puny weakling among emerging viruses. It takes HIV eight to ten years to kill. Ebola can do the same thing in eight to ten days."

"New viruses probe man like an invading army looking for a weakness in enemy fortifications. Ebola strains, like the one I work with, are filoviruses. We didn't even know that family existed until a 1967 outbreak in Germany."

"The Bearing Works in Marberg was converted to a vaccine manufacturing plant that used kidney cells from Ugandan monkeys. Thirty-one workmen were infected and seven died for a kill ratio of one to four. To put it into perspective, yellow fever has a kill ratio of one to twenty."

"The next probe was in Zaire, when Marberg's big brother tried to wipe out the rift valley. The Ebola is a tributary of the Congo or Zaire River. In September of 1966, the infection swept through fifty-five villages with a kill ratio of nine out of ten. Hundreds die. Then, mysteriously, it left without crossing over permanently and infecting humans on a mass scale. Why? No one knows."

"A few years later, it struck Cairo. Same kill ratio, and it stopped again. Survivors suffered a low grade fever, and later, converted their skin tests to positive. The epidemic fizzled out after a few secondary cases. It is simply a matter of time until a virus crosses over and is carried around the world in six weeks.

"I'm sorry, Detective, I've digressed from your question with a mini-lecture. It's a bad habit of mine I'm afraid."

That's okay, professor. The more I know, the better off I'll be."

"Seven days after the alien organism invades, the patient develops a persistent headache. Three days, later stomach ulcers bleed. Their eyes turn red from subconjunctival hemorrhaging, and their skin will turn yellow as the virus digests liver tissue. The tissue beneath facial skin starts to liquify from the onslaught of virus producing a mask-like expression."

"Bright red blotches on the skin congeal into mature bruises, and the lungs become congested as the fluids from digested tissue cannot be cleared. Virologists call this condition extreme amplification. The patient is now a viral bomb of nuclear proportions."

"The patient is not in pain, because, in one of nature's dichotomies, they will be bleeding and clotting at the same time. The clots produce a series of merciful strokes as the brain liquifies. The strokes diminish the pain in other portions of the body."

"At this point the patient goes down or crashes and bleeds out in the parlance of the virologist. The gut lining tears loose from the muscularis and pours itself out as explosive, bloody diarrhea. Occasionally when this happens, there is an audible sound that has been described as tearing a strip of cloth from a bed sheet. That sound is the explosion of the viral bomb."

"Blood erupts from every orifice, and the patient goes into profound and irreversible shock and dies. More importantly, every person who came in contact with the blood or fluid of the victim is now a potential victim themselves. Biological Armageddon," Bell repeated.

Stunned by the grizzly details of viral death, Marty felt uncomfortably warm. Pulling at his collar he said, "Thank you Doctor. That was very graphic. Could altered immunity in the street people account for what you saw on the slide? I know I'm way out of my league here, but their diet and hygiene are deplorable. Maybe they're weaker to start with and can't fight off the infections as well."

"I suppose," Bell answered, his gaze boring into Marty "Of course we'd have to know the T-cell subsets and helper-killer ratios."

"Helpers? Killers? Sounds like what I'm used to," Marty said.

"The white cells are not a homogeneous population. There are subsets. Like the beat cop, B-lymphocytes are for generalized defense. For every B-Cell there are three specialists, like your homicide teams, robbery teams called T-cells. They handle specific malfunctions in the immune system. This group contains the immunologic swat team, the CD8 killer lymphocytes. They attack noxious agent with the intent to kill. There are a few natural killer cells here too, who attack invading organisms at random. I'm sure you've run across natural killers in your profession, Sergeant." Bell's tone was strangely challenging.

"That explanation was perfect, Doctor. Those terms I understand." Marty saw a look of defiance in Bell's eyes. Why was it there?

Nora smiled at Bell. "I was looking for encouragement before I started subset testing."

Bell fiddled with his pipe again and said, "Consider yourself encouraged."

"One more thing, Alex. I can't fit all these findings into any known viral syndrome," Nora said. "It has some of the changes you'd expect with the tropical hemorrhagics, but I wasn't aware that severe, pulmonary changes were associated with them."

"That's not totally correct," Bell replied. "The pulmonary component fits either the Marberg or the Cardinal subset of the Ebola. Cardinal has airborne transmission and causes pneumonia, however the respiratory changes you have look more like Hanta. Ebola *can* produce severe lung pathology, but the patients don't live long enough for it to matter. Maybe you've come up with the Akron Virus."

"I certainly hope not," Nora said.

"I read about the Hanta virus, but what's Cardinal?" Marty asked. "Do you call it Cardinal because it's airborne."

"This has nothing to do with birds, Detective," Bell chuckled. Viruses are named for where they are first recognized, such as Ebola or Marberg, or from their first victim. The Cardinal subset was isolated from a fatal case of Ebola in a Danish boy named Peter Cardinal who lived near Lake Victoria. He came in with pneumonia and was on a respirator within twenty-four hours."

"Where do these viruses come from, Dr. Bell? Why haven't we seen them before?" Marty asked.

"Contagious infections have always been with us, Sergeant. We just gave them different names. Smallpox was one of the first. In the 1700's, it all but wiped out some Native American tribes. What smallpox didn't do, measles nearly did when it was dumped into the same population who lacked immunity. The pandemic of 1918-19, that was just a new strain of influenza, killed twenty million people world wide.

"Infections were local in the beginning because people didn't travel far from home. It took effort to get smallpox to the Indians. By 1918, people were sailing all over the world, carrying killer infections with them. The influenza pandemic significantly reduced the world's population at the time. Imagine what something as lethal as Ebola could do."

"Gradually, we developed vaccines to influenza as well as things like rabies and polio. Then, we developed faster means of transportation, and started to violate the isolated rain forests and unexplored areas of the world."

"The inhabitants of the rain forest have been there long enough to develop natural immunity to the viruses in their environment. By clearing the jungle, burning millions of acres of timber, uprooting native people and forcing migration to new regions viruses spread. That's without considering the mutational effects on viruses that pesticides and defoliants may have produced."

"There's a very good chance that the Human Immunodeficiency Virus that causes AIDS comes from our primate cousin the Green Monkey. The monkeys have a lethal virus that is only a couple of amino acids different from the human variety. Some researchers believe that mutational forces rearranged the gene and allowed permanent crossover."

"The filovirus I'm studying has probably been around for a long time, but we only found it in the 1967 German outbreak."

"Why doesn't everybody who was exposed get sick?" Marty asked.

"Natural immunity. Take tuberculosis for example. If you expose a given number of people to active TB germs, a given percentage of them would overcome the infection without medicines. These people are now immune through their natural reaction to the germ. We only know that they were infected if we check antibody levels in their blood. That's what a TB skin test does. Attenuated bacteria is injected under the skin, and if the patient is immune, a red lump develops as the body fights the infection."

"Other people exposed to the same dose of bacteria will get clinical TB in the lungs, kidneys, bones. Some of these survive and have immunity against future attacks. Others die. If our imaginary population lived in an isolated rain forest with TB in the environment, and never came into contact with anyone else, in a few generations the group as a whole would be highly resistant to their local brand of TB. We presume that's how the natives coexist with the filovirus."

"How dangerous is the one you're working with, Dr. Bell?"

"The worst recorded filoviral outbreaks occurred almost simultaneously in Zaire and the Sudan in 1976. Those were the ones I mentioned in the lecture this morning. Two subtypes of Ebola were isolated from five hundred-fifty cases, four hundred-thirty died. Viruses of that magnitude would be too dangerous to handle here.

I use Simian Hemorrhagic Fever virus that comes from the Philippine Maccac Monkey. It's extremely lethal to the monkeys, but doesn't infect man. I'd need a level-four containment unit to handle human Ebola, and level-two is about all I can muster here. The only scare with my virus occurred in Rustin, Virginia in 1989 when some animal handlers sero-converted. Except for a low grade fever, they suffered no ill effects."

"Exactly what are you doing with the viruses, Alex?" Nora asked.

"Ebola is an RNA virus with a filamentous envelope. It's a simple virus with only seven proteins. We know a fair amount about three of them and little to nothing about the other four. The SHF virus is very similar and shares those four mystery proteins. I'm sequencing the protein strand amino acids in an attempt to assess their function."

Turning to Marty he said, "All genetic material is a series of amino acid building blocks hooked together by chemical bonds. A series of these makes a protein. Proteins combine to make genetic material. Sequencing means we are identifying each block to determine exactly which acid they are and what order they're in. Once that's accomplished, I'll start lopping off the amino acids on the ends, deleting or changing their sequencing along the chain, do whatever I can to find out what makes it pathogenic and where the messages that trigger its reproduction originate."

"For a dumb gum-shoe like me, that sounds like science fiction."

Bell chuckled as he refilled the bowl of his pipe with dark, shag tobacco. "In science fiction, things are exciting, and you have space-age gadgets to do the work. I'd give my grant money for one of McCoy's tri-corders."

"Another Trekkie?" Marty asked with surprise.

"I've always been fascinated by the advanced thinking that went into those scripts. It's an interest I share with Nora. "In my world, there are no tri-corders or transporters . . . just a lot of tedious trial-and-error with a thousand failures for every success. It's not glamorous at all, Sergeant."

"Nora, if you will keep me up-to-date on what you find, I'll be glad to help you in any way I can. Has the body of the latest victim been embalmed yet?"

"Unfortunately, it has. He was already ripe when they found him."

"Too bad. If fresh tissue becomes available, please call me."

"That's one call I hope we never make, Professor," Marty interjected. "But, if this madman follows the typical pattern of the serial killer, there will be more murders, unless I stop him."

"You sound very determined, Mr. Cox. What if he's not a madman? Would that make him harder to catch?"

"Could any sane man do what he's done?" asked Marty.

Bell didn't answer. He stared at Marty for a few seconds, then said to Nora, "If you have a few milliliters of blood to spare, I'll do some testing for you; see what I can find."

"I have some frozen plasma. When I got suspicious, I removed all the blood that I could. I even collected some blood clots and froze everything. I'll send some over with the courier this afternoon."

"Now, if you'll excuse me, I have to get a sample ready for this afternoon's run in the lab." Bell stood.

Extending his hand to Bell, Marty stood. "Thank you, Doctor. It's a relief knowing that we have an expert like you on our side."

"I'm not sure how much help I'll be, but I'll do my best," Bell said, creating a fresh cloud of smoke as he talked.

Outside, Nora ran a hand through her hair and shook her head. Taking a deep breath of the clean air she exclaimed, "Eech, I hate that. Everything reeks of smoke. If you spent much time with Alex, you'd get lung cancer for sure. I don't know how his research assistants handle it.

"It is a disgusting habit, isn't it. What's level-three containment?"

"There are four levels. Level-one is a sterile room. Level-two is bounded by ultraviolet light banks. The U-V light disrupts the genetic material of the virus and sterilizes it. These require negative pressure as well. When you open a door into level-two, the air sucks in to minimize losing virus to the outside. AIDS is handled in level two. In level-three, there's all of that, plus you use gowns and gloves and full operating room type sterility. Level-four requires an airlock, space suits . . . the whole nine yards. We don't need . . . or want . . . a level four-unit here. The whole world only needs two or three level-four units."

Stopping suddenly, Nora spun him around by the arm to face her."Wait a minute. What do you mean disgusting habit? From a Camel smoker, isn't that the pot calling the kettle black?"

"I don't smoke anymore."

"Since when?"

"This morning. Smoked my last one. Not buying anymore."

"What brought this on?"

Marty shrugged and stuffed his hands into his pockets. "You did of course. The other night at Tangiers, I realized you were an ex- smoker. If I smoke, you'll want to smoke. It isn't good for either one of us, and since I plan on spending the rest of my life with you, I thought I should quit, so you won't be tempted to smoke either."

Nora hugged him, hooked her arm in his, and they turned toward the parking lot. Marty felt uneasy, as if he were being watched. Looking back over his shoulder toward the research building, Marty thought he saw the curtain in Bell's office window move.

CHAPTER 12

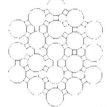

arty drove Nora back to her office so she could pack the blood samples for shipment to Bell and keep an appointment that she hadn't been able to reschedule. It would mean another trip to the medical center later, but Marty didn't mind. Nora's sample case had seen better days, and she had to wrestle the sticky catch at the end of the frayed strap into place. Straining down on the lid, Nora seated the catch with a grunt of satisfaction.

"Got to get me a new one," she said after she had kissed him.

"Don't do that. That would be a great Christmas present."

"I'll give you better ideas than that, buster. I can deduct the case if the office buys it. Let's see if the mad Frenchman is ready for us yet." Tapping in Jacque St. Jean's number, Nora switched on the speaker phone so Marty could hear the conversation.

"'Ello, Electron Microscopy, St. Jean speaking," answered a jaunty baritone voice, heavily accented in French.

"Afternoon, Jacque, it's Nora."

"Nora, darling. I 'ave just finished with your samples. Please come. It is exciting, cheri."

"I'm leaving now." Hanging up the phone, Nora said, "There's something in the tone of Jacque's voice that bothers me," she said. "Beneath the usual veneer of Jacque's joviality, I hear something else. Let's go see what it is."

When they arrived at the medical center and entered the main building, Nora said, "Let's walk," and started toward the stairwell.

Starting up the stairs, she continued, "I told you the school is beefing up its research. Jacque is one of the best electron microscopists in the world and has contributed more to the world's literature than any three men in his field."

The red light above his office door was blinking. "In most labs, a blinking light means there's an examination in process. In Jacque's case, it means he forgot to turn off the light again. When he gets excited about something, Jacque forgets about little things, like food, sleep, or turning off the signal light," Nora said rapping sharply on the metal door.

"Come in, cheri."

A weak shaft of red from a darkroom safe light illuminated the room. A tower-shaped electron microscope sat among the shadows to their right. A work bench occupied the wall opposite the door. It was littered with materials used for sample preparation, and spanned the space between the electron microscope and an imaging control panel that reminded Marty of the bridge of the Starship Enterprise. Multi-colored displays blinked in irregular fashion creating a surrealistic atmosphere in the blood-red back lighting. Banks of dials and switches illuminated with glowing red and green lights, surrounded the main console.

Hunched before the screen sat a portly man with square frame glasses. His hair was in a disheveled state, and his glasses were slipping down his sweaty nose. When the glasses were one millimeter from plunging off the end of his Roman beak, he unerringly sent them back to the bridge of his nose with the sweep of a manicured hand.

Leaping to his feet, Jacque kissed Nora on each cheek. When he realized Marty was there, a scowl darkened his face. The expression on his face said he was not happy to see Marty. "I was unaware you would be bringing a guest," he said sternly.

"Jacque, I want you to meet Sergeant Martin Cox of the Akron Police Department. Marty is no guest. He's in charge of the investigation and knows everything about the autopsy reports, including the possibility of viral infection. He's one of the good guys."

Jacque's expression softened immediately, and he shook Marty's hand. Excitement returned to his eyes, and he said with animation, "Nora, you 'ave really got something this time. At least in two of the three samples you sent me. I'm preparing the last sample now. Let's fix it before we start."

Scurrying to the bench, Jacque turned off the high speed centrifuge. It slowed with the hushed whisper of well-oiled metal against metal as the computerized breaking system kicked in. Double checking to be certain the tub had stopped spinning, Jacque opened the circular door in the top of the machine. Removing a test tube containing a minute button of amorphous material covered by a pale liquid, Jacque decanted the liquid with an automatic micro-pipette.

"These are the liver cells from the unfortunate man of this morning. I 'ave the second one in the homogenizer. It will not be ready until tomorrow. I hope that will be all right."

Jacque located a tube of resin from the back of the cluttered work bench. Scrounging among the debris he produced a balsa wood stick the size of a kitchen match. Placing a drop of the resin on the wood, he poured the button of material from the bottom of the tube into the tacky plastic. With a deft swirl of his wrist, the ball of material was firmly trapped in the quickly hardening plastic. Adding a second drop of resin, Jacque stuck the balsawood into a piece of clay. "Perfect," he said. It came out, pear-fect.

"Bravo," Nora said, clapping, as he bowed gracefully from the waist. Marty joined in the applause.

"Please," he said, with staged humility. "It has been a curse upon the men in my family for seven generations." They all laughed.

"We'll let that cure while we go on. I 'ave much to show you from the earlier cases." Expressive, brown eyes danced behind the glasses as he guided them back to the bridge of the Enterprise and plunked Nora down in Mr. Sulu's chair. Pulling another chair from the corner of the room, he positioned it to Nora's left. Jacque indicated that Marty should sit there, in Chekov's chair. Or was it the other way around?

"These are from the liver of the first unfortunate," St. Jean explained. Jacque flipped switches and turned knobs.

The central monitor glowed with a bluish tint as an enlarged cluster of five cells took shape on the screen. They were arranged in a neat, orderly line, disrupted only by smudges of processing artifact.

With a control element that reminded Marty of a joy stick used to play computer games, Jacque manipulated a single cell image to the center of the screen and zoomed in on it like a fighter pilot on a strafing run. He turned another switch, another dial, and the details of their cellular structure began to enhance. "Here they come," Jacque said with the exuberance of a child who had just spied the first element of a circus parade.

Nora's jaw went slack, and she brought a hand to her open mouth. The disorganized cells were literally blown apart. Snake-like virus spilled in clumps from the shattered cell walls like a thousand diminutive Medusa heads. Jacque increased the power and unmistakable rope-like tangles of filovirus slithered onto the screen.

"Oh, my God!" Nora hissed, clamping the hand tighter over her mouth as though she could change the reality of what she said by physically restraining the words.

Shifting the view to an adjacent cell, Jacque exclaimed, "That's not all." All the humor in his voice was replaced by anxiety.

The cell on the screen was still intact, but its walls bulged out at irregular intervals like an overloaded grocery bag. Imminent rupture seemed apparent. The source of the internal pressure was readily visible. Inside the cell were neatly stacked piles of crystalline-coated packets that reminded Marty of transparent bricks.

"Inclusion bodies," Jacque said grimly.

"What's that mean?" Marty asked.

"As the virus replicated inside the liver cells, the production of the virus was so rapid that the only way to store the finished threads was to compress them into tight, lethal tangles and stack them on top of each other. These transparent rectangles are blocks of pure virus. The runaway production of virus fills the cell until it can't hold any more. The internal pressure splits the cell open, and the deadly cargo is dumped into the blood stream. Each virus looks for a new cellular host, and the process begins again," Jacque explained.

"Extreme amplification," Nora said louder than she intended. "That's the stage we are seeing. A nuclear bomb ready to go off. Seth Mancuso was ready to crash and go down with a filovirus infection."

"One man, with an infection like this, closed the Nairobi Hospital for six weeks. Can you imagine the disaster if he came into one of our local emergency rooms? The epidemic would make Zaire look like a minor outbreak."

Jacque was silent for a moment, then said, "You realize, cheri, that we 'ave been exposed to it, too." His voice was calm, matter of fact, yet the words echoed from the walls of the cramped chamber like a cheerleader's voice in an empty gymnasium.

"I guess we have," she answered grimly. "Marty was there for the autopsy. I'm sorry, Jacque. I shouldn't have exposed you until I knew what I was dealing with.

"It's alright, cheri. I would have done it, even if I had known. Besides, the tissue was fixed when you brought it to me. I'm in less jeopardy than the two of you. I don't suppose you could get your hands on some antibody could you? We could do our own immuno-florescence."

"I don't have any. That stuff's as precious as gold. But, I know someone who might have some. At least he'll know how to get it without raising too many eyebrows. If we go asking for antibody, people are going to want to know why, and I'm not ready to tell them yet."

"If it's Zaire, aren't we taking a terrible risk?" Jacque asked.

"I don't think so, but I don't know. The material from these autopsies has been around the labs for weeks, and none of the lab folks are sick. My assistant cut his finger with a contaminated knife blade, and he's okay."

"Do we call Atlanta?" Jacque asked.

"Not yet. I don't want C.D.C. here too soon. If the first two victims had the disease, and they were posted months ago, why aren't more people sick? We should be in the middle of a plague. For now, let's isolate the samples and sit tight."

Jacque's effervescent grin returned. "I guess it doesn't matter for us now. As we say in my country, 'E.Coli happens'. I won't sleep until next week. If we're healthy then, the incubation will be over."

"In my country we say, 'Shit happens', and I won't sleep either," Marty said.

Returning to Nora's office, she dialed Bell's number and clicked on the speaker phone. After a dozen rings, she was ready to hang up when a breathless voice answered. "Doctor Bell's office. Anton Polovski, speaking." The accent was middle European. "How may I help you?"

Remembering the men in the projection room, Marty wondered if this was the tall one or the overweight one? From the level of wheezing Marty voted for bulk.

"This is Doctor Nora Daniels. May I speak with Doctor Bell?"

"I'm sorry, Doctor. He's been in the containment facility all day. I can leave a message, and he'll call you back . . . if he sees it. Doctor Bell doesn't always check his messages."

"How long do you expect him to be in containment?"

"Anywhere from five minutes till next Tuesday. He gets involved."

"Can you call into the facility? I need to speak to him."

"I'm ready to defend my dissertation. I'm not about to lose my job now. We don't call into containment."

So, Bell was a tyrant, thought Marty.

"Then, I'd like to leave him a message, please. Tell him that later this afternoon, I'll be bringing some samples over that I told him about."

"Of course, Doctor Daniels. Will there be anything else?"

"No, thank you."

Nora hung up and flipped through the Roladex. "One of these days I'm going to get an electronic directory. My staff gives me a hard time about my card system, but I refuse to give in."

"I'm worried about Clarence. That call, that we didn't answer last night was from Clarence. I checked with him first thing this morning, and he said he was okay. I'm going to call him back. That cut on his finger could be as deadly as if he had slit his own throat."

He answered on the second ring. "Clarence Mackey speaking."

"Hello, big guy, it's Doctor Nora again. How are you feeling?"

When he realized who was calling, his voice grew excited. The speaker phone added a tinny quality to his voice that made it sound comic. "Clarence is just fine, Doctor Nora. It was only a teeny cut."

"Do you have any fever? Do you feel hot or sweaty?"

"No."

"How about a headache or pains in the joints?"

"No, nothin' like that. All gone, Doctor Nora."

"Do you have . . . loose bowels, going more than usual?"

Clarence had a crush on Nora, and Marty could hear the poor man blush at the mention of anything as personal as a bowel movement. "No," he muttered, embarrassed. To change the subject he added, "Clarence ain't had nothin' like that. No pukin', nothin'. Can Clarence come back to work now? Clarence ain't sick no more, honest, Doctor Nora."

"I miss you, Clarence and I need your help. It's not the same when you're not there. Get a good night's rest. See you tomorrow."

The enthusiasm in his voice was unmistakable. "Thank you, Dr. Nora. Thank you. Clarence will be there first thing."

Pushing her chair back from the desk, Nora took a deep breath and sighed as if the weight of the world had been transferred from Atlas' shoulders to hers.

"Marty, are we making a cataclysmic mistake?," she asked. "These men were ready to crash. What if a virus *has* broken through into the derelicts? Three cases are more than coincidence. Is this damn virus spreading in my blood stream, or Jacque's, or yours? Does it matter if I wait another few hours before I call in the cavalry? Is there enough cavalry out there for all these Indians?"

When Marty held out his arms to her, she launched herself across the room and flew into them, hugging him with such ferocity that it made him wince. She covered his face with kisses.

"I spent half the night asking myself the same questions, and I'm nowhere closer to an answer now than I was yesterday. A general panic won't change the situation. Until people start to get sick, they wouldn't believe us anyhow. Let's sit tight and see what happens. Did you get a chance to go over the material in the envelope?" Marty asked.

"No, but I'll do it later. "What time is your plane?" she asked.

"Akron-Canton to Chicago, then to the bay area. I should get there about seven-thirty Pacific time."

"Marty, be careful. Are you going to the hospital?"

"If I can. Patrick says the place is locked tighter than Fort Knox on Sunday. I don't know how much good it will do."

"I'm afraid for you. I'm afraid for myself. I just found you, and I don't want anything to happen to you . . . to us."

Tilting her face to his, he kissed her gently. "I'm afraid too, Nora, but we have to work through this. If it's contagious, we've been exposed. Nothing we can do about that, now. All we can do is keep looking for answers." Irrational as it was, he felt nothing could harm her if he was there. "I'll miss you."

"I'll miss you, too," she responded, and kissed his forehead.

"You know, Marty, this has been a monumental few days. I've been dumped into the middle of a murder mystery. I've gotten to know you, and I may be falling in love with you. And, I may be witnessing the birth of a plague that could wipe out half of civilization. Aside from that, it's been an average few days. I'd say that's a fair load to ask a girl to handle."

"What's this girl stuff. Thought you were a macho feminist?"

"I don't feel like roaring right now."

"I agree. It's been a hell of a few days. I've been through it all too, and the only important part was the falling in love business." He kissed her lightly on the nose. You don't ever have to do anything alone again. Neither do I. Bring on your wimpy, old plague. Together, we can handle anything," Marty added.

Passion exploded between them. Breathing heavily, Nora pushed him back. "Hurry back, Marty," she said.

CHAPTER 13

arty boarded the plane with Spellman and his wife, Shelia, an unattractive, anorexic woman who looked old enough to be Spellman's mother. Her features were too sharp, and everywhere curves were required she sported angles. Shelia weaved unsteadily, as if she had been drinking.

When he had guided Shelia into her seat in the first class section, Spellman opened his briefcase and handed Marty a folder. "This is a report that Andrew Carson sent about Rosewood's death. Read it before we get there." It was a command, not a request.

Taking the folder, Marty made his way back to the coach section. Settling into the window seat, he loosened his tie. After the smooth take-off, he opened the thick folder and began to read.

A color photograph of Hayden Rosewood, a handsome man who looked younger than his sixty years, was clipped to the top page. The spotless white tennis clothes he wore accentuated his deep California tan. A white headband held back thick, sandy hair that was graying at the temples.

Clipped to the second page was a photo of Joe Worthy, a squat, beefy man with the florid face of someone with chronic hypertension. At five-feet-ten, he was at least thirty-five pounds overweight, with most of it sequestered about his midsection like a spare tire. An unkempt, graying beard, thick glasses, and thinning hair gave him a grandfatherly appearance.

The narrative phrase under this picture read, While Rosewood is a natural and glides to the ball, Worthy leaps at it like a cat going for a mouse. The result is the same, both get to the ball. While Rosewood makes the game look easy, Worthy makes it look hard. When Worthy misses a shot, the sportsmanship and good nature that Rosewood displays is not shown by Joe Worthy, who is a fierce competitor who hates to lose.

I wonder who did these little character sketches? Marty thought. *They are certainly revealing.*

On the next page, was a brochure advertising the Southern California Senior Men's Open Tennis Tournament. A picture of the Coronado Bridge and the Hotel Del Coronado graced the cover.

Most of the towns in Southern California had grown. There were more shops, more people, more traffic. One constant from bygone days was the Hotel Del Coronado. Marty and Janet had gone there for a vacation the year after they were married, and he remembered it with fondness. The red turrets of the sprawling Victorian building reached skyward like those of a baronial castle. Its white wooden sides fought a perpetual battle with the ravages of salt air and pollution, and it was a toss-up as to whether the painters or the elements were winning.

The next page contained a detailed account of the weekend, supplied mostly by Joe Worthy. Rosewood and Worthy easily won their first match on Saturday morning. They had a stiffer challenge in the afternoon, but won the tie-breaker and the match.

Later, they met on the patio and had drinks. Rosewood drank his usual vodka and tonic with a twist of lemon, while Worthy had Scotch. They had eaten dinner at the hotel, and both of them had had the same things to eat, except for desert. Worthy had apple pie, while Rosewood had a brandy. After cigars and a second brandy on the patio, Rosewood complained of a slight headache and went to his room.

About midnight, the hotel operator had awakened Worthy and called him to Rosewood's room.

Rosewood was burning up with fever, and Worthy rang for the house physician. Rosewood possessed an inherent fear of doctors. He hated needles; he despised the annual physical required by the partnership, and felt doctors might use the opportunity to get even with him for making their lives miserable.

Shortly before the doctor had arrived, Rosewood had begun to vomit blood-tinged material. The doctor diagnosed acute viral gastroenteritis, and he gave Rosewood an injection to stop the vomiting and ice bags to bring down the fever. When the fever had broken an hour later, the physician promised to return in the morning.

The next morning, Rosewood was worse. Diarrhea had joined the vomiting, and the whites of his eyes were tinged with yellow. The house physician had insisted that Rosewood be hospitalized, but he refused, demanding instead to be flown to San Francisco. The house physician had arranged the transfer.

Rosewood began to complain of joint pain, and by the time the paramedics had arrived, he was having difficulty breathing. Intravenous fluids were started, antibiotics administered, and the paramedics brought Rosewood out the door on the lower level and drove him to the waiting airplane.

On the way to the airport, Rosewood had suffered a respiratory arrest when he vomited a significant amount of blood. An endotrachial tube was inserted, and the doctor had ridden the plane with them to San Francisco.

By the time they had reached the hospital, Rosewood was in a coma and the jaundice had progressed. Later that afternoon, he had begun to hemorrhage from his nose and ears, and his joints had began to swell. Around midnight, he yanked out the endotrachial tube. His wife, Shirley, had rung for help and tried to calm him down. Screaming wildly about demons and hemorrhaging from every orifice, Rosewood had punched his wife in the face and vomited pure blood all over her. By the time the attendants arrived, Rosewood was dead.

The last three pages were character sketches of the other partners in the firm, Everett Goldman, Andrew Carson and Tom Gordon.

By the time he had finished reading the report, Marty was perspiring heavily, and his hands were shaking. Rosewood's death sounded exactly like Bell's description of a viral death. But, if it was one of the deadly organisms Bell had described, why was nobody else infected? As he contemplated the ramifications of his thoughts, the flight attendant arrived with the drink cart, and Marty ordered a double Scotch.

A nap after dinner helped Marty feel refreshed as the plane made its final approach to the San Francisco International Airport. Spellman waited for him, and they left the plane together.

A tall, immaculately dressed man stood waiting near the gate. From the description in the folder, that would be Andrew Carson, one of the a younger partners The ex-basketball star was six-feet-nine, and his rigid posture and broad shoulders made him seem even taller. A shorter, black man stood next to him.

Hugging Shelia, Carson firmly shook Aaron's hand and led the way toward the baggage claim area. Spellman introduced Marty to Carson. As they shook hands, Carson's huge hand swallowed Marty's.

"Folks, I'd like you to meet one of our new law clerks, Eshan Roberts. Eshan, this is Aaron and Shelia Spellman and Detective Martin Cox." The man's muscular arms and chest were impressive. His tailored suit looked as if it had been sculpted.

"Pleased to meet you," Roberts said with a quick, insecure smile. When Spellman shook the black man's hand, the expression on his face betrayed the judge's bigotry. Did Spellman just hate blacks, or was he an equal opportunity bigot and hated all minorities equally.

"Eshan was an All-American tailback at Penn. If he hadn't blown out a knee his senior year, we might have lost him to the Philadelphia Eagles. Give Eshan your claim checks and describe your bags. He'll pick them up and meet us at the limo stand," Carson said.

"There are five matching pieces of Dunhill black leather. Two garment bags, two medium pullmans and a make-up case," Shelia said.

"I just have this," Marty said, pointing to the tan leather bag he was carrying. Roberts nodded, took the tickets and hurried ahead of them, following the baggage claim arrows down the escalator.

"Nice to see you have a boy to handle the chores," Spellman said in his most condescending tone.

Carson frowned his disapproval. "Be careful how you use that term out here, Aaron. Not only might Eshan sue for discrimination, he might beat the hell out of you for good measure; works out regularly. He's a karate black-belt and bench presses four hundred pounds. While you're here, Eshan will be your bodyguard."

"Bodyguard," Shelia whined. "Why do we need a bodyguard? What's wrong? Is there something you haven't told me, Aaron? Are we in danger? Aaron . . . Aaron."

"God damn it, Shelia, will you shut up. There's no need for hysterics," Spellman replied disgustedly. Shelia dropped her lower lip in an angry pout.

"Until we find out about the threats," Carson interjected, "find out what the notes mean, and who sent them, we've agreed not to take any chances. Eshan *is* a law clerk with us. Most of the other bodyguards are professionals. If the fact that Eshan is black bothers you, we can get you one of the pros. Do you feel as strongly about Italians? I think a couple of the new security guards use to work for the mob." It was Carson's turn to let his sarcasm show.

"This is crazy," Aaron growled. "I'll be damned if a spook in a five-hundred dollar suit is going to baby sit me! That goes for some over-sized dago as well. I can take care of myself. Besides, I have my own bodyguard, Detective Cox." Spellman curled his lip into a sneer, and Marty felt the sting of the condescension in his voice.

"Keep your voice down," Carson growled, shrugging his shoulders in frustration. "Your choice. I was told to make the offer. My conscience is clear." They walked out of the terminal to the limo waiting at the curb in silence.

Driving across the Golden Gate Bridge into Marin County, they turned up the winding drive to the Rosewood estate in the hills overlooking Sausalito. The modern, concrete and glass edifice sprawled across the side of the mountain near the entrance to a small canyon and providing a breath-taking view of San Francisco Bay from the two decks that wrapped across the front of the house.

Red-eyed and dressed in black, Shirley Rosewood greeted them at the door. When she saw Shelia, she burst into tears. The two embraced, and Shelia expressed her condolences. They introduced her to Marty, and she showed them to their rooms.

"Please join us on the deck after you've had an opportunity to freshen up," Shirley Rosewood said.

Marty called the station and left Rosewood's phone number. When he called Riley's number, he got an answering machine and left a message that he would call back after the memorial service tomorrow.

When Marty came out onto the deck, Everett Goldman was the easiest to identify, as he marched majestically back and forth along the patio rail. The man looked like Buddy Ebson, the actor, who had played the Jed Clampett character on *The Beverly Hillbillies* T.V. show. According to the character sketch, Goldman's detractors called him Jed behind his back. He was a shade over six-feet-two with an aristocratic mane of silver hair, a slouching gate and easy-going manner that probably caused opponents to underestimate his strength and aggressiveness.

Greeting Marty in a mellow baritone, Goldman looked at him through blue eyes that were as cold as a winter sky. Currently between wife number four and five, he was alone. Or was it five and six? Marty couldn't remember from the report.

Andrew Carson and a woman who was likely his wife, were talking with another couple who had to be the Gordons. Andrew Carson didn't fit his tall, plain wife, Ann Marie. With her gaunt, stark features and no make up, she reminded Marty of the woman from the painting, American Gothic. Plain, circular glasses completed the likeness.

At five-feet-five, Tom Gordon was thin and wiry, and seemed only half Carson's size. Balding, with a weak chin, Gordon reminded Marty of a turtle. Thick glasses magnified his eyes.

In contrast to Tom Gordon's homeliness, his wife, Denise, was a knockout. Pert, vivacious and busty, she was an outrageous flirt, and wasted no time going to work on Spellman when he came onto the deck.

Joe Worthy arrived as darkness was descending. And, Marty thought that the man looked sallow. If this was a viral illness, why hadn't he developed any symptoms?

Marty turned to look at the extraordinary view from the deck rail. The sun, now a brilliant orange ball in the Western sky, smudged the horizon with crimson and purple and pink as it plummeted behind the edge of the mountainside. The twilight crept down the canyon like a magenta stream of water followed by a rapidly developing darkness.

Movement from the shadows at the end of the hedges caught his eye. It was hard to see in the wanning light, but he could make out two figures. Marty's pulse quickened, and his mouth went dry. As the security lights came on, flooding the yard in light as bright as day, Marty reached for his weapon, then remembered it wasn't there. Two men stood by the hedge talking nonchalantly, undisturbed by the lights. One of them was Eshan Roberts. The other was a hulking brute that had to be one of the professional bodyguards. Roberts waved to the group on the deck, and Goldman waved back.

A fog horn sounded in the distance. Looking in the direction of the sound, Marty could see the edge of the Golden Gate Bridge that was enveloped in an impenetrable fog that surrounded the rust colored columns like a cocoon.

Escorting Marty around the deck, Spellman introduced him to everyone. Denise Gordon looked at him as if he were a raw piece of meat and it made him feel uncomfortable.

"Telephone for Mr. Goldman," said a servant with a British accent who appeared at the door.

Denise Gordon was in the process of working on Marty when a pale, and obviously shaken, Goldman came out onto the deck. Trying to keep his voice calm, Goldman said, "Would everyone come inside the house, please?" When no one moved, he shouted, "Get inside now!"

Inside, Goldman held up his hand for quiet. "I don't want to unduly alarm anyone, but I just had a phone call from a man who said that he was glad to see us all together, and that he was glad Aaron made it out for the funeral. He also said that we made wonderful targets out on the deck."

A chorus of questions erupted from the group. Marty pulled Andrew Carson aside. "Get to your security people. Whoever it was has to be in site of the house. Leave Roberts here with me, and send the rest of them out to look for him." Carson nodded and reached for the phone.

Marty met Carson at the door, and they secured the house before taking station at the two major entrances.

After a tense hour, the security team returned empty-handed. Shirley Rosewood insisted that everyone stay together for security purposes, and they all agreed.

When the others were finally able to get to bed, Marty and Roberts double checked the house, and made certain that the external security men were in position. Marty decided to sleep on the couch in the living room that faced the doors to the deck, surrendering his room to the Carson's who had previously planned to go home. The perimeter lights were left on outside.

Unlacing his shoes, Marty sensed a figure in the doorway. It was Spellman. "Detective Cox, I've just talked to your supervisor. You are to provide Mrs. Spellman and me with personal security until we are back in Akron."

"That's fine, Your Honor. I only need a few hours to check with Sergeant Riley tomorrow," Marty said, marvelling at Spellman's gall, calling the chief in the middle of the night in Akron.

Spellman's voice took on an aggressive tone. "I don't care what kind of business you think you had, you are to *stay with us.* Is that understood?"

"Sure," Marty grumbled as Spellman stomped back to the bedroom.

The memorial service attracted a who's who of the San Francisco legal community, including Mayor Clara Johnstone, who had been a successful prosecuting attorney. Marty watched from the rear of the chapel as Goldman delivered a stirring eulogy amid a bank of cameras.

At the end of the remarks, Goldman's voice cracked, and tears formed in the corners of his eyes. At first, Marty was impressed with Goldman's sincerity, then silently applauded the man's theatrics. As Goldman's eyes swept his audience, the ice blue gaze held no compassion. It was all an act.

A shaken, but effective, Shirley Rosewood thanked everyone for their kindness and announced a memorial law scholarship in her husband's name at his alma matter, Stanford, funded by the firm. She thanked everyone for coming and invited them to the brunch at the Spring Hill Country Club.

Marty mingled with the group of reporters who were standing at the side of the aisle when Worthy came up to him. "Anything suspicious?" he asked.

"Not that I can see," Marty answered.

Carson came over to them and touched Worthy on the shoulder. "The final autopsy reports will be ready shortly after noon. I've reserved the smoking room. We'll can go over it as soon as I have it." Carson nodded to Marty, turned and hurried from the church.

The Country Club was crowded, and Marty joined the hired security force working the crowd. A waiter approached him and offered him a glass of champagne. There was something familiar about the waiter, but Marty couldn't quite place it. The tag on the man's jacket said his name was Jose, and Marty made a mental note of that.

Half-an-hour later, Marty saw Carson wave to him as the partners moved toward the smoking room. When they were all seated, Carson said, "I have finally tracked down the quotation from Shakespeare on the notes that we received. It's from Henry VI. The full quote is, 'First thing we do, let's kill all the lawyers.' That's the end of the good news. The bad news is, each of the letters in the message were cut from different newspapers or magazines. Nothing traceable. The only prints on them were our office staff's and the postal workers'. That's a dead end."

"Do any of you have any idea who might have written them? Think hard. No matter how far-fetched it seems, we need to give the investigators somewhere to start," Goldman interjected.

"We all have enemies," Worthy said. "You can't do what we do and not make them. I'm sure a lot of the doctors Rosewood took to the cleaners are happy he's dead. I have a couple of lifers, from my days with the prosecutors office, who swore the usual vendetta. One of them was recently stabbed in the heart with a homemade knife, and the other is dying of tuberculosis. The three of us have discussed it among ourselves. That's the only kind of thing we can think of. What about the two of you?"

Goldman said, "I have a lot of hostile physicians I've beaten in court over the years. One poor bastard threw himself off the roof of the hospital after he lost the case."

"Most doctors have a ton of insurance. Hospitals force them to carry it. That's why I sit on the boards of two hospitals." The others laughed nervously. "It's no skin off their noses. Their insurance premiums go up. They pass the premiums on to the patients, so I don't see any of them as real threats."

"Likewise," Spellman said. "I'm not willing to take this thing that seriously. I think these notes are a bad practical joke, and that Rosewood's death was a coincidence."

"I haven't been on the bench long enough to make any new enemies," Aaron added. "Like Ev, most of my detractors are disappointed doctors. I worked on the jumper's case with Ev, but he was lead attorney. Besides, if this had anything to do with my work in Ohio, it makes no sense that all of you would be threatened, or that the note would be sent to me here."

"The autopsy results are on the table in front of you." Carson said. Take a few minutes to scan them, and we'll go over them."

After they had time to digest the documents, Gordon said in a voice that sounded like fingernails on a blackboard, "The autopsy says Hayden died of an infection. The initial tox screen doesn't show any evidence of drugs or poisons. At least none they usually look for."

"For obvious reasons, I'd like to know what the infection is and the degree of contagion. I spent the weekend with him when he was the sickest. Do they have any ideas how infectious it is?" asked Worthy, a quiver of uneasiness in his voice.

"If you're worried, what about Shirley?" Goldman's displeasure at Worthy's weakness was obvious in his tone of voice. "That last night in the hospital, Rosewood vomited blood all over her. If his blood was infected, she'd be polluted with whatever it was."

"The bacterial cultures have incubated for a couple of days, and they're all negative. They don't know what kind of infection it is."

"I guess there's nothing to do but wait," Goldman said . How long till they're finished with all the tests?"

"Because of the possibility of infection, they're going to rush it. We should have a detailed report in a week to ten days. Are you feeling okay, Joe?" asked Carson. "You look a little peaked."

"Yeah. I have a headache from all the wine I drank with you boys last night, but I expected that. Red wine does that to me these days, but I still can't resist a good Bordeaux." The tone of his voice told Marty that Worthy *hoped* it was the wine.

"Well, let's get back to the luncheon. Since I'm here, I might as well score a few points with Councilman Whitehead," said Goldman.

"Are you still trying to get the fags to let you rezone your Castro property?" Spellman inquired. "You were working on that before I left the firm."

"So, it's been a while. Besides, we don't talk that way out here," Goldman replied in his snootiest tone of voice. "Councilman Whitehead simply lives an alternative lifestyle in a neighborhood where such lifestyles are commonplace. I simply wish to tear down a couple of rotting Victorian townhouses that would cost more to renovate then they could ever be worth, and put up a nice heavy-metal bar that will appeal to the leather crowd and make me a pile of money. The houses are nothing but old fire traps. But, to improve their neighborhood for them, I need the council-man's assistance."

"Jesus Christ, Ev, you sound like a senatorial candidate," Gordon chided him.

"Absolutely not. There's not enough money in government. I'll stick to what I do best." They all laughed.

In the dining room, Marty saw Denise Carson standing on the terrace talking to a woman Marty didn't recognize. The waiter, Jose, intercepted Spellman, who was boring in on Denise like a great white shark, and did his best to persuade Spellman to take a glass of champagne. Spellman re-fused.

Marty watched the waiter move toward the other partners who were emerging from the smoking room. None had a drink, and it appeared to Marty that the waiter was hell-bent on changing that.

When the waiter was almost to them, a woman grabbed him by the arm. Spinning around, the waiter looked into the scowling face of Mayor Clara Johnstone. Shirley Rosewood stood beside her.

"We would like some champagne, please." She looked down her nose at him from behind unattractive half-glasses, as if he had something un-desirable smeared on his face.

The waiter hesitated, then smiled. "Of course, Your Honor."

The mayor took her glass and started to reach for a second to give to Shirley Rosewood. Before she could reach the glass, the waiter escaped into the crowd. Walking to the partners he held out his tray, and each of them took a glass of champagne. From across the room Marty could see Mayor Johnstone talking to the club manager.

It was almost two, and their plane left at nine. There would have been plenty of time to meet with Riley, but Spellman refused to allow it. Marty was to stay with Spellman, and the judge refused to go to a meeting with Riley. Finding a telephone, Marty dialed the number Riley had given him. A woman answered.

"Riley residence, Corin speaking."

"Hello, this is Detective Marty Cox, from Akron, Ohio. I was given this number to call when I got to town."

"Oh yes, Patrick is expecting your call. Just a minute please."

Riley's booming voice came on the line. "Welcome to San Francisco. I saw the note in the paper about the memorial service. Figured that's where you'd be. Sorry I wasn't home last night. I had to go with the little woman to a shindig her company put on. She's an executive with an ad agency."

"No problem. I couldn't have met with you last night anyhow." Mar-ty quickly related the events of the previous night. "The whole thing spooked the judge. He woke my boss up in the middle of the night and had me assigned to be the judge's personal security. I'll have to go back on the plane with him. My orders are not to let him out of my sight till he's back home."

"Too bad. Your street people thing jogged something in my memory, and I had arranged for you to research it on the computers."

"I can come back. Since Spellman changed the tune in the middle of the song, I don't see how my boss has any choice but to let me come back."

"Good. Just keep me posted. I'm relatively flexible."

They rang off and Marty went in search of Spellman.

CHAPTER 14

By the time the red-eye from San Francisco landed in Cleveland, it was six in the morning.

Marty followed Spellman home, where his personal security people had been beefed up by two uniformed members of the Akron department. After he showered, Marty tried to call Nora, but she wasn't at home. On the way to the station, he was about to call her at the office when the car phone in his hand rang.

"I didn't know if you were back from your trip to fairyland or not, but I thought I'd try to reach you anyhow," King said. "We got another one, Marty. They found him in a doorway on Exchange street about ten minutes ago." Marty copied down the address.

The patrol cars, flashers winking, were blocking the street. Parked next to the middle car was the forensic van, and Dorsey's red Corvette was at the curb. The area was ringed with yellow tape to keep curiosity seekers at bay. Marty ducked under the tape as Dorsey walked over, removing a surgeon's mask from his face.

"Got another sidewalk citizen with his identity rearranged. Big forty-four behind the right ear."

Dorsey guided him to the body. A forensic team measured, bagged, taped, photographed and dusted. Marty recognized Denzil Alberts, one of the deputy coroners. Alberts' people wore protective garb.

"Real mess, Marty. Doctor Daniels's on the way over.

"What's with the outfits?" Marty asked.

"Doctor Daniels said if we got any more of these, we were to treat it with full body precautions," he said handing Marty a mask and rubber gloves. "You won't need to suit up unless you want to help us with the dirty work," Alberts added.

The victim was between fifty and sixty years old with the puffy look of a chronic alcoholic. The man lay twisted at an odd angle, as if he were trying to do a horizontal pirouette. The alcove swarmed with flies feeding on the blood. Some were more interested in the corpse than they were the blood.

The wall and the doorway behind the body were flecked with bits of bone and brain. The odors were a combination of the man's life on the street, the rusty odor of blood and the sickening smell of ripening flesh as the morning heat seeped into the alcove.

Marty turned to see Nora duck under the tape. "Morning, gentlemen," She said. When her eyes meet Marty's, they conveyed what she didn't say out loud.

While she put on her mask and gloves, Alberts filled her in on the status of the investigation. In the alcove, she ordered the body to be photographed from three more angles and had blood and tissue samples collected from a dozen more places.

When they turned him over, the man's face looked hideous. The head shot was devastating and there were no other injuries.

"Notice anything different?" she asked.

E.L. shrugged. "Looks like the same perp to me. Single shot, right ear. Exit wound wipes out the face, making it harder to give him a name," E. L., said, looking pointedly at Marty.

"Not quite the same," Marty said. "No jaundice. No red streaks around the eyes, and a lot more blood at the scene.

"No bruising either. There's the usual postmortem pooling of venous blood, but no fresh bruises." Nora added. "I want to do a post, before the embalmers get to him. You guys coming?"

"I have more important matters to attend to, like breakfast," E.L. said. "If I come with you, eatin' will be out of the question. Besides, I only work till noon." With a wave, he walked away.

"I'll be there as soon as I wrap things up," Marty said,

When Marty arrived at the morgue, the autopsy was well underway "It's good to see you back, Clarence. Are you feeling better?"

"Doctor Nora told Clarence what to do, and now everything's okay."

Nora hesitated while she pulled back the flap and inserted the retractors. "Marty, the mask is on the shelf above the sink. We may be a day late and a dollar short with these, but wear one till we figure this thing out."

"I have the final autopsy reports on the lawyer in San Francisco." Nora glanced up at him and nodded.

Slipping the smelly, composite mask over his face, Marty pinched the adjustable, metal strip tight on his nose. The mask made Marty look like a praying mantis.

"Something's wrong, Marty. Take a look." Nora moved aside so he could get in closer.

Steeling himself against what he was going to see, Marty peered into the man's abdomen. When he realized that he was biting his lower lip very hard, it made him feel foolish. Nora directed his attention to a purple mass of tissue under the right rib cage.

"There's not a damn thing wrong with this liver, other than early changes of cirrhosis related to alcohol intake. There are no petichial hemorrhages on the wall of the abdomen, the mesentary or the bowel. This bowel is normal." For emphasis, she picked up a loop of intestine and ran it through her fingers.

Which wall had the cracked tile on it? When he had forced the contents of his stomach back down, he said, "Then, he's not infected."

"I don't think so. It's liable to get gamey in here. Why don't you wait for me in the office? "

Marty didn't argue, and when Nora came in forty-five minutes later, he closed the door and took her in his arms. Her lips were soft and sweet, and they lingered on the kiss for a moment. "I love the sweet smell of formaldehyde in the morning. Do you wear it often?"

"Most of the time, so get used to it." She moved around to the coffee pot, poured herself a cup and offered him one.

"Does that mean you're going to keep me around awhile?"

Smiling, she sat down at her desk. "More than likely." The smile faded when he told her about the trip. "I get the felling that we're working against time. Now, about today's killing. None of the changes are present in the bowel. The internal organs are normal, and there's fluid in the lungs. There were acute changes in the brain this time."

"Just a straight homicide then," Marty said. That strange feeling crept into his gut again. "Are we over-reacting with the infection theory. Clarence cut himself with a dirty knife and he's okay. People have handled the autopsy material, the bodies and there's no epidemic."

"I know," Nora said, frustration in her tone.

"When do you plan to take the samples to Bell?"

"I'll call him later this morning. He's always there. Let me see the material from San Francisco."

The pager on his belt went off, and he called Sergeant King.

"I have a message from Riley. They took Tom Gordon to the hospital this morning. Gordon isn't as sick as Rosewood was, but they've hospitalized him as a precaution."

"Did Riley say what the symptoms were?"

"Fever, chills, aching joints. Sounds to me like the flu," King said. "Don't see why they're all bent out of shape about it."

"Keep me posted if you hear anything else. I'm at Doctor Daniels' office. She just finished the post from this morning." Marty rang off.

"Tom Gordon, another lawyer from the firm, is in the hospital with the same symptoms as Rosewood," he told her.

"I'll look over this material before I see, Alex. I sent Jacque the samples by courier. Do you have to go back to San Francisco?" Nora asked.

"Yes, I've got to see Riley. If Spellman hadn't been a prick, I could have done it all while I was there. Riley has a lead for me from their computer file that I'll have to look into personally."

"Can't you get into their computer from here?" Nora inquired.

"I could, but the impressions of an experienced officer are as important as what the computer has to say."

The office door opened after a brief knock, and Clarence stuck his head in the office. "Mr. Detective, some man wants to talk to you on the phone. It's the one where the light is blinking."

"Thank you, Clarence," Nora said, and Clarence went out. She punched the blinking button and handed Marty the receiver.

"What's up?" Marty asked, expecting to hear the voice of Sergeant King. Instead, it was E. L.'s Virginia twang.

"Must be the spring two-for sale."

"The what?"

"You know, two-for, two-for-one. Buy one, get one free. We got another body. Found him next to the dumpster behind the Canal Place condominiums. Wino with a forty-four caliber face-lift."

"Meet you there." Marty handed Nora the phone and recited the conversation to her.

"Guess I'll have to read these later," she said, tossing the autopsy material on her desk.

The scene was a replay of the earlier call. The body was stuffed between a dumpster and a concrete retaining wall. There was blood and tissue everywhere, but there was no jaundice, bruising or splotching. The inevitable flies were at him. "Why didn't Noah swat the primal pair when he had the chance?" Nora asked.

"This is out of character," Marty said, as much to himself as to Nora. "He's never killed twice in one night. Serial killers tend to stick to their pattern. The ritualistic nature of their killings is as important as the killings themselves. They don't deviate."

The post on the second body was like playing a favorite movie again. The words were familiar, the characters the same, and the outcome predictable.

In her office again, Nora said, "I took samples from everything." She sighed heavily, as if the effort would remove some great weight she was carrying from her shoulders.

Looking at his watch, Marty said, "I'll go back to the office and see if I can get through to Riley."

"I'll be giving a lecture to the med students at four, and I'll take the samples to Alex after that. What are we doing for dinner?"

The simple question warmed Marty's heart. "I know a great little Italian place in Kent called, Ristorante De Gianni-Johnnies' Place. Best Italian food in the state. You'll love it. John and Judy are our kind of people. Besides, it's close to the med center." Taking her hands, he pulled her to her feet. When he kissed her gently on the lips, she hugged him warmly.

As he drove back to the station, Marty mulled over the events of the morning. Two more men were dead, and there were no witnesses, no new clues, nothing. Why did the killer change his pattern? What was different about thses killings? Was the killer aware that the men were sick? Maybe Riley would have some answers.

Sitting in his office impatiently flicking a pencil between his fingers, Marty waited as the long distance call was being placed. Riley's voice sounded tense.

"The second lawyer is worse. The guy is yellow as a Chinaman. A group of eggheads from Fort Detrick Maryland called USAMRIID roared in here like a swarm of locusts and sealed off the place. Very hush-hush. You didn't hear it from me, mind ya."

"The local scientist who is helping us with the investigation worked there for awhile. It's the army biological research center where they dream up germ warfare weapons. They also help the C.D.C. with infectious disease outbreaks."

"Well, I hope your scientist helps real soon. Shortly after the boys from Maryland arrived, the lawyer started to hemorrhage. He's acting just like Rosewood did."

Crashed and bled out. Went down. Marty felt sick at his stomach.

"I got my info second hand."

The boys from C.D.C have joined the feds from alphabet place, and they have him buttoned up tighter than an old maid's corset. Place looks like a bee hive. Folks comin' and goin' constantly."

Viral Armageddon loomed in his memory like the featureless monster from a childhood nightmare. Had some killer organism broken through into man and was ready to unleash the viral apocalypse? Was the biblical description of Judgement Day, with liquid flesh dripping from skeletal frames, a description of the havoc caused by a killer organism released on mankind by its own stupidity?

"Sounds like things are getting tense out there. I'm up to my shield in new corpses. Our boy was busy last night. Two more bodies this morning. Getting so I'm afraid to answer the phone. Every time I do, it's another street soul headed for the great soup kitchen in the sky."

"This perp ever pop two in the same day before?"

"Nope."

"Sounds like he's raisin' the ante."

"I've got one of those feelings. You know, the kind of feeling you get when things just don't fit. I get the impression he's trying to muddy up the water. Maybe we're getting too close."

"Could be." Riley said. "I checked the computer to see about your street people." Riley's voice didn't have the same, cold tone Dorsey used when he talked about the unfortunates. "Seven years ago, before we had a lot of street people here, an epidemic of sorts broke out among the winos on Polk Street. There were a series of strange illnesses and reports of a phantom stranger. The press dubbed him The Death Angel. He scared the winos to death.

They credited this Death Angel with five kills and two probables. Then, eight years ago, it all stopped with the death of Joseph Carbone, affectionately know by his colleagues as, Refer Joe, because he lived in a refrigerator shipping carton. Somebody slipped him a lethal dose of something, and he died of a massive bowel hemorrhage."

"Why was he in the hospital?"

"I don't have enough time to check out the hospital records of every wino who's been in the hospital for the past decade," Riley said.

"I'm sorry," Marty apologized. "I don't mean to impose. You've already been a great deal of help. I'll try to book a flight later today."

"You don't have to apologize, Riley said, his voice softening. "Goldman's firm is the biggest malpractice group on the coast, and they have a lot of political muscle downtown. Besides, all these feds running around talking contagion makes me nervous."

If you really knew the potential danger, my friend, you would be more than nervous, Marty thought.

"Let me know when you've made your reservations. I'll pick you up at the airport. I got a spare room at my place, and the little woman loves to entertain. You can stay with us. We don't get many out-of-town guests."

"That's kind of you, Sergeant Riley, but I don't want to impose."

"You won't be, and the name is Patrick."

"Thanks, Patrick. I'm Marty. I'll call you back in an hour."

Forty-five minutes later, Marty told Riley, "I'll be there about nine your time on United flight 4055," Marty told him.

"I'll meet you at the gate," Riley said.

"How will I recognize you?" Marty asked.

"Easy. I'll be the biggest damned Irishman in sight." Riley laughed and hung up.

Picking up the phone, he dialed Nora's number. "Department of pathology, Doctor Daniels' office. Miss Purdy speaking."

"This is Detective Cox. I know Doctor Daniels is at the medical school, but can you get a message to her for me. Tell her that I will be unable to keep our evening appointment. I'm leaving for the airport in about an hour, and I'll call her tomorrow."

"I'll be sure she gets the message."

"Thank you, Miss Purdy." Marty hung up and went home to pack.

CHAPTER 15

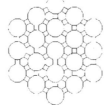

ayor Clara Johnstone started the morning with a headache. Leaning back in her desk chair, she rubbed her temples with both hands in an attempt to relieve the blinding pain. Removing two extra-strength Tylenol from the bottle, she washed them down with coffee from the cup that sat on the edge of the desk blotter. Despite taking nearly a whole bottle in twenty-four hours, her head still thumped.

Unbuttoning the top buttons of her blouse in an attempt to cool the flush she felt proved to be an effort. When the intercom buzzed, the sound caused pain to course through her temples like a shower of hot sparks. Before the electronic Banshee could wail again, Clara punched the button. "Yes, Melissa."

"Mr. Worthy is here for his nine o'clock appointment."

"Give me a second, and then send him in," she replied. Her schedule was always tight, and this damned headache made it seem worse. "Melissa, I feel like dog dirt. Send Worthy in and cancel the rest of the day. Tell Raymond to have the limo ready in ten minutes." Clicking off the intercom, she closed her eyes for a few seconds and massaged her temples again.

Mellisa ushered Joe Worthy in, and she stood to shake his hand. The pain in her head made her dizzy.

"Afternoon, Clara. Pardon my asking, but do you feel all right?"

"I have a killer headache, Joe. Started early yesterday morning. I didn't sleep much last night."

"I hope you're not getting what I had. Right after Hayden's memorial service, I got the worse case of the flu I've had in twenty years. I had to go to bed for twenty-four hours. But, I feel fine now. It only lasted twenty-four hours."

Clara motioned him into the padded leather chair across the desk from her. A sour rumbling coursed through her stomach as she sat down. "What can I do for you, Joe?"

"I'll be brief, Clara. Ev Goldman asked me to see if you could support the zoning change for his Castro property. Councilman Whitehead is willing to introduce the request at next week's council meeting. He's convinced a couple of the immediate neighbors that it's a good idea. They'll be there to speak on behalf of the proposal."

"How much did that little maneuver cost?" she asked. The pain in her head made it hard to concentrate.

"Your Honor, these are merely civic-minded citizens who understand how best to serve their community."

"Cut the bullshit, Joe. Give me one good reason why I should go out on a limb, politically, to help Ev Goldman."

"Let's just say that our firm would be doubly grateful when you start raising funds for your re-election campaign next summer."

"Since you make such a logical and persuasive argument, counselor, I'll do what's best for the neighborhood. If the folks down there want it, who am I to stand in their way."

"Thank you Clara. I'll leave the particulars with Melissa. You can look them over when you're feeling better. If you need any further background material, please call me at the office. You take care of that headache now, you hear."

The nausea came back, and as soon as Worthy was gone, she dashed to her adjoining bathroom. The effort made her head throb, and the pain drove her to her knees. Kneeling before the bowl, bathed with sweat, she vomited into the commode like a drunkard, and she collapsed against the cool porcelain rim. With alarm, she noted tiny flecks of blood in the disgusting mess in the bottom of bowl.

Pulling herself shakily to her feet, she flushed away the embarrassing residue. Holding her head as still as possible, she went back in the office and called Melissa. "Is the car ready?"

"I've canceled the rest of the day. The car will be here by the time you get downstairs. Will you need help getting to the car?" Melissa asked with concern in her voice.

"No thank you, Melissa. I'll be alright." Sitting down gingerly in the chair, she was burning up and loosened another button on her blouse. Reaching for the bottle of Tylenol, she decided against taking more of them and put the bottle back on her desk. She would call Tony Benedetti. Maybe he could call her out something?

She dialed Benedetti's number from the phone in the back seat of the limo, and the discomfort caused by the ringing of the phone forced her to hold the receiver away from her ear. She was one of the few people who could get by the troll who manned the phone at the office of San Francisco's most popular internist.

"Clara my dear, what seems to be the problem?" Benedetti's voice sounded like it belonged to a television game show host.

Describing her symptoms briefly, she finished with, "And, when I vomited, there were flecks of blood in it."

"You probably strained a little blood vessel in the back of the throat. Don't worry about that. My diagnosis is viral flu. I'll phone in some potent antibiotics for you and something for the nausea. Do you still use Livermore's Pharmacy on Division?"

"That would be fine, Tony. Thanks a million. Could I have something for the headache, too? It's killing me."

"No problem. And, Clara, when are you coming in for that complete physical you keep putting off? You're already three months overdue. You need to have that pap smear redone. We had the questionable cells last time, remember?"

"Consider me scolded. Next week, I promise. I'll tell Melissa to set something up." Leaning back, she closed her eyes.

After a stop at the pharmacy, the limousine pulled to the curb in front of Clara's Nob Hill, Victorian townhouse. The driver opened the door and helped her out. As she stood up, the combination of the bright sunshine in her eyes, the pain in her head and the exertion of the movement made her dizzy. She staggered against him. "I'm sorry, Raymond. I'm really shaky."

"That's okay, Mrs. Johnstone. Is Rosa home? I don't think you should be by yourself." He handed her the bag from the pharmacy.

"Yes, she lives here full time since her mother passed away last fall. I'll be fine, Raymond. Don't you fret."

Raymond helped her to the door and rang the doorbell. With a look of profound relief, he turned her over to the rotund Latino housekeeper who answered the door.

"Thank you, Raymond." She pronounced it Ray-moan, in her heavily-accented English. The expression in the enormous, brown eyes that dominated her tiny nose and round face filled with concern.

"Senora, let Rosa help you." Fussing Clara into the master bedroom, Rosa laid out a nightgown and bathrobe. "You get undressed and ready for bed. Rosa will make you a nice cup of tea to take your medicine with."

"I don't know about the tea. I've already thrown up at the office, and I still feel queasy. I'm not sure I can keep anything down." Clara was having trouble putting sentences together. Her tongue felt like it was coated with molasses.

Undeterred by reasonable argument, Rosa replied, "Si, Senora, but the tea is good for you." Turning, she waddled from the room.

Gritting her teeth, Clara made her way to the bathroom. Pulling off her soaked dress, she let it fall at her feet. She didn't dare try to pick it up.

Even her bra was wet, so she shucked it, toweled herself dry and slipped on a nightgown. Looking into the mirror, she looked even worse than she felt.

Her skin had a sallow cast, and the whites of her eyes were bloodshot and tinged with yellow. Black circles surrounded the eyes, and she looked as if she had been beaten. Splashing cold water on her forehead, she went back to the edge of the bed.

This was one of the times that Clara missed Jim the most. He was always so kind, so loving when she was sick. Why did he have to die? Reaching for a tissue, Clara dabbed at her eyes then dried her nose. She stared dumbfounded at the tissue. It was covered with blood.

"Senora!" Rosa cried, as she came in with a wooden tray containing the tea. Setting the tray down so hastily that she slopped tea into the underlying saucer, Rosa helped Clara into the bathroom. Tilting back Clara's head, Rosa pinched the bleeding nose with her chubby fingers. With the other hand, she ran a wash cloth under cold water and placed it on the back of Clara's neck. It took nearly ten minutes to staunch the flow of blood.

Mercifully, the nose bleed had eased the pain in her head. Rosa gave her the antibiotic that Benedetti had ordered, a Demerol tablet for the pain and a Compazine suppository for the nausea. She was chilling so badly that the bed was rattling, and Rosa covered her.

Putting the back of her hand on Clara's forehead, Rosa said, "You have bad fever, Senora. I take your temperature." Removing the thermometer, Rosa looked at it and gasped. "Jesu, it's one hundred and three." Clara closed her eyes, and Rosa pulled the drapes.

Rosa made another trip to the bathroom for a cold compress and two aspirin. As she washed down the tablets, the water felt good to Clara's parched throat. Checking the covers to be sure they were at her throat, Rosa said, "You sleep. I come back and check on you later." Tiptoeing out, Rosa softly closed the door.

Plagued by feverish dreams of monsters and blood, Clara slept fitfully. In the dream, a creature that looked like a lizard with rows of chainsaw teeth bit into her right leg sending a throbbing pain all the way to the hip. Pushing through the web of the dream to consciousness, she realized that the pain was real. Her right leg felt like it was on fire. "Rosa, come please!" she cried.

Pain stabbed at her calf like a charlie horse, only worse than she had ever experienced. When she tried to move the leg, it wouldn't respond. Panic seized her. Bursting into the room, Rosa snapped on the light.

"Madra Mia!" Rosa gasped, putting the back of her hand over her mouth. "I call nine-one-one!"

"No, my leg! The pain!" Clara shrieked.

Pulling down the covers, Rosa staggered back at the sight of Clara's leg. Clara looked at the leg and gasped. The skin was a golden yellow, as was her hand on the cover. From the knee down, the leg was mottled in the front, and the calf was almost black. Crumpling back into the pillows, Clara began to cry.

When the paramedics lifted her onto the stretcher, it felt as if every joint in her body was on fire. The bandage over the I-V site in her arm was saturated with blood, and her nose started to bleed again. The ride to the hospital was a blur of incoherent images, and the wailing siren compounded the pounding in her head.

Benedetti was waiting at the emergency room. Examining her swiftly, he began barking orders. They drew blood, added vials of medication to her I-V, took a portable chest x-ray, and wheeled her into the C.T. scanner. The narcotics Benedetti had given her in the I-V kicked in somewhere on the way to the scanner.

When she awoke, she was in a private room connected to a bank of monitors. Benedetti and a nurse were at the bedside. They wore surgical caps, gowns, masks with plastic face shields and rubber gloves. Clara was having trouble focusing, and her entire body felt numb. The pain was gone from her head and her joints. Now, she was having trouble breathing. "What's going on, Tony? What's wrong?"

Scratching his chin pensively, he said, "You have an infection. Exactly what kind of infection . . . ." Shrugging his shoulders helplessly, he turned his hands palms up. "Have you been out of the country in the last six months?" She shook her head. "Around anyone with diarrhea, jaundice, hepatitis.? Think hard, Clara. I need all the help I can get."

Her face felt like it was made of Jello, and it was hard to form her mouth into words. "None of those things?"

Pulling a chair to the bedside, Benedetti sat down and placed his gloved hand on top of hers. The rubber glove on his hand felt alien. Hesitating, he fidgeted nervously. "Is there any chance, even a remote one, that you might have been exposed to AIDS?" The pain that asking the question caused him was etched in his sweaty face, and she felt sorry for him.

Clara closed her eyes. "No, I haven't been with a man since Jim died, or a woman either," she added, attempting a feeble joke. "Do you think that's what I have?"

Taking a deep breath he blew it out slowly. "Okay, I'll lay it out for you. No, I don't think you have AIDS. This isn't like anything I've ever seen before. I asked our infectious disease man to take a look at you. He's not sure what it is either. The C.T. shows an area of infarction in the middle of your liver. You're jaundiced, and you're liver is failing. The lab studies paint a picture that's consistent with hepatitis, but hepatitis doesn't progress this fast."

A low moan escaped her lips, and she closed her eyes.

"That's not all. You have a blood clot in the artery to your right leg. We can't thin your blood to break up the clots because you're bleeding internally. If you survive, we'll have to take the leg off at the knee. There's blood in your urine, in your ears, and you have either blood or some other fluid in your lungs."

"Am I going to die, Tony?"

"Not if I can help it, Clara." She didn't think he sounded as if he believed he *could* help it.

"Is that all?" She was afraid of the answer.

"Your white count is down, and your immune system is giving out."

Tears filled her eyes, and she couldn't see. Tony wiped her eyes clean with a gauze sponge. "This has to be some bizarre nightmare, and I'm going to wake up any time."

Clara looked helplessly at Benedetti who was staring at the sponge he had used to wipe her eyes. It was covered with blood.

CHAPTER
16

lexander Bell was feeling the strain of the past hours. He had been working for over three hours, and that was pushing the amount of time that he could work safely. The purified air inside the orange Raycal space suite made his throat feel as if he had just marched across the Sahara Desert.

The hissing sound made by the air as it circulated inside the suit seemed louder now. A feeling of claustrophobia would soon follow, and he would have to quit. A thin layer of moisture was beginning to fog the lower portion of the face plate from the perspiration trapped inside the suit. One more bottle, and he would be done.

Bell activated the automatic pipette.

Manipulating it carefully through the impervious orange gloves that covered the white cotton gloves against his skin, he deposited the liquid in the pipette into a three ounce pharmacy bottle that contained an ounce of holding medium. It looked as clear and as harmless as water. The clumsy gloves made it difficult to screw the cap into place.

With a pair of tongs, he dipped the closed bottle into a sterilizing alcohol-ammonia bath and wiped it dry with a white cloth. He placed the bottle into a rack with a half-dozen similar bottles.

Disconnecting the umbilical hose that attached him to the air exchange system in the containment lab, Bell relished the instant of blessed silence inside the helmet. Then, the metallic whine of the back-pack generating system kicked on, and the annoying rush of filtered air returned. He moved to the far end of the lab like an astronaut roaming the surface of an alien planet.

Inside the cramped room, Bell placed the rack of bottles into a sub-zero freezer. Now, all he could do was wait.

He went to a thick metal door sealed by a rubber gasket and a dogging ring, like a water-tight hatch on a ship. Spinning the ring, he opened the door. Beyond it was a standard wooden door that led into the main area of the containment facility.

After securing the inner and outer doors, Bell crossed the room, turning out lights as he went. He felt weary to the bone. A hot shower and a glass of brandy was paramount in his thoughts as he spun a larger dogging-wheel on the outer steel door that opened into the level-two area of the lab. Nora Daniels, dressed in street clothes, was standing just outside the door with her hand poised on the intercom button. Jumping back with a bewildered look on her face, she caught the heel of her shoe in a grate in the floor and nearly fell.

"Get out of here and go to my office now! I'll join you there." He mouthed the words carefully, because she would have trouble hearing him through the face plate and above the whine of the back-pack's fan. Turning abruptly, Nora hurried away like a child who had just been scolded and told to go to her room.

Standing in the decon shower, Bell's mind whirled. So much planning. So close to the end. Why now? Grinding his teeth in frustration, he waited for the timed shower to finish. Was she alone? Where was the damned detective?

When the chemical shower stopped, he rinsed the suit with clear water and ripped off the velcro straps that sealed the outer gloves to the suit. Peeling off the outer gloves, he checked the cotton gloves beneath for wet spots. Finding none, he unsnapped the velcro neck collar and removed the helmet. Bell climbed out of the Raycal suit and hung it on a peg to dry.

At his locker, he removed the adhesive tape that held his long underwear sleeve to the white cotton gloves. He did the same to the tape that attached the white cotton athletic socks to the trouser legs. Since the Raycal suit had boots attached, he didn't wear shoes. Removing the sweat-stained long-John's he went into the regular shower. Making her wait would give him the advantage of time to think.

When he was dressed, Bell opened a box marked "hazardous biologicals" in the rear of his locker and removed a nine millimeter Berreta pistol. Checking the clip, he found it fully loaded, and pocketing the weapon, he slammed the locker door in frustration.

Pausing at the outer door, he forced his breathing to slow down. Calling upon guided imagery skills that had served him well in the past, he closed his eyes and focused on his anger and frustration until he could visualize them as colors. Visualizing pure white energy, he watched it enter his nose and mingle with the red rage and green frustration until they were washed away. Walking into the office, he was perfectly calm.

"My dear, Nora. How nice to see you. Sorry if I frightened you with my haberdashery." Seated behind his desk, he saw the yellow post- it note describing her call, and frowned.

"I was startled. Full suits are only necessary in a level four lab." The tone of Nora's voice carried an inquisitor's inflection.

"I'm sorry to be so abrupt, my dear. Although I didn't believe I had contaminated the suit, one never knows."

"What kind of work are you doing?" she insisted.

Nora, don't ever try to deceive anyone. . . . You're as transparent as cellophane, he thought. "I handle live cultures of virus every week." The lightness was gone from his voice, and his eyes narrowed as he spoke.

"This strain of the simian virus is nearly identical to the human Ebola. I should be highly embarrassed if one day I became the portal of entry of a mutated monkey filovirus into the human race. There is already a disease called Bell's Palsy. I don't need a Bell's virus." Pressing his fingertips together, he looked intently across the desk into her eyes. Her disbelief was obvious.

"I never expected to see something from a moon-walk video wander out of a low-level containment unit," Nora said, her tone pinched.

"Now, what was so important that you risked contamination to venture into the facility?"

"The most important things are on the E.M. that Jacque will send over tomorrow. We photographed the plates, and he's put them in the autoprocessor. The cells from the first three men show a filoviral infection that's undergone extreme amplification. They're loaded with inclusion bodies." Her voice quivered at the enormity of it.

"There were two more victims. I have blood and tissue samples for you, but I don't think they were infected. Jacque's doing E.M. on them, but they won't be ready until tomorrow," she blurted out.

He went about the ritual of filling and stoking his pipe. Where was that troublesome detective? When he was wreathed in smoke, he said, "Are you aware of what you're postulating, Nora? Three cases of filoviral infection would be reason enough to call in the Marines. Have you called in the Marines, Nora?"

"Not yet. I wanted to see what you thought."

"Did you bring serum from the three victims? I have all four major types of filoviral antiserum. We can confirm the infection and identify the strain."

"Can we run the samples now?"

Bell's best plans were always the product of decisions he made when reacting to what the scenario dictated. "They will need to incubate for at least an hour. We should use the incubator in the containment lab. Are you sure you don't want to wait out here?"

"This stuff has been around the pathology department and the coroner's office for months. I can't believe it's dangerous. My prosector cut himself with a contaminated knife and never got sick. I can't explain that, can you?"

Bell allowed an uncharacteristic smug look of satisfaction to cross his face. "Sometimes such things have simple explanations, once you have all the facts," he said cryptically. "Your detective would never forgive me if I contaminated you with live virus. By the way, is he coming by?"

"Marty has to go back to San Francisco. The officer in charge of the case out there did some preliminary digging for him. Riley found a string of deaths in derelicts around the bay area a few years back that are similar to the ones here. Marty wanted to check them out."

"I'm sure if there is a connection, he'll find it. Your young man seems to be as good at his job as we are at our science." His voice was cold and hard. The detective was getting too close.

"The deaths may have happened while you were still at Berkley. Do you remember anything about them?" Nora asked.

Removing his glasses, Bell rubbed his eyes and sat motionless for a few seconds. "Periodically, some divinely-directed plague weeds out the derelict population, just as wolves purify a herd of elk. It's of no consequence."

His callousness registered with a surprised look on her face. "Could this be a spontaneous viral outbreak in an immuno-compromised population? One that runs its course when the more seriously compromised are eliminated. But, why *doesn't* it infect others?"

A twisted smile lifted the corners of his mouth as he struck another match to his pipe. *She was as dogged as that damned detective.* "Those are ponderous questions, my dear," he answered, enigmatically.

"One more thing." Digging into her briefcase, Nora withdrew the manila envelope that Marty had given her. "This is the autopsy reports from San Francisco. I think you'll find them interesting. The results are nearly identical to my findings on our men," she said, handing the envelope across the desk.

Placing it among the piles of papers already there without looking at it, he said, "Let's get on with the sero-typing."

Bell led her through the deserted hallways to the third floor. In the locker room, he nodded toward a locker in the bank to the right. "We don't stand on ceremony here," he said as he hung his lab coat on a peg and began to undress. "There are scrubs inside the locker. If you're shy, keep your back to me while we change."

Turning toward his locker, Bell undressed. He glanced over his shoulder once. Nora had turned away and was stripped down to her bikini briefs and bra. He admired her as he might appreciate a marble statue. Even if he were interested in her physically, he refused to be distracted now.

When he had finished dressing, he slipped the Berreta into the waistband of his scrub suit as visions of painted-faced women danced in his memory. They should all have died. He quelled the developing anger with breaths of white light. Maybe when he finished his present task, he would rid the world of whores.

"I'm ready, Alex." When he turned around, she was dressed in a scrub suit that hung from her like an oversized sack. They moved to the shelves at the end of the room and donned disposable plastic boots, surgical masks and plastic face shields that covered the exposed skin above the mask. Reaching for a plastic surgical gown, he put it on. "Double glove and tape the cuffs of both the gloves and boots so nothing can get inside. Standard procedure for level-two. Did you see the lab before it went online?"

Nodding, she followed his instructions.

"It will be different now. If you feel any degree of uneasiness, talk to me. People have been known to panic inside a sealed facility." Her brow knotted with concern, and she took a deep breath.

Bell led her across the locker room to the door at the opposite end. "I always feel like John Wayne in a World War II movie when I open one of these." As he turned the wheel, the door opened with a hiss, and air was drawn into the negatively pressurized room beyond.

Banks of ceiling-mounted ultraviolet lights cast an eerie purple glow over the room. A series of shower heads ran down the middle of the room from the sealed door at the opposite end of this rectangular space to the doorway in which they stood. Multiple drains were embedded in the floor.

"I'm sure you remember from the tour, Nora, that these ultraviolet lights are automatically activated when the containment door is opened and remained on for ten minutes after the unit is shut down. The ultraviolet light deactivates the proteins in the genetic structure of the virus and is able to sterilize most varieties. These lights, and those in the locker room, are added precautions to prevent viruses from getting out of the contained environment. My staff calls these two rooms the tanning parlor, because of the tanning effects of the ultra violet lights on their skin."

"Although the showers appear to be ordinary, they are not. The regular showers are in the locker room behind us. This is the decontamination facility, and the shower heads spray a mixture of chemicals and water that completely saturate everything in the room."

"The shower runs continuously for seven minutes, and the locker room door automatically locks while the shower is running to prevent a panicky individual from compounding an already serious situation by running out of the facility."

"This room, along with the negative pressure environment, is the main safeguard for our level-two facility. The air in this room and the next is on a separate air handling system from the rest of the building. The pressure of the rooms is kept negative so that when we open the door, outside air is sucked in and the resultant flow keeps infected particles from drifting out. The air is changed, filtered, purified and recirculated every three minutes.

As Nora looked around the room, her eyes drifted to the conduits that carried the heat, light, water and negative pressure system through the wall. "Those look different from when I saw them on the tour. What's that viscous-looking material smeared around the ducts where they perforate the walls?" Nora asked.

The damned woman didn't miss a thing, Bell thought. "When a unit goes on line, the duct work perforations are sealed with a chemical sealer to keep the organisms from finding the pipeline and following it out of the room. At times, microbes seem to possess an intelligence of their own."

They moved to the inner containment door. When Bell tapped in the access code, the door swung open with a hiss of the negative pressure. The inner portion of the facility had an open area to the right with sinks, refrigerator, a work bench and an operating-dissecting table with surgical lights suspended above it. An operating microscope was mounted next to the table. To the left, and at the far end, was a series of small rooms. Some of the rooms on the left contained incubators, racks of tubes, shakers, pipettes, and a variety of miscellaneous laboratory paraphernalia. Others held cages for rats, mice, and other experimental animals.

Bell went to the refrigerator and removed a metal case. Inside were five vials of clear plasma. Removing them one at a time, he identified each of them. "This is from Marberg. This is Zaire. This is Sudan, and these are Cardinal and Rustin." He handled them reverently.

Bell opened a new plating sheet. Small wells in the sheet accommodated a few drops of liquid. Taking the plasma samples from Nora, Bell placed a drop from each sample into five different wells on the plate. Adding antibody containing serum from his samples to the appropriate well, he mixed each gently with the tip of the automatic pipette. Carrying the wells to an incubator, he checked the thermometer and placed it inside.

Describing the function of the rooms along the left wall, he led her to the rooms at the far end of the laboratory where he had been working earlier. Opening the door to the middle room, he stepped aside so she could go in. It was a cramped store room filled with boxes of new laboratory glassware. Removing the pistol from his waist-band, he pointed it at her back.

"I don't understand," she said turning around. When she saw the weapon, her expression froze in alarmed confusion. It gradually changed to recognition, then anger.

"I'm terribly sorry, Nora. I should have know my little ruse with the last two subjects wouldn't succeed. It was a feeble gesture on my part to throw your detective off the scent. I didn't expect to fool either of you for long. Now, if you please, turn around." He motioned with the barrel of the gun.

When she hesitated, he grabbed her by the shoulder with his left hand and rudely turned her around. Fighting to control his exasperation and the urge to hurt her, he still dug his strong fingers painfully into her shoulder. Her tiny yelp of pain pleased him. "I don't wish to hurt you, but I must keep you out of the way for another few days. Then it won't matter."

Returning the pistol to his pocket, he forced her hands behind her back, and taped them together with adhesive tape from the shelf beside her. "Put your feet together, please," he said, gently pushing her to a sitting position on a box of glassware. When her ankles were firmly taped together, he checked to be sure that her circulation was not impeded.

"I trust that's not too uncomfortable. It won't be necessary to gag you. You may scream all you wish. No one will be able to hear you. I've changed the access code so the graduate students can't blunder in. I've sent them away for a few days, but you can never predict how inquisitive young people will behave. Just look what *your* inquisitiveness has done for you."

"Why, Alex? Why are you doing this? Have you lost your mind?"

Instead of Nora's face, he saw the face of the Berkley psychiatrist who had asked him that same question, just before he smashed the man's face beyond recognition. Eyes blazing, he bellowed at her, "I'm not crazy! Don't ever say that I am crazy! It's their fault, not mine! It's judgement day for them, and I am the judge, jury and executioner!"

Balling his fists, teetering on the brink of losing all self- control, he closed his eyes and breathed deeply, gulping in the healing, white light. Slowly, the fury dissipated. "It's unfortunate that you and your detective are so clever. If he's as quick as I think he is, he may find out enough to come for me before I finish. I can't allow that. You're my insurance policy against such an occurrence. I have to leave you for a time, but I'll be back. Please forgive me, Nora. I'm sorry you have to be involved. You won't be harmed unless there is no other choice." Closing the door, Bell plunged Nora into blackness.

When he had changed back into his street clothes, he went to Jacque's laboratory and slipped a small, leather case from his pocket. Removing a holding wrench and a lock pick from the case, Bell inserted the wrench into the bottom of the lock. Holding it firmly he wiggled the angled pick over the top. In seconds, the last tumbler clicked and the door opened.

Locating the autoprocessor, Bell shut the machine down and removed the rolls of film from the spindles inside. Next, he removed the stack of finished prints from the dryer at the other end. Leafing through the stack of photographs, he nodded his approval. Jacque had captured extreme amplification in award-winning fashion. Unfortunately for him, no one would ever see these photographs.

CHAPTER
17

arty's eyes felt like they had been sandpapered, and his throat was scratchy and dry. He started to straighten the tie he had loosened after the plane took off from Chicago, then thought better of it. It seemed like a week since he had seen Nora, and he missed her. Rubbing his eyes, he collected his carry-on and joined the exiting passengers. Passengers exiting a plane reminded Marty of prisoners on a chain gang marching in lock step.

At the end of the jetway, the usual throng of greeters crushed the entrance to welcome home lovers, parents, children or friends. To the right of the surging throng, standing like an oriental temple guardian, was a jovial looking giant who had to be Riley. When he noticed Marty looking at him, a grin spread across his expansive face.

Standing a shade over six-feet-eight, Riley carried his three hundred pounds on a heavy-boned frame that conjured up brick walls and immovable objects.

Patrick was likely a little older than Marty, and although Riley was not really over-weight, the pounds had rearranged subtly to create a grandfatherly brick wall. Strategically placed wrinkles decorated his florid face, adding additional character to a countenance already filled with it. Silver threads infiltrated the temples of his auburn hair, and as he moved toward Marty, he limped noticeably favoring his left leg.

"You must be Patrick Riley," Marty said with a smile and extended his hand. "You *are* the biggest Irishman at the gate." Riley extended his hand, and it was even bigger than that of Andrew Carson.

"And, you must be Marty Cox. Welcome to San Francisco. How was the flight?"

"Not bad. Connection in Chicago was on time. The best kind of flight, as many landings as take offs."

"Can't always be sure of that these day," Patrick replied, his blue eyes twinkling. "You don't look like it was a good flight. If you don't close your eyes pretty soon, you're gonna bleed to death."

"Haven't slept well the last few nights," Marty grumbled.

They moved toward the baggage claim area, and Riley's eyes sparkled. "Case keeping you awake?"

"Partly," Marty said, thinking of Nora.

Collecting Marty's suitcase, they crossed the street to the parking garage. Riley obviously loved his wife, Corin, and babbled effusively about how glad she was to be having a house guest.

"Corin likes to have company from back east. We've been out here for over fifteen years, but she still misses Chicago."

"Chicago? You're from Chicago?" Marty asked in disbelief.

"Yep. I worked metro homicide for over ten years. Then, Corin had this great offer to move out here in upper-level management for her advertising firm. My boss was kind enough to call the folks out here and tell a few lies for me. They simply had to find a spot for a man of my immense . . . ability, and I fell into a job with the department here. " Riley laughed heartily as he patted his ample girth.

"Of course . . . Riley!" Marty said, clapping his forehead with the palm of his hand. "I knew when you told me your name that something clicked in the back of my head. I was with the force in Chicago for a time. You left three years before I got there. Your name was still a legend in Precinct Five. Something about a brawl on Rush street. They say that you cleaned out a bar full of bikers single-handed."

Riley laughed good-naturedly again. "That's an exaggeration. There were only three of them, and two were so drunk they couldn't stand up. No problem for an old Notre Dame tight end." Riley tapped his left knee. "That's why I limp. Designer knee, courtesy of a U.S.C. linebacker."

As they walked through the parking garage, they exchanged small talk about common acquaintances in Chicago. Patrick unlocked the back of a bright-red Jeep Cherokee and put Marty's bag in the car.

"Hop in," Riley said. "I'm sure the little woman will have a snack for us at home, but I want to talk to you for a while first. We'll stop by a place I know on the way home."

Marty felt comfortable with Riley, "Nice car, but I understand that these babies are number two on the car thieves' hit parade."

"No perp in his right mind would come close to my little baby. This vehicle is protected by giants, and if I can't beat the crap out of 'em, Corin will."

It was easy to laugh with Riley, but Marty wondered how Riley's little woman could be a deterrent to car thieves.

"Besides, I'm getting ready for the big one." Riley continued. "Everybody out here thinks the big one will be an earthquake. It's actually going to be a snow storm, and I'll be the only one able to get up and down these damned hills. I'll make enough to retire before it melts. You remember how it was in Chicago?"

"Do I? Snow up to your ass," Marty agreed.

"That would have been up to my knees," Riley said playfully as they climbed into the Jeep.

Circling out of the airport, Riley pointed the Jeep down Highway 101 toward South San Francisco. A dark ridge of hills loomed on the horizon as the four lanes of traffic meandered beneath a warren of intertwined concrete arches that conveyed traffic in all directions. Marty didn't get a chance to enjoy the scenery on the limo ride with Spellman, so he sat looking out of the window.

A line of steel towers marched resolutely up the side of the dark hills carrying high-tension power lines to the communities on the other side. The car radio, that was tuned to a country music station, snapped and cracked as they passed, interrupting another somebody-done- somebody-wrong song. Entering a flat stretch of highway, the bay splashed against oil-stained rocks to their right and the lights of Candlestick Park visible at the point.

Interrupting Marty's contemplation of the scenery, Patrick switched off the radio and asked, "Why did you decide to leave Chicago?"

The simple question brought memories flooding back to him, and he hesitated a few minutes before he could answer. "My wife was killed in a pile-up on the Eisenhower. When it happened, she was pregnant with our first child and was on the way to the gynecologist."

"I'm sorry," Riley said, "I didn't mean to get personal."

"That's okay. I couldn't talk about it for years. I can now. Anyhow, I came unglued and started to hit the sauce. Quit the force and went home to get my life back together. It took a while, but I'm back on track now. I think I've met someone who could bring me back all the way."

"That's good," Riley said sincerely. "I don't think I could stand loosing Corin."

Looking out the window again, Marty watched the orderly rows of multicolored townhouses that constituted Daley City drift by. Breaking the awkward silence, Marty said, "I suppose, since this is San Francisco, you'll take me to a veggie bar and stuff me with tofu burgers and sprouts."

"No way. Friends of mine only get the very best in bay area cuisine, and we have a lot of cuisine here."

The Jeep climbed the hill past Vermont Avenue

They leaned into a gradual, right-hand turn, followed by a gentle left.

"Get ready for one of the most spectacular sights you will ever see, Marty. This makes it fun to come home to the city." There was a touch of pride and excitement in Riley's voice.

Sweeping through the turn, the city of San Francisco burst from the magenta twilight like a diamond-studded tiara sparkling in candlelight. The Embarcadaro, South of Market, China Basin and Potrero Hill exploded in a sea of lights that reflected onto the water. The ramp to the Bay Bridge was topped with bulbs, like the garlands on a Christmas tree, and the stately buildings, dominated by the familiar Trans America Pyramid, was a vista that took Marty's breath away.

"Magnificent," was all he could think of to say.

Patrick took the Fourth Street exit past the gingerbread front of the Hotel Utah. A fresh coat of brightly-colored paint in various hues accented the architectural relic. Marty was glad that San Franciscans didn't tear down everything connected to their past as the city expanded into the future.

In minutes, they entered the chaotic world of Folsom Street's contribution to the city . . . Hamburger Mary's. The diner was a throwback to a time of flower children and free love.

The noisy bistro was filled with old photographs and assorted collectables, all hung at different, dizzying angles, giving the soberest of patrons reason to doubt their sobriety. They were led to their table by an aesthetic, bespectacled youth who looked as if he would benefit greatly from a regular consumption of the house specialty. Marty mused at the mix-and-match decor of crystal chandeliers, in need of a good dusting, and tables covered with mismatched table cloths and milk in baby bottles.

They moved past well-scrubbed college kids, over-dressed tourists with southern accents, a grubby giant in full motorcycle leathers and his equally-portly, leathered mama. Marty felt compassion for the middle-aged couple at the next table who were down-wind from the fragrant bikers.

When they were comfortably seated at a table in the quiet corner of the diner, a tall, effeminate boy in his late twenties, with eye shadow and a vacant expression, sashayed to the table. "Hi, Patrick," he said in a throaty falsetto. "Who's the hunk? He's not one of the usual dip-shits you hang out with."

"This is my bro from the Midwest, Marty," Patrick replied with an evil grin. "Marty, this is Josie. His mamma named him Joe, but he grew up to be Josie. Marty's one of your straight old boys who still prefers holes to poles."

Cocking his head, Josie appraised Marty and shook his head sadly. "Too bad. Real waste. What you boys drinking tonight?"

Marty replied, "A frosty cold one sounds good to me."

"Do you drink the piss in the green bottles, too?" Josie asked.

Marty looked at Riley whose twinkling eyes didn't match the sober tone of his voice. "Of course he does, darlin'" Patrick said.

"Two Heineken, coming up," Josie replied.

"Bring us two plates of my usual, too" Patrick called out as Josie slinked away. Acknowledging the order, Josie flipped his hand into the air and pointed a manicured index finger toward the ceiling.

The look on Riley's face told Marty he should explain. "What I said at the airport, about the sauce, when I got myself squared away, it wasn't the alcohol at all, it was the depression over Janet's death. I'm not now, nor ever was an alcoholic."

Waving a big paw in the air, Riley said, "Hey, that's okay. I never try to tell another person how to live. Besides, the Irish advising about alcohol would be a real oxymoron." Riley laughed, but he was obviously relieved.

"I like you, Patrick, and I don't want any misunderstandings," Marty said seriously.

They exchanged quips about the other patrons until Josie came back with the burgers and beer. Marty lifted the top section of bun and inhaled. "Ambrosia," he murmured.

"Hell, this is better than ambrosia," Patrick grunted. "This here is one-third pound of your choicest beef, grilled to fat-dripping perfection, served up on a Giusto's nine-grain role with lettuce, tomato, thousand island sauce, grilled onion and sprouts."

"You're right. Ambrosia doesn't stand a chance," Marty agreed. "But, you still had to throw in the friggin' spouts, didn't you?"

They dug into greasy bites, sauce dribbling over fingers and down chins. After they had finished half of the repast, Riley wiped his chin and reached for a paprika-covered French fry.

Leaning forward in conspiratorial fashion, he said, "You didn't fly halfway across the country to admire the scenery and wangle a date with Josie, even though he is cute. Let me bring you up to speed on what's happened," Riley said.

"We have the makings of a major league crisis. Rumor is, another partner at Goldman and Associates was admitted to what they've named the special unit. Looks like the infection has taken a shine to the lawyers in that firm. This one's name is," Riley paused to fish a scrap of paper from his pocket, "Andrew Carson."

Remembering the face of Andrew Carson, Marty hesitated then forced the last bit of burger into his mouth. Licking the grease off his finger tips, he washed the burger down with a swallow of Heineken. "I met Carson last week. This is creepy," he said.

"Creepie ain't half of it. That leaves only Goldman, who resumed his world speaking junket after the memorial service, and," consulting his paper again, Patrick added, "Joe Worthy, who was in San Diego with Rosewood. Worthy isn't sick, yet. But, since you were at the memorial service, you probably know all that."

"Not about the new casualty. The fact that Worthy isn't sick is understandable. The scientist who's helping us back home said not everyone exposed to a given disease will get it. Maybe this Worthy has natural immunity." Marty explained the concept to Patick. "And, there are six people involved in this. We have a judge back home who used to be a member of that firm. He got a letter too."

"Letters?" Riley wrinkled his brow in a puzzled fashion.

Marty explained about the notes that the lawyers had received in San Francisco, and the one Spellman showed him.

"I'll be diddly-damned," Patrick snarled. "The bastards downtown didn't tell me about the notes. I checked the report on the computer. It should have mentioned those notes, but it didn't. Why the hell would they do that?"

"Maybe they don't want to give some other crazies ideas about bumping off lawyers," Marty suggested. "Or maybe it's the clout you mentioned.

"This fucking city has too many unique groups if you ask me," Riley snapped, anger dominating his expression like a sudden, summer thunderstorm.

Finishing off his last bite of burger, Riley wiped his chin and said, "That's not all. We have a sick mayor, and she's worse off than either of the lawyers. They've moved her to the special unit, too. My sources tell me she's not going to make it."

Remembering the mayor from the memorial service, Marty realized that his hands were sweating. Three people who were at the memorial service were hospitalized. More sick lawyers didn't surprise Marty as much as Mayor Johnstone's illness. If it was an infection, and all three of them had it, the exposure had to occur at the service, because that's the only time they were with the mayor. And, if the mayor was infected after such a brief exposure, then whatever it was had to be virulent. The waiter, Jose, and his unusual behavior popped into Marty's consciousness.

"I know this sounds off the wall, Patrick, but I want you to do me a favor. Check with the manager at the Spring Hill Country Club and get me a background on a waiter who works there named, Jose. It may be nothing, but he acted a little strange at the reception. It was the only thing out of place that I can remember"

"No problem," Riley said, taking a pen from his shirt pocket and making a note on the scrap of paper.

"Any chance I could get in to see the mayor, or talk to her doctor."

"Like I told you, the special team from the C.D.C. and that experimental bunch from Maryland are all over that place like white on rice. It's crawling with army sentries and plain-clothes security. Absolutely no visitors."

"I'll check in with Nora tomorrow. She's with the coroner's office back home. Maybe she knows someone out here I could talk to about our Midwest version of this infection."

"From the sparkle in your eye when you mention her name, I'd say she's a little more than the coroner," Riley said.

"Is it that obvious?" Marty asked.

"You got that doomed look, boy," Riley answered.

Patrick took the time to fish a particular paprika-coated fry from the pile on his plate and dipped the end in a dab of ketchup. "I thought you said all your boys checked out from lead poisoning? You said they might have been sick, but what's this about an infection?"

"The first three were sick, but the cause of death is still gunshot wound to the head. I've seen a copy of the autopsy report on your dead lawyer, and our victims showed similar autopsy changes," Marty hedged, and it made him feel uncomfortable. What if Nora was wrong and they were infected? Did he have a right to expose Patrick and his wife? Was Patrick exposed already when he visited the hospital?

"The kicker is the last two victims. Neither of them showed any sign of the disease, although the final tissue reports aren't in yet," Marty continued.

"Maybe the last two were decoys. Maybe they were supposed to throw you off the scent." The look on Patrick's face told Marty that his new friend sensed Marty's evasion.

"I've thought about that. Either way, I think we'll find the answer in that special unit. I can handle a serial killer, but I'm not so sure about the plague," Marty responded.

"You think we may be dealing with a serious infection?" Riley's eyes were cold and all lightheartedness was gone from his tone.

"Could be. Nobody who's handled the bodies or tissue samples back home has gotten sick. Nora's prosector cut his finger on a scalpel blade that they used for the third autopsy, and he's okay, so far. I'll level with you, Patrick, if it is a serious infection, I've probably been exposed." Saying it out loud made Marty cringe at the reality it represented. "If you're concerned, I could check in at a motel: stay away from you and Corin."

Contemplating another fry, Patrick said, "I was sent over to see Rosewood just before he died, and, later on, I interviewed Gordon when he was jaundiced. I wondered why they sent me to check on guys who were sick when no crime had been reported. Now that you've told me about the notes, it makes sense. Since we don't know what they have, or how it's transmitted, I suppose I've been exposed to it, too. If this is something that serious, sounds like we got a leg up on our own plague without crossbreeding with yours. Make you a deal. You don't give me what you got. I won't give you what I got."

"Deal. Us midwestern boys don't cross-breed with nothin' from San Francisco," Marty answered gravely. Riley's expression lightened, and they both laughed.

"I've arranged for you to use the computer in the lieutenant's office. We'll hit it early in the morning. I made a cheat sheet to get you in and out of the files. They have the newspapers on optical disk with a reader file.

You should be able to get what you need," he said pushing a piece of paper across the table. I'm sure it's not much different than what you're used too. Might be a little more powerful and sophisticated. You can access the library files, newspaper, our files, the F.B.I., almost anything."

"The back of the sheet has the data on the derelicts. The file extensions are on the print out. That should save you a shitload of time. Outside of that, there's nothing else I can do."

"Thanks, pal. Now, if you don't get me some rack time, it won't matter what you've done. My fried brain won't be able to understand what I read." Marty reached for the check, and Riley slapped his hand.

"Your money is no good out here. Let's go. Corin has the spare room all spruced up, and she's dying to meet you. I wanted a little time with you first. All the newspaper talk about infections has her antsy. She goes bonkers when someone coughs in the same room. Let's keep this little plague chat among us boys." Marty nodded his assent.

Riley lived in an immaculately restored Victorian townhouse in Pacific Heights. Corin was waiting for them and hugged Marty so tight that he was afraid she would pop one of his vertebra.

His little woman, as Partick called her, was six-feet-one, and had been an All-American volleyball player at Southern Cal. They had met during a fraternity party after the annual S.C.-Notre Dame game, and it was love at first site. Corin was a marvellous combination of overwhelming female, grace, and centerfold pulchritude.

Corin made Marty feel welcome and asked him non-stop questions about everything from his trip to the coast to his family while feeding him cheese, fruit, water crackers and warm, sourdough bread. Despite the stop at Hamburger Mary's, Marty polished off his share, as well as a measure of the wine she served with it.

When they finished, it was nearly two. Marty thought about waking Nora, then decided it was too early in Akron. Corin showed him to a cozy room on the third floor where he climbed into bed, turned out the light and slept like a stone.

CHAPTER
18

pening the door of Nora's make-shift cell, a shaft of light bore past Alexander Bell and assaulted Nora's dark-adjusted pupils, causing her to wince with discomfort. Stepping into the room, Bell turned on the single bulb with a pull chain, and Nora blinked rapidly as her eyes slowly adjusted to the new level of illumination. She channeled her obvious discomfort into fury directed toward her tormentor.

"Damn you, Alex! Untie me right now! This has gone on long enough!" Her voice trembled with rage.

Ignoring the outburst as if she had merely said good morning, Bell said, "I know you are uncomfortable, my dear, and I'm truly sorry. You have missed your evening meal, so I've brought you a late supper. I hope you're fond of Big Macs. I'm not much of a cook I'm afraid." He shrugged his shoulders sheepishly. "There's also some coffee and Coke. You may have either or both."

When he placed the bag of food on the floor, the smell of onion wafted through, evoking a growl of hunger from her stomach. "Do you need to relieve yourself?" he asked gently.

For several seconds she stared angrily at him, before moving her arms and legs as if they were stiffened with starch. The tracks from fresh tears mingled with the oil on her cheeks, and her hair was greasy and matted with perspiration. Her miserable appearance made him feel momentarily sorry for what he was doing to her.

"Yes," she whimpered pathetically.

She's good, he thought. *She was trying to sound as if she was beaten. That is poorly disguised anger. I must think of a way to frighten her. Frightened, she's malleable. Angry she's dangerous.*

"I brought a portable commode with me and placed it in the closet next door. If things go as I have planned, I'll be able to return frequently enough that you won't get too uncomfortable," he said, bending down to untape her ankles.

As soon as he released the tape, she brought her knees up sharply into his face, and he tasted the rusty flavor of blood from his damaged nose. The move caught him off balance, and he toppled over backward, striking the back of his head on the wall. Pinpoints of white light streaked his vision like a meteor shower. The blow temporarily stunned him. Shaking his head helped to clear his vision, as she bolted past him into the hall. Bell lunged for the door, but she kicked it closed in his face.

The door locked when she slammed it, and he furiously rattled the knob in vain. Fighting to control the anger her attack had produced, Alex closed his eyes and breathed until he could make his voice infuriatingly calm.

"Nora, you cannot escape. Even if you free yourself, you cannot get out of the containment facility without the code. I've closed the override mechanism. Now, will you please open this door before I lose my temper?" He gritted his teeth in an effort to remain calm.

Nora didn't answer him. There was the scrape of furniture and the sound of breaking glass from beyond the door. If she got both hands free, she might find something to use as a weapon. Damn the woman.

Centering his energy into a closed, right fist, Bell smashed it into the panel in the center of the door. The wood splintered on impact, and he stepped forward, adding his weight to the left-handed strike that took out a third of the door panel.

He could see Nora, who jumped at the sharp crack that had accompanied the sound of the splintering wood. She had been able to get her hands in front of her and was frantically sawing through the last vestige of the tape that bound her wrists on a piece of broken beaker that she had trapped between her knees.

The tape on her wrists separated, and she dashed toward the exit door. Reaching through the splintered door panel for the knob, Bell burst from the room as Nora yanked on the dogging wheel of the chamber door with an effort that reddened her face. The wheel didn't budge.

To the right of the door was a lever resembling a fire alarm pull handle. Red letters above it identified the bar as the emergency manual override. Nora grabbed the handle and pulled down with all her strength. The handle snapped down. Nothing happened. Panic set in, and she rapidly jerked the handle up and down.

She turned to face him as he stormed down the hall toward her. The fury that he had been fighting to control for years, urged him to hurl himself down the hall like a rampaging bull and smash her to pieces. It took

all of his considerable self-control to remember that she was not the enemy. As he approached, she looked frantically around for something she
could use as a weapon. There was nothing.

Grabbing her by the shoulders, he slammed her against the metal
door. It felt good to punish her. He spat out the blood that seeped down
his throat from his nose. The circular handle on the door dug painfully
into her back. His face was inches from hers, and she tried to turn her
head.

Releasing her right shoulder, he grasped her mercilessly by the hair,
forcing her to face him. As he talked, he sprayed her face with droplets of
blood-tinged spittle.

"Nora, you are forcing me to hurt you. Don't you *ever* try anything
like this again. If you do, I will have no choice but to kill you! Do you understand?" The shouted words echoed through the steel chamber.

Breathing heavily, he dug his fingers painfully into her shoulders
when she didn't answer. "Do you understand?" he asked again, shaking
her so hard that her head snapped back, and her teeth clanked together.

Tears of pain burned down her cheeks. Nodding, she allowed herself
to go limp. Bell breathed in the white light and eased his grip, pushing the
anger beneath the surface.

Putting his arm around her in grandfatherly fashion, he dabbed her
cheeks with a handkerchief from his breast pocket and said, "My dear
Nora, you are a brilliant young scientist. I have no quarrel with you. I
wish you and your young man nothing but happiness . . . after I am finished. I simply cannot let you stop me until I have completed my work."

"What work, Alex?" Nora sobbed. "Why are you doing this? Those
men were just homeless creatures with nowhere to go."

"That's quite correct, Nora. They did nothing to me. They were just
that-nothing. Don't you understand?" The frustration of her ignorance
caused him to raise his voice. He disliked raising his voice. There were so
many brilliant people in the world. Why did they have so little common
sense?

Finally, he was able to answer her through teeth clenched in a struggle for self-control. "They were my living laboratory, experimental animals, to be used to develop safeguards for those who mean something to
society. I gave their miserable existence what little meaning it could ever
have when I sacrificed them. In their deaths, they proved beyond the
shadow of a doubt the validity of my work. Society should erect a monu-
ment to them. Their deaths were a noble sacrifices for the advancement of
science."

"What scientific advancement? Why did they have to be sacrificed,
Alex?" Nora asked, lowering her voice in a transparent attempt to sooth
him. It succeeded in making him more angry.

"That will be evident in due time. Come, you've been a bad girl."
Turning her roughly around, he guided her back towards the room. It

made him feel better to dig his fingers deeper into her shoulders than was necessary. Wincing with pain, she bit her lip so she wouldn't cry out. Smiling, he squeezed harder.

"May I go to the bathroom, Alex? Please?" she asked as they neared her cell.

"I'm sorry my dear. You have abrogated your right to the social graces. You have been very naughty and must be punished."

Marching her into the closet, Bell pushed her to a sitting position on the stool and taped her ankles together. This time the tape was tight, impairing the circulation to her lower legs. Next, he taped her left hand above her head to an exposed hot water pipe. The arm stretched away from her at an awkward angle. After securing her to the stool by running several lengths of tape across her lap and under the seat of the stool, he placed the McDonalds bag within reach of her right hand.

"If you are hungry, you may eat. I do not believe you can free yourself, but with some ingenuity, you should be able to retrieve the food. If not . . . it is fit punishment for your shameless behavior."

"Please Alex, let me use the commode. I feel like I'm going to explode. Please, Alex."

"Next time, if you're a good girl."

Turning abruptly, he walked outside and closed the shattered door. In the outer room, he snapped off the overhead light, and backed away from the light that seeped through the hole in the door so he could watch her without being seen. The aroma of the food in the McDonalds bag drifted toward him.

Nora's plight reminded him of the classic white rat experiment from Psych I at the university. The class subjected the poor creature to two, equally enticing choices. Regardless of the choice the rat made, it was rewarded with an electric shock. Each time the rat was shocked, its frustration increased exponentially. Finally, it decompensated and cowered in the corner of the maze box, unable to move. Nora now knew what that white rat felt.

Taking a deep breath, she reached for the McDonalds bag. Unrolling it with her free hand proved easy. Opening it, she extracted the Big Mac, laid it on her lap and unwrapped the burger. Nora bit into it ravenously.

The Coke was her next obstacle. The lid came off easily. Polishing off the sandwich, she ignored the fries and drained the soda. Her ingenuity impressed him.

Turning her attention to the bonds, she tried wiggling her toes and stamping her feet. Good. Decreased circulation in her limbs would discourage her from another physical assault. Her taped hand was going to be as numb as the leg. A painful expression crossed her face, as she sucked in a breath.

Gritting her teeth, Nora pushed off with her feet, tugged downward with her fettered arm, and hopped the stool closer to the bound arm, relieving some of the pressure. Stopping to rest, she leaned forward in her chair, causing him to silently applaud her determination. Resourceful, ingenious, determined and brilliant. Doctor Daniels was a very special person.

Despite himself, Bell found her torment exciting, and he felt the stirring of a partial erection. The painted faces of the Vietnamese whores flickered into his consciousness like photographs from an album. The only time he had ever had an orgasm with a woman was when he killed one of the filthy sluts. Would killing Nora give him that kind of pleasure? But, that had been another life. He was too civilized for that barbarism now. Besides, he didn't need women for anything.

Nora tugged and tore at the lap tape to no avail. She hopped the stool further to the left to get as much pressure off the arm as she could. A look of dismay crowded out the pain on her face, and she squirmed as though there was something unpleasant on the chair beneath her. Nora stretched toward the taped arm. With a burst of movement, she tried to swing all her weight on the tape. Instead of breaking, the tape only tightened.

Closing her eyes, Nora gritted her teeth and gasped for breath through clenched teeth. No longer able to dam the flow of urine, she emptied her bladder down her legs onto the floor of her cell. As she howled in anguish, it collected in a puddle by her feet. When she started to whimper, Bell quietly left the containment area.

CHAPTER
19

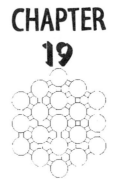

ight streaming in the window through paisley curtains pulled Marty to consciousness. Sitting up in the strange bed, he looked at his watch. It was nearly ten o'clock. Throwing back the covers, he leaped to his feet. The sudden movement made his head swim. Then, he remembered that he was in the Riley's spare bedroom, and he hadn't reset his watch yet. It was seven in the morning.

A delicious odor of bacon permeated the air, and he detected muted sounds from the kitchen directly below his bedroom. Shuffling into the attached bathroom, he turned on the shower.

As he toweled himself dry, there was a knock on the bathroom door. "Are you decent?" asked Corin from the hallway.

Wrapping the generous bath towel around his middle, he opened the door.

"As decent as I ever get. Good morning."

She looked radiant, and smiled warmly as she handed a mug of coffee across the threshold. Corin was barefoot, without makeup, and had her silken, blonde hair pulled back in a bun. She wore a mauve sweatshirt and looked like a goddess from Norse mythology. "French roast black. It's our favorite. I hope you like it. Breakfast in ten minutes. There's a hair dryer in the cupboard under the sink."

"French roast happens to be what I drink every morning. Thanks."

After running an electric razor over his chin, he splashed on Polo Crest, then dressed in a pair of tan Dockers, Topsiders with no socks and a cranberry turtleneck. Marty glanced in the mirror and decided that if he had more tan, he could be taken for a native Californian.

The airy breakfast nook stood before a bay window that looked out on a central garden filled with blooming perennials.

Colorful orange and yellow patterned curtains accented the chocolate colored counter tops. Tasteful accent pieces gave it a cheerful, spring look. It reminded him of Nora's kitchen.

Seemingly engrossed in the morning paper, Patrick sat with his glasses perched precariously on the end of his ample nose. Wrinkling his nose, the glasses teetered but didn't fall. "Damn, Corin. It smells like a French whorehouse in here. Are you using that cheap perfume again?" A smile danced in Patrick's eyes, and he studiously avoided smiling or looking at Marty.

"Maybe you should tell Corin how you know what a French whorehouse smells like, Walking to the stove, where Corin was working on something that smelled wonderful, Marty peered over her shoulder.

"Smells good, " he said.

"I think you're going to like it. Do you like to cook?"

"Let's just say that I've developed a keen interest in it lately."

"He's got a new sweetie, Corin. You know how young lovers are, Patrick interrupted, then told Corin all he knew about Nora, as Marty listened, blushing.

"How'd you sleep, Marty?"

"Like a log," Sitting down opposite Patrick, the place setting was white china trimmed in yellow and orange that matched the draperies. Two-toned napkins of the same color were looped by monkey wood, napkin rings. It looked like a picture from *House Beautiful.*

"I hope you're hungry," Patrick said. "The little woman has rustled up enough grub for a scout troop."

Corin nudged Patrick with her hip as she walked by and poured Marty a glass of fresh-squeezed orange juice. "Two big hulks like you should be able to polish off this little ol' breakfast and ask for more."

"I think we just got challenged," Patrick said. "Nothing new for you in the news. They transferred the mayor and both lawyers to the critical list. Thome homered in the last of the ninth, and the Indians beat the Twins two-zip." He shoved the front section of the paper to Marty, and he read the update on the lawyers.

Corin returned with plates in each hand. "How do you like the way these women jocks use both hands, Marty. Ain't it great?" Patrick said with a leer as he twisted an imaginary mustache.

Partick was a fun-loving man, and Corin seemed to be a good sport, and was well suited to Patrick's whimsical nature. Marty wondered if the absence of children meant they couldn't have any, or had chosen not to. The size of the offspring these two might have produced would have been something to see.

"Here you go, *boys, "*Corin responded, frowning at Patrick. She set the plates down and punched Patrick in the shoulder. "Behave yourself, animal," she added. "Wait till Marty gets to know us better before you drag all the family secrets out of the closet."

"Remember darlin', this is San Francisco. When you talk about coming out of closets, be sure Marty knows what you're referring too." Watching the Riley's made him miss Nora more than he already did.

The plate Corin sat before him was smaller than the one already at his place and coordinated beautifully with the larger one. Two wheat crepes filled with sweetened, ricotta cheese, peaches and blueberries, sat on a bed of sweetened, peach puree dotted with fresh berries. She returned with a side of crispy bacon for each of them.

Eating heartily, Marty complimented the chef again. When he was finished, he begged off seconds and asked, "May I use your phone to call Nora? I'll put it on my credit card."

"The phone is in the den," Corin said, "but if you put it on a credit card, I'll track you down and break your fingers."

"Don't you love the way the little woman sweet-talks? When you're finished making long-distance ga-ga, brush your teeth and we'll head downtown. I'll just have another crepe while you're busy. Got to work on my girth," Patrick said, patting his abdomen.

Marty carried his coffee cup into the den off the living room. One wall was lined with books, and the window overlooked the steep street in front of the house.

When he got the answering machine, he felt a little silly. Of course, it was 11 o'clock. Nora would be at the office. No, this was Sunday. She should be at home. Maybe she went to church. Marty realized that he didn't know how Nora felt about religion. He didn't know how Nora felt about most things, but he wanted to know how she felt about everything. Marty left her a message, promising to call.

Marty was frowning when he came back to the kitchen.

"What's the matter, Marty?" Corin asked. "Is anything wrong?"

"Nora wasn't home. I hope there hasn't been another killing."

"Young love," Riley grumbled. "Come on, Marty. Let's hit it."

Patrick wasn't working today, and he introduced Marty to the duty crew, showed him where the bathroom and coffee pot were located and ensconced him in the lieutenant's office in front of the computer. He scribbled his phone number on the top of Marty's computer cheat sheet. "Call me if you need anything, or if you get lost bumbling around the computer files. I'll be back around noon, and we'll grab some lunch."

Food was the last thing on his mind at the moment. Filling the coffee mug Patrick had given him, he set to work.

Marty negotiated his way into the central records file. They were arranged into segregated computer files identified by code names. Consulting Patrick's cheat sheet, he punched in the file titled DEATHANG. EXE. The records had been upgraded to optical disk files, so crime scene photographs, pictures of suspects, coroner's sketches and any other pertinent data could be viewed rapidly.

This was a far cry from the stacks of paper files that he would have had to wade through five years ago. Of course, the paper files were probably still in packing crates somewhere in the bowels of the station house. Marty thought about Nora's description of storing autopsy materials. The police departments of the world were worse.

The cases were sequenced in order of occurrence. Marty read the entire file to get an overview of what happened. Then, starting at the first, he read them again, pausing to take notes and write down the questions that came to him.

Despite the well-arranged files, Marty's plodding style had eaten up the entire morning. It was nearly noon. Much to his surprise, he was hungry. At the pay phone across the squad room, he dialed Nora's number. The recorder answered again. He left another message.

Marty hung up and called the homicide desk in Akron. Mort Peckum was the duty sergeant on King's day off. "Mort, Marty Cox. Have there been any calls for me today?

"Hi, Marty. Nope, nothing. You expecting something?"

"Not really. Doctor Daniels was supposed to call me after she met with Dr. Bell. Anymore street folks bite the dust?"

"All quiet on the western front. No, I guess it's eastern front from where you are, and no, Doctor Daniels hasn't called."

"Thanks, Mort. If she does, take a message. See ya."

Placing the receiver back on the cradle, he frowned. That little grumble that told him things weren't right surfaced. Marty called her office number and gave up after ten rings. Something was wrong. Where was she? *Get hold of yourself old boy,* he chastised himself.

Walking through the office door, Patrick waved at him. "How is she? Finally get in from her date?"

"She's still not home," Marty said glumly.

"Don't worry. I'm gonna take you to lunch at the Cliff House. It'll take your mind off things."

Corin was waiting in the car, and they bantered as they drove along Geary past the Japan Center and into the Richmond District. The houses thinned as they rounded the curve and started down the hill toward the ocean. Parking against the curb on the steep hill above the Cliff House, they walked down the hill past the remnants of the Sutro Baths to the San Francisco landmark.

The Cliff house looked magnificent as it stood poised on a rock precipice facing the Pacific Ocean. The proud piece of San Francisco's history dated back to a gentler time, when Sunday afternoon picnics by the sea, and swimming in the protected pools of the Sutro Baths was a pleasure shared by families and lovers. It was a time when Victorian principles and architecture ruled the city.

Though the glass window facing the ocean, they were able to see the waves dashing against the protruding rocks and could watch the antics of a colony of sea lions that inhabited the rocks. Occasionally, their barks could be heard through the glass as they squabbled over possession of a particular spot on the rocky roost.

They dined on perfectly fried calamari rings, french fries and Caesar salad, accompanied by an excellent Fume Blanc. Corin gave most of her fries to Patrick. Pushing back from the table, Marty patted his waist. "I knew I should have brought the slacks with the expandable waistband."

"You're still skinny," Patrick said with a chuckle. "How's it going, Marty? Have you come up with anything helpful, yet?"

"Not yet. I don't want to jump to conclusions. I just finished the first go-round. When I get home tonight, we can chat."

"Cigars and brandy in the den," Patrick said, clapping his hands together with glee. "That's what I like to hear."

"You like to hear anything that gives you an excuse to smoke one of your smelly stogies," Corin said. "Just get all the shop talk done *before* we go to dinner."

"Yes, Corin," the men answered, like repentant school boys.

When he got back to the office, Marty entered the next file marked, DEATHANG. EXE. and scanned it. This file contained clips of newspaper articles describing the crimes. A comment in the article about the death of the first victim caught his attention:

The mysterious stranger connected with the epidemic of gastrointestinal disease among the street people in the Embarcadaro region may have escalated to murder.

The article described the first of the five confirmed victims of the Death Angel. The man had been found in an alley beside his worldly possessions, a shopping cart filled with old bottles, cardboard and rags. His body was badly bruised, and multiple needle marks were found on his arms.

How could this man afford drugs? Marty added that to his list of questions.

Pulling up the pictures from the autopsy, he reread the coroner's report, and reviewed the sketches and report of the crime scene officers again. No drug paraphernalia was found on the body or among his possessions.

Carefully, he repeated the sequence with each of the five confirmed cases. An obvious pattern was evolving, but he resisted the temptation to start analyzing things. The last two men both died in the hospital from acute gastrointestinal hemorrhage. In the autopsy data, Marty found something that gave him a chill.

Splitting the screen, he brought up both autopsy reports at once and started to compile a list of similarities between them. By the time he had finished, Marty was perspiring. The autopsy reports of the first five deaths showed the same thing. There it was, plain as day, and he had missed it the first time.

It was almost five. Walking to the phone, he dialed Nora's number again. When the answering machine responded, Marty slammed down the receiver before the message ended.

Drumming his fingers on the phone box, he extracted a handkerchief and wiped the perspiration from his forehead. Dialing information, he jotted down the number, hung up and redialed.

"Peters' residence," a young female voice answered.

"This is Detective Martin Cox. I'm sorry to bother you at home, but it is imperative that I speak with Doctor Peters. Is he in?"

There was a scratching sound as she covered the receiver and spoke to someone. He couldn't understand what was said.

"He's not available at the moment. May I take a message?"

"I'm trying to contact a member of his staff, Doctor Nora Daniels. I have an important message for her."

A hand went over the phone again, and a man's voice said, "Detective, this is Doctor Peters. I just came in. What can I do for you?" Marty repeated the request.

"I've been out of town, Detective, but I stopped by the office to retrieve messages. I had one from Doctor Daniel's assistant. Doctor Daniel's mother was involved in an automobile accident, and Nora's gone to Columbus. I don't believe it was serious, but Nora, as an only child, wanted to be there with her. May I give her your message when she checks in?"

"Thank you, Doctor. I have her mother's number," Marty lied. He wasn't ready to tell Peters what was going on yet. At least she was all right, and he could stop worrying about her.

Feeling relieved, Marty went back to the desk and sorted his notes. Then, he remembered the gastrointestinal flu epidemic noted in the article. There was mention of the dark stranger. Marty went to the newspaper file and brought up the menu. Under search, he inserted the words gastrointestinal flu and dark stranger and pressed "enter."

The screen blinked and the message, out of range, appeared. Puzzled, he tried again with the same results. He manually started to page back through the file from the date of the first murder. After two months, when the date read January 1, he got another end of file message. That was evidently as far back as the computerized data went.

Returning to the original case file, Marty went through the data one more time. When Patrick arrived about six, Marty was ready to go.

They seated themselves in the den, sipping glasses of mint flavored, iced tea. Dinner was set for eight at Aqua, an upscale seafood restaurant on California Street.

"Let's talk shop. We can't tick off the boss lady, or she'll kill us." Marty said. Patrick smiled and nodded.

"Before we start, I checked with Spring Hill Country Club and they had extra help that day. No less than four Joses that day. Since you didn't have a last name it'll take a while.

"I think I see a pattern," Marty began. "Before you measure me for a rubber room, hear me out. Okay?" Patrick nodded.

"The first five cases are interesting. Body one was found near the water south of Market on Third. From the amount of bleeding and bruising, hemorrhage under the skin, puffy face, blood around both eyes, they figured he was beaten to death. The autopsy report mentioned needle marks on the arms, so they wrote him off as a dead junkie. They only made the connection after the next two deaths."

"He could have been a junkie," Riley said. Moving to a teak box on the corner of his roll top desk, he extracted a thin cigar. "Want one? The little woman lets me have two a day."

"Nora quit, and if I smoke she will too. Thanks anyway."

"Damn, I got to meet this girl."

"I would like that. Let's hold your question about the drugs for a second. Number two turns up exactly three days later, north of China Basin on Townsend. This time, more needle marks but less bruising.

"Then there was a gap of . . . " Marty paused to look at his notes, "fifteen days before number three turns up on the Embarcadaro near the Ferry Building. Exactly three days later, number four is found a block further up the street. Each resembles a smash and grab, except there's nothing to grab from these guys, and there are needle marks."

"The detectives thought it was a bad batch of heroin. But, these gentlemen of the gutter had no money to support a habit with that many needle marks, and they never found any drugs in the tox screens. There were never any kits. Not a single needle, syringe, or tourniquet was ever found."

"What are you driving at, Marty?"

"In a minute, buddy. Number five shows up almost a month later. Twenty-seven days to be exact. He only has damage to the organs internally. Nothing outside. There were changes in the liver, heart and lungs, reminiscent of our Akron boys."

"Now comes the clincher. Exactly ninety days later, the first man dies in the hospital. The post findings are a carbon copy of number five. This bird lived long enough to talk about a strange figure, a Dark Angel, who gave him liquor."

"A vampire on shore leave?" Riley interjected.

Marty scowled at him. "Be serious. Sixty days later . . ." he went back to the notes, "Mr. Joseph Carbone buys the farm in San Francisco General of gastrointestinal hemorrhage, after a three day illness that looked just like victim three. Carbone also babbled on about a shadowy stranger. Then, the killings stop."

Draining the last of his tea, Marty changed his mind and took one of Patrick's cigars. When he had finished lighting it, he continued. "The killings stopped until six months ago, when they started again in Akron, Ohio." Looking at Riley, Marty tried to gage his reaction.

Wrinkling his brow, Patrick blew three perfect smoke rings toward the ceiling. He went to a decanter on a corner shelf and poured a Jamisons, neat. "Want one? I got to have something stronger than tea if I'm going to buy into this. How does it connect with what's going on in Akron and our local shysters in the special ward?"

Accepting the glass from Riley, Marty took a sip, and the warm liquid burned his throat. "That's where the holes are. I'm not sure. Are we dealing with a certifiable looney-tune or a calculating maniac? There was a reference to an epidemic of stomach flu and a dark stranger in the article about the first murder. I want to check it out tomorrow. Think you can stand me for one more night?"

"You bet," Riley said, grinding out the cigar butt in the ashtray next to him. "Let's get the little woman and tackle some fish to die for."

"Poor choice of words, buddy," Marty said as they stood.

"What do you make of the needle marks, Marty? If it's not drugs, what is it? If we're not dealing with some sick fucker, what the hell's going on?"

Marty felt the weight of his answer. "I'm almost afraid to say it out loud. I've got this terrible feeling in my gut that a genuine Dr. Frankenstein is out there, and he's about to turn a real-life monster loose in the world that's worse than any nightmare Mary Shelly could ever have dreamed up."

Radiant in a cheery, yellow, sun dress with a brown and yellow, flowered jacket, Corin brought the sunshine of her presence into the smoky room and drove away the depression of their conversation.

"How do I look?" she demanded.

"Good enough to eat," Patrick said, twisting the imaginary mustache again.

Aqua was on California Street next to Taddish Grill, another San Francisco landmark. It was California panache at its best. The vaulted dining room was utilitarian, with a bank of mirrors on the wall opposite the wooden bar. The tables were too close for intimate conversation without involving those at the next table in the dialogue. The tinkling of glasses, intermingled voices and waiters who glided efficiently though narrow passageways from table to table added an air of excitement to the room.

The black mussel souffle appetizer that he ordered was both delicious and unusual, and he chose steamed John Dory with a sauce of wild mushrooms and truffles, served on a pastry shell filled with parsnip puree. Corin chose Aqua's version of surf and turf, a delectable white fish and squab dish, while Patrick groused over the lack of real meat on the menu, then polished off his nut-crusted salmon in dill sauce without a whimper.

Sipping Cakebread Chablis after dinner, they reminisced about Chicago and traded war stories. They gave him plenty of chance to talk about Nora and to sing her praises. The more he talked about her, the more he missed her.

Marty felt tired on the ride home, but when he went to bed, sleep was elusive. He desperately wanted to hear her voice and talk to her about the wild theory he had developed. Turning over on his side, he pounded his ear into the pillow.

Suddenly, like the light bulb in the balloon over the comic strip character's head, Marty remembered his own answering machine. Nora had teased him mercilessly about it when he told her he had bought one. Perhaps she had left him a message.

Pausing to pull on his pants, he tiptoed down the stairs to the den. When his recorded message started, he pushed five on the key pad. The pre-recorded message of greeting was interrupted by three electronic beeps. There was a crackle of static on the line and then an uninterrupted series of beeps. There were no messages on the tape. When he hung up the phone, his hand shook. Something was very wrong.

CHAPTER 20

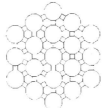

t was early in the morning when Alex Bell opened the door to Nora's prison and went inside the cramped space. When he cut the tape suspending her arm, it fell like a dead weight into her lap. The skin of her hand was the color of fish-flesh, and as the blood surged back into collapsed veins and capillaries, she yelped with discomfort. He cut the tape around her feet and over her lap.

"I'm sorry my dear. I know your arm feels as if you have stuck your fingers into a light socket, but the pins and needles sensation will go away when the circulation is restored."

He kept his voice gentle; filled it with kindness. "I hope we can avoid any more frightful episodes like the one last evening. I'm going to let you get up and walk about. You may use the lavatory and freshen up at the sink in the animal lab. I've brought you a clean scrub suit to replace the one you soiled. I have food, too. I thought we could share a meal together. If you're ready to be more civil about your circumstances, I will leave you relatively unfettered when I go. I shall have to minimally restrain you. No surprises when I come back."

Nora thanked him and used the porta-potty. Her panties were stained with dried urine, so she left them off. She gave herself a sponge bath in the scrub sink. From the look on her face, it was as good as a bubble bath in a luxury hotel. Ignoring his presence, she cleaned the encrusted urine from her pubic hair, labia and the insides of her thighs. The skin was irritated and burned by the irritating urine. Bell watched her as he would watch a cat preening itself, turning discreetly away before she was finished and looked up. Women didn't interest him physically, anymore.

"I hope you like Mexican," he said cheerfully when she was done. "I stopped at Taco Bell."

She nodded. "I am hungry, Alex."

He had previously placed two chairs opposite each other in the center of the chamber. Between them was a surgical stand that passed for a table. He had draped it with a scrub towel and had spread out tacos, bean burritos, tostadas and large Pepsis.

Unwrapping a burrito with green sauce, Nora took a bite. Filet mignon could not have been better. "This is kind of you, Alex. Thank you. What time is it?"

"It's very early in the morning. I'm afraid I've been gone for quite some time, but I had a great deal to do. Another twenty-four hours and your confinement will no longer be necessary."

"Alex, I'll be missed. Marty will come looking for me."

"I left a message with your department secretary, informing her that you had gone to Columbus to be with your mother who was injured in an auto accident. I accessed your personnel file from the hospital computer to get mama's address. There's no reason for them to doubt. If they check Riverside Hospital, the computer will tell them that your mother is resting comfortably in their observation unit and will be released shortly.

By the time Detective Cox returns from the coast and uncovers the charade, it will be too late."

"Too late for what, Alex?"

When he looked at her, his eyes were devoid of expression. Did she think her feigned sincerity fooled him? How could she have so many attributes, yet be so stupid about some things?

"What did you mean when you said the sacrifice of the street subjects was necessary? You said that monuments should be erected to them. Why, Alex?" she asked.

Bell ate half a tostado in silence, save for the crunch of the crispy tortilla. The unruly sauce made a mess of his fingers, and he wiped them on a napkin.

"In any scientific experiment, controls are necessary. When the military tested nerve gasses, or sought antidotes for communist block poisons, they used human subjects. Condemned prisoners and political captives were sacrificed like laboratory animals in the name of national security."

"In the forties, when the government wanted to assess the effects of atomic energy on human beings, unwitting military personnel were subjected to crippling and even lethal doses of radiation, this time in the name of national defense."

"My work is no different. I needed human subjects. Because of lawyers, human subjects are no longer available. I could not use primates. I hate to work with the filthy beasts, and besides, I could never risk the chances of public contagion should one escape. A public outbreak would be unthinkable. I could never do that, never."

"So, I turned to the living dead. Men who had stopped living and were taking up space on the streets until some quirk of fate ended their lives. I didn't use any of the retched women from the back alleys, because I didn't want to contaminate the experiment with the different reaction that women might have to my inoculations. To use only men required less sacrifice. I provided a service to society and advanced my work simultaneously."

"What kind of research?" When he frowned sharply, she hastily added, "If you care to discuss it with me."

Unwraping another burrito, she began to eat. Pondering her for what seemed an eternity, he began haltingly, "I suppose if something should happen to me, someone should understand the basic tenets of my work in order to avoid widespread panic and an unnecessary waste of resource trying to prevent that which needs no prevention. I will share with you what time permits."

"I told you that the Ebola virus has seven proteins in its matrix. I said that we know a little about three of them and nothing at all about the other four. Well, my dear Nora, I lied." An impish look danced across his face, like a schoolboy who had just put one over on the teacher.

"There is no way for you to know, but I worked with nucleic acids and nucleic acid sequencing when I was at Berkley. When the filovirus wriggled from the primordial slime of Marberg, USAMRIID made me a lucrative offer to help develop the military potential of the virus."

"Jesus, they don't even know how to keep the stuff from killing people, and they're looking for military uses?" There was outrage in her voice.

"Remember, child, that not all people view the world from the same perspective. We are not as free from atomic-age mentality as you would like to believe. Some still find a threat under every rock. They just have new names."

But, they gave me a blank check, that I could also use to support more humanitarian labors, so I went to work."

"When did you move to Maryland?"

"I didn't. The lab came to me. My family resided in Palo Alto, so I refused to leave." His eyes narrowed, and for a brief moment an immense pain tore from its mooring in his subconscious and roared into his conscious. It was some time before he could trust himself to continue.

"I identified the three proteins of the virus. They are of no consequence. They regulate the mundane functions of the cell. Once the virus infects the lymphocytes, they take over the normal cellular function, the sodium pump, endoplasmic reticulum and so on. They readjust host cell functions to benefit the virus. It is the other four that are the keys to the deadly nature of the virus."

"The precise alignment of the other four control the lethal effects of the virus, its survival mechanism, and its ability to replicate. By judiciously rearranging the sequence, by terminal binding or deletion, subsets of virus may be created that will do any number of things. I have solved the riddle, Nora!"

The enormity of what he told her made Nora gasp. "Alex, you've found the key that may unlock viral diseases and given a weapon of unimaginable destruction to those lunatics in the military."

"That's right, Nora. It could be a weapon. But, I had wonderful things planned for it. By rearranging one of the proteins, I found I could speed up or slow down the length of time it took the virus to infect the subject."

"Even more exciting was controlling its reproduction. It proved to be the easiest, and was the first of my discoveries. That allowed me to safely test the first subjects. I could dose the subjects without the worry of an epidemic. By switching the places of the two end proteins and doing something else that I will not reveal to you, the virus is sterile. When the host dies, the virus dies. There is no possibility of an epidemic. What do you think governments of the world would pay for that secret, Nora?"

"Once I had controlled the length of time it took the virus to infect, and was sure it would kill only when I wished it to kill, the last thing I needed to do was to control the destructive effects of my magical threads."

"That proved most difficult, but I solved that one, too. I can down-regulate the destructive process so there is no external trace of the infection. The patient will appear to have died of natural causes, unless there is an autopsy. Then, some bright young scientist like you will uncover my secret."

"What about inoculation, dose, delivery mechanisms? Does natural immunity develop, or does resequencing change that, too?" Nora asked.

"The virus is cooperative. Every three days a new subculture can be made and adjusted. A thimbleful of holding medium could easily infect five-hundred people. Filovirus are susceptible to heat, cold, strong acids or alkalis. They are easily killed outside of the body.

"I have tested this on ten humans so far, and only one showed natural immunity. My germs have a kill rate of ninety percent."

If she was shaken by the fact that he had just confessed to nine sacrifices, she did not let it show. She was as tough as he thought she might be. Instead she asked, "How do you inoculate the subject?"

"I used direct inoculation at first. One-hundred percent effective but terribly cumbersome. It took me several years, but now I have the ideal delivery system for mass audiences."

"The first is drinking water. Unfortunately, not everyone drinks water. What was it that W.C. Fields said?

'I never drink water. Fish fornicate in it.' By a precise alkalinization of the terminal protein, my virus can swim all day in an alcoholic solution that is fifteen percent by volume. I haven't conquered the heady concentrations of the bourbon or scotch that Fields preferred, but beer and wine do quite nicely, as do fruit juices."

"My God, Alex. What did the army do with your data?"

"The army? I never gave the army my data. They would have turned my discoveries into a weapon of mass destruction. Millions could be slaughtered. History would brand me as a monster. No, that would be unthinkable!" How could she think he would do something that horrible? He wasn't a butcher. Only a few unfortunates were sacrificed who were better off dead. That didn't make him a monster.

"Then why, Alex? What are you planning to do?"

Flushing, he clenched his fists and leaped to his feet, knocking over the surgical tray and spilling the soft drinks onto the floor. "Not all the people in this world are innocents, Nora. Some of them are parasites that feed on the sweat and the very bodies of decent people. They don't deserve to live. Think of my discovery as rat poison for human rodents."

"Human rodents? For God's sake, Alex, what are you talking about?"

Refusing to answer any of her questions, he lead her back to the room with the porta-potty and locked her in.

CHAPTER
21

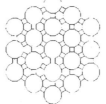

ell left the containment area and went to his office. He had been up half the night using his computer to burrow into airline and hotel files. An ache had developed behind his eyes, and his mouth was so corroded with tobacco that his breath would cause flowers to wilt. At exactly five past seven, he picked up the phone and dialed the judge's office number.

"Good morning, Judge Spellman's office, Janell speaking."

"This is Howard Tompkin, from the law offices of Goldman and Associates in San Francisco. What time do you expect Mr. Goldman to arrive in Akron?" he asked. He had already reversed the process by calling Goldman's office to find out the day, now he needed the time.

"Judge Spellman is on the way to the airport to pick him up now. Say, isn't it the middle of the night out there?" she asked.

"Yes, it is," Bell said evenly. "It is very urgent that I get in touch with Mr. Goldman at once."

"If Judge Spellman checks in with me before then, may I tell him the nature of the emergency?" Suspicion crept into her voice.

"No, thank you. I'll need to speak with Mr. Goldman directly. You've been very helpful," he said, and hung up.

In the bathroom, Bell applied a second layer of make-up cement to his upper lip and waited until it was tacky to the touch before attaching the black mustache. The tinted contact lenses changed his eyes to brown, and body padding added a modest beer belly to his frame. It was time to go to work.

The City Club was located on the top floor of one of Akron's tallest buildings and provided a sweeping panorama of the city. From his post behind the bar, Bell watched as Spellman and Goldman were ushered to a window seat in the grill room by an attractive, brunette hostess with a tight fitting skirt and maroon uniform jacket. The sight of Everett Goldman brought bile to his throat.

The ability to harness his emotions was the secret to his success with disguises. He could be an Amish farmer or a Chicano waiter, or anything else he chose to be. It simply required him to bury Alexander Bell's feelings and emotions and to become an actor playing a role.

Originally Goldman's law firm was his only target. Mayor Johnstone had helped him realize how short-sighted it would be to limit his revenge. There were lots of others who needed to be purged from society. And, he had the perfect means to do it.

Three days ago, Eddie Alvarez, the club's grill room attendant had left suddenly for Alabama on an emergency. Alex had arranged the "emergency" with a ten-thousand-dollar cash payment to Alvarez, who was desperately in arrears with his bookmakers. Disguised as Jose, he was introduced as Eddie's cousin, who would fill in until Eddie returned.

Jose was a splendid bartender with a soft, polite manner and the required degree of humility. The grill room was small and empty at this time of the morning, so he could easily hear their conversation.

"Thank you, Sally," Spellman said. "This is my friend, Everett Goldman. Ev, Sally Kellerman."

"Pleased to meet you, Mr. Goldman." She gave him a toothy smile and extended her hand.

Taking it, Goldman held it a fraction longer than necessary and said, "Pleased to meet you, Sally."

As Sally walked from the room, she nodded for Bell to lean closer."The judge and his guest get special attention."

"Yes Ms. Kellerman. I'll take special care of them. You can count on that," Bell finished filling two glasses on the tray in front of him with orange juice. When she was gone, he added half the contents of the small vial in his pocket to each glass.

The morning sky was overcast and the color of braided steel. Occasional breaks in the clouds allowed patches of blue and streaks of sunshine to permeate the canopy covering the city. "The view is spectacular up here, especially with those clouds," Goldman said.

Spellman grunted with agitation, obviously unimpressed. "Have you heard anything new about Gordon or Carson?"

"What are you talking about?" Goldman asked, arching his eyebrows.

"Before he could answer, Edward Jackson, the grill room waiter, interrupted. "May I get you some coffee, gentlemen?" he inquired, laying menus before each of them.

"Thanks Edward," Spellman said, and the gaunt waiter nodded and shuffled off to get the coffee.

"Did they tell you Gordon was sick? The same symptoms as Hayden.

Next day it was Carson."

"No, I had a last minute change of hotels in Vienna, thanks to a cooperative young woman I met in the bar. How sick are they?"

They turned toward Bell as he came to the table with two tulip glasses. "Mimosa cocktails, complements of Ms. Kellerman," he said with an impeccable Southern draw.

Spellman frowned. Bell set the glasses on the table and smiled amiably. "Are you new here?" Spellman asked. He seemed to be trying to decide if he had seen Bell before.

"I'm Jose, Your Honor. I'm filling in for my cousin Eddie, your regular grill room attendant. His mamma is sick in Georgia. You enjoy, compliments of Ms. Sally."

Walking back to the bar it was difficult to control the rage that simmered beneath his subservient smile. Breathing in the white light, he resumed his station.

"Here's to what's her name," Goldman said as they clinked glasses in an impromptu toast and drank.

"He name is Sally, but forget it. Janell would castrate me if I let you skate away with another skirt."

"Got to protect the family jewels," Goldman laughed as they toasted each other again.

Spellman eyed Bell suspiciously, then said, "Damn, that man looks familiar. I've seen him somewhere before. It'll come to me."

Jackson returned with the coffee. "I'm sorry, Judge. I didn't know you wanted juice."

"It's a Mimosa from Sally," Spellman snapped.

"Oh . . . .." Edward said. He took their breakfast orders.

"I talked to Joe last night. Gordon's as sick as Rosewood was, but Carson just has fever and nausea. The real panic started when Clara Johnstone got it. She's comatose, and they don't expect her to live. I don't think she had time to push your real estate deal through before she collapsed."

Visibly shaken, Goldman nearly spilled the remnants of his Mimosa as he gulped it down.

"There's obvious concern about an epidemic of whatever this is. The Center for Disease Control is there, as well as some high-tech biology team from the military."

"Any connection between this outbreak and that note we got?"

"At first, Worthy said that they thought there was, but when Clara came down with it, it changed the police's thinking."

Goldman was pensive, watching the cloud show through the window for several seconds before he spoke. "If it's an infection, we've all been exposed. It could have been passed around at Rosewood's wake."

Sobered by the conjecture, Spellman said, "What if they quarantine everybody? That would fuck up everything."

It was just like that bastard, Spellman. Nothing mattered except his precious convention, and his own selfish interests. Bell vowed to make certain that it was one convention that no one would ever forget.

"What if it *is* an infection, Aaron?," Goldman asked. Think of the ramifications. How many people have you exposed since the funeral? I could have taken the stuff to Austria and Germany. I could be a damned Typhoid Mary. So could you. There's a hell of a lot more at stake here than your God damned convention!" Goldman's voice was strident.

"Of course, Ev. Of course," Spellman said patronizingly. The whole thing has me on edge, too. I was just trying to be practical."

"Practical? Aaron, you're the only person I know who is more selfish than I am," Goldman said coldly.

Jackson brought their breakfast orders, and Goldman glanced at his watch. "What time is it here? My brain is scrambled from too many time zones."

"It's nine twenty-four."

Thumbing the stem on his watch, Goldman reset the proper time. "There goes six hours. There have been a lot of times in my life that I wished six hours could have gone by that fast," Goldman said wistfully.

"When are you going to get a new watch? You've had that Timex ever since I practiced with you."

"Judges can get away with vulgar displays of prosperity," Goldman said. "It makes the suckers think you're harder to bribe and raises the ante for those who try. A plaintiff's attorney has to make them feel sorry for him."

The phone at Bell's elbow rang. "Grill room, Jose," he said with the drawl.

"Call for Judge Spellman on one. It's his office," said the operator.

"Judge, it's your office on line one." Punching the button under the blinking red light on the panel, Bell handed the phone to Spellman.

"Yes, Janell, he's here. No, not yet. What did he say his name was? Okay." Frowning, he handed the phone back to Bell.

"That was Janell. Tompkin from your office called. Said it was urgent and they'd call you here at nine."

"It's well past that now," Goldman said.

"Janell probably screwed up the time. Maybe he's going to call at nine coast time."

"That makes no sense. There are at least a half-dozen law clerks in the office by seven-thirty every day."

Getting up, he stomped to the bar. "Where's the telephone?" he demanded.

Handing him the phone and indicating a button with a green light, Bell said, "Just punch this button. The operator will connect you."

At the table, Bell asked, "Did you enjoy the cocktail, Judge?"

"Yes," Spellman growled, his eyes locked on the Bell's name tag.

"Haven't I seen you somewhere before?" Spellman asked.

"Not to my knowledge, Judge," Bell said affably.

"You don't look Spanish, and why the southern accent?"

"My mother was Chicano and won the battle of the first names. The last name is Kelly. My friends call me, Joe, and I was raised in Georgia." Picking up the empty champagne flutes, Bell said. "If you will excuse me, sir."

"What's the word, Ev?" Spellman asked as Goldman slumped heavily into the chair across from him.

"Carson started hemorrhaging from the bowels this morning. He's stabilized after massive transfusions, but they don't expect him to make it through the morning. Gordon is worse, too."

"Damn!" Spellman sputtered, lookin as if he had just bitten into a sour lemon.

"A priest just gave Clara Johnstone last rites." Goldman's voice was shaky.

"Any talk of quarantine?" Spellman asked anxiously.

"Voluntary in their homes, so far. They're in the process of tracking down everyone at the funeral and the brunch. The plans are to ask them to do the same."

"Damn," Spellman muttered again.

"Something else peculiar," Goldman said, wiping his forehead with a handkerchief that he produced from his pocket. "We don't have anyone at the firm named Tompkin and no one from the office called here today."

Behind the bar, Bell whistled softly to himself as he washed out the champagne flutes with Clorox.

CHAPTER
22

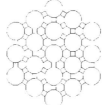

"here's nothing new in the paper about the lawyers, except that all of them, particularly the mayor, are worse," Marty said, as Patrick dug into a bowl of oatmeal with raisins and brown sugar.

"This whole thing makes me nervous," Corin said, turning on the small television set on the counter and finding a channel with a news broadcast in progress. "What if some incurable infection other than AIDS, that's easier to transmit, got loose in the general population?" She visibly shuddered.

The news anchor man with power hair and the frozen smile of the profession looked puzzled and stared off camera. "We're going to break away for a live report from Kevin Marsden at city hall." A younger clone of the anchor man, standing on the sidewalk in front of city hall, filled the screen.

"Yes, Joel, we've been advised that momentarily there is going to be an announcement about Mayor Johnstone's condition. Our cameras are inside." The young man brought a finger to the barely-visible earphone he was wearing. "Let's go inside, Joel. The mayor's press secretary Hillary Graham is at the podium."

A grim-faced woman, obviously struggling to keep her emotions in check, stood gripping the edges of a wooden podium so tightly that her knuckles were white.

"Ladies and gentlemen," she began. "At five minutes past eight o'clock this morning, Mayor Clara Johnstone died as a result of a virulent infection." She struggled harder to keep back tears.

"The organism responsible for the infection has not yet been identified. Details of the memorial service will be supplied to you when they are available."

The woman fled toward the door at the side of the room as the reporters exploded with a barrage of questions she wouldn't answer. The screen faded and Kevin Marsden's face reappeared.

"There you have it, Joel. Mayor Johnstone, one of the most popular mayors the city has seen in recent years, *dead* from an unknown illness. The mayor's personal physician, Doctor Anthony Benedetti, and the Center for Disease Control will supply us with more information shortly. We'll interrupt our current programming to bring you further updates as available. Live, from city hall, this is Kevin Marsden." The studio anchor returned, and, with a sad face, extoled the virtues of the late mayor over a film clip of her political career. Anticipating her death, the station was well prepared to report the story. When the clip concluded, the anchor man smiled and began a report on the parking woes facing fans at Candlestick Park.

Marty got to his feet. "I think I'd better get to the library."

The brilliant blue sky was dotted with wisps of cotton-candy clouds and the warm breeze promised a glorious afternoon. It was the kind of day that made him wish that he didn't have to spend it inside, but Mayor Johnstone's death overshadowed that.

At the library's information desk, he obtained directions to the microfilm file. After working with the computer, the microfilm files were cumbersome. Pages of the paper were stored on large reels. The film was threaded into a reader that passed each frame into the beam of a projection bulb.

It took Marty fifteen minutes to find the first murder, and the article contained only an oblique reference to the Dark Stranger. Page by page he framed back. Forty minutes later, he found it.

After skimming the article, he reread it slowly, jotting notes and questions on his pad. Footnotes at the bottom of the column cross-referenced other articles on the same subject. Finding the referenced article, Marty repeated the procedures. The chain of articles was four links long, and when he finished the third, the pattern was clear.

In March, the emergency department at San Francisco General began to see a trickle of derelicts with debilitating gastrointestinal infections. The trickle increased to a stream, and by the end of July, a flood. A staggering two-hundred-six patients received treatment.

Two similarities between the epidemic and the murders convinced him they were connected. The outbreaks of new cases were separated by multiples of three days. That meant that the incubation cycle of the infecting agent was three days. Likewise, each new outbreak was less severe than the last. Marty was convinced that the stranger who visited the derelicts prior to the outbreak of flu was the same person described by the two men who died in the hospital.

Reviewing the notes from the descriptions, Marty pieced together a composite of the Dark Angel. He was of medium height, average weight and medium build with no identifying marks or scars, and he may or may not have worn glasses. In short, he could be half the men in the library, since at least that many fit the description.

Marty paged back to the first article on the flu outbreak, but found nothing. At least he felt sure that the street people had been systematically infected like guinea pigs in a laboratory. Was Spellman right? Was someone using a lethal organism as a weapon? Could anyone handle anything that lethal and not end up with a generalized pandemic?

Absently thumbing the wheel that turned the film canister, he scanned the pages as they flipped by. A familiar name caught his eye, and he backed up to the article. Two smiling men in Tuxedos flanked an angular woman in a bridal gown. "Goldman and Associates lose case to Cupid," the banner proclaimed.

Marty straightened in his chair, and read the body of the article.

Aaron Spellman, a senior partner in the firm of Goldman and Associates is leaving the practice following his marriage to Ms. Shelia Kauffman of Akron, Ohio. Mr. Spellman will be entering the private practice of law in Ohio, and will manage the affairs of the bride's family, Kauffman Enterprises.

On a hunch, Marty went to the central file and found a dozen more articles listed for Goldman. The first three articles were mundane accolades concerning Goldman's charity work. The others were reports of a sensational malpractice trial involving Goldman and Associates. Four articles referenced both Goldman and Spellman. In the second article that he accessed, Marty found it.

"Goldman says victim deranged", the banner read. Goldman had been the plaintiff's attorney in a malpractice suit. A young vascular surgeon, Nicholas Bellangier, had been on duty at the Pacific Medical Center when the trauma team responded to a twenty-seven-year-old welfare patient named John Henthorn. High on heroin, Henthorn had smashed his motorcycle into the back of a pickup truck.

Henthorn's hip had also been shattered and the femoral artery supplying the blood to his leg badly shredded. Using a novel technique involving artificial graft material, in a seven hour operation, Bellangier restored blood flow to the leg.

Five days later, the artificial graft became infected and the leg become gangrenous. Amputation was required. Despite expert testimony on behalf of Bellangier, supporting his excellent judgement and surgical skill, the jury awarded Henthorn eight million dollars. Everett Goldman and Associates took half the settlement. Co-council Aaron Spellman, was also quoted. Marty's pulse quickened.

The judgement exceeded Bellangier's malpractice insurance, and when the appellate court upheld the judgement, Bellangier had to raise four million dollars from private sources. Five months later, Doctor Bellangier jumped from the roof of the Pacific Medical Center to his death in the street below. Spellman stated that the doctor had been severely depressed and emotionally unstable. Spellman was not surprised at this irrational action. After expressing his condolences to the family, Spellman concluded that at least Bellangier would not be able to harm other patients.

The original article on the suicide was on another reel. Threading the spool onto the reader, Marty's hands were trembling. The headline screamed, "LOCAL PHYSICIAN LEAPS TO HIS DEATH."

According to his friends and co-workers, Bellangier had been despondent over the loss of the malpractice suit, even though the four million dollars had come from family resources. His mental condition had steadily deteriorated. One Thursday afternoon, he had gone to the roof of the hospital, walked to the edge and jumped without hesitation. Since there was no other living family, the body was claimed by his brother Alexander Bellangier.

A picture of Doctor Bellangier was on the second page, and Marty felt his skin crawl when he looked at it. Doctor Nicholas Bellangier was an exact duplicate of Alexander Bell.

CHAPTER
23

lexander Bell, drove down Market Street toward Quaker Square. When they had started the project, he wondered if they would ever get the place finished. It took forever to cut through the silo walls. They were four feet thick. Only in Ohio, or perhaps California, would people think it perfectly sane to turn a derelict grain silo into a hotel with round rooms. The complex had originally belonged to Ferdinand Schumaker, the oatmeal king, and was one of the first Quaker Oats factories.

Parking next to a caboose that was part of the restored train station complex across from the Quaker Square Hilton, he got out of the car. An Italian eatery now occupied the refurbished train station.

The spring evening was muggy, and the oppressive air suggested the possibility of a storm. With a last-minute check of his makeup in the car window, Bell crossed the parking lot that was dominated by massive tan colored grain silos that now sported windows. Patting his breast pocket for the tenth time to be sure the vial was still there, he went into the hotel.

Walking down the hall, Bell entered the utilitarian ballroom where the One Hundred Club dinner would be held. He was surprised at the amount of information about the club on the interntet. Founded fifteen years earlier by a dozen trial attorneys from Columbus and Cincinnati, it was originally called The Lawyers Club of Ohio. Its purpose was to form an elite cadre that the founders hoped would be considered the most prominent and influential trial attorneys' organization in the state. Bell wondered how long it had taken them to establish the criteria for admission, given the egos of the founders.

By the end of the year, twenty-five lawyers were members of the snobbish club, and by the end of a decade their number had swelled to one hundred. It had been decided that no further members should be accepted, and they had changed the name to its current stylish moniker. When a member retired from practice, they became an emeritus member, and the group elected the replacement to keep the number at one-hundred.

According to the computer, a one hundred percent attendance at the annual dinner was the rule. Every chief justice of the state supreme court had been a member of the club since it was founded.

Likewise, the president of the Trial Lawyer's Association was the traditional guest speaker, and since Spellman was not yet a member, he was an invited dignitary. Spellman was the first alternate on the club's list, and his membership was a given with the next vacancy. After this weekend, there would be a considerable number of vacancies, and, if there was a God, which Bell sometimes doubted, Spellman would not be alive to accept it.

The more elegant ballrooms of San Francisco and his brother's haunted eyes tormented him. It wasn't good to think about his brother. This was a night to be relished, free from the turmoil caused by the ghost that had driven him here.

Three walls of the ballroom were decorated with red, white and blue crepe, and a poster-sized picture of a grinning Spellman, with the legend "Akron's Own" beneath it, dominated the fourth wall behind the podium.

In the kitchen, he reported to the catering manager who had hired the extra servers from the City Club to work the banquet and was given an assignment at a back table, far from the podium. It was what he had expected.

"Excuse me, Mr. Davenport," Bell said with all the deference he could force himself to muster. "I know you don't know me from Adam, but I'm from California. I'm using my vacation time to fill in for a cousin of mine who had to leave town on family business."

Davenport raised one eyebrow and stared intently at him.

"I'm the head waiter at the Spring Hill Country Club in San Francisco," Bell lied with a perfectly straight face. "Mr. Goldman is a member there, and I always serve him when he comes in. I would consider it an honor if you would allow me to serve him tonight." Bell's lies flowed in subservient tone.

"I realize he's at the head table, but I am experienced, and I'm sure he would be pleasantly surprised. You have heard of our club?" Bell held his breath.

Davenport looked at him warily. "Yes, of course I've heard of it. We'll see. I'll watch you work the floor during the cocktail hour. Now, get cracking. The reception line is forming up."

"Thank you, sir. I'll see to the members of the receiving line at once."

Almost bowing, Bell scurried off to collect a tray of wine. When his back was turned to Davenport, he gritted his teeth. *Nicky was a lot better at groveling than I ever was,* he thought. *Maybe if Nicky had more fight, . . .* he didn't finish the thought.

The receiving line had been on station for fifteen minutes when a lull occurred, and Bell approached his quarry with a tray of wine. He could feel Davenport's eyes boring into his back.

"I thought you might be getting thirsty by now, Judge. May I offer you some refreshment?" He kept his voice cheery, and he smiled.

He was counting on the fact that Spellman and Goldman would be surprised to see the waiter from the City Club. Their reaction would cement his deception with Davenport, who would think that Goldman knew Jose from the coast, not breakfast this morning.

"What are you doing here?" Spellman demanded in a voice loud enough to be heard by the manager.

For the sake of Davenport, Bell smiled affably while fighting the urge to strangle the arrogant bastard. "I need the dough, Your Honor. I got an expensive ex. This is my night off at the club, and the hotel folks asked me if I would fill in for your special party." Spellman took a glass of white wine; Goldman chose red. It was overkill to dose them again, but he wanted to be absolutely certain that these two died. The president of The One Hundred Club, Roosevelt Edwards chose white.

As the elite of Ohio's trial bar filed into the dining room, Bell was everywhere, with a fresh glass of treated wine, a bite of Brie or a cracker. At seven twenty-five, they dissolved the reception line and went inside. In the kitchen, Bell added a little something to each of the water pitchers.

Calling Bell over, Davenport said, "You did a good job. Take the head table, but no screw ups."

"Yes, sir. Thank you, sir. You can count on me." It worked! There was a God, at least a God of revenge.

The occupants of the head table settled into their places, and Bell came by to fill their water glasses. "The appetizers will be here in a moment, gentleman," he said with a twinkle in his brown eyes.

The meal was excellent, making Bell wish he could join them. Quiche Lorraine was followed by French onion soup and a mixed green salad with fresh tomatos. He might have skipped the prime rib with dutchess potatoes and steamed asparagus and gone straight to the apple tart and vanilla ice cream that was dessert.

Spellman only pushed at his food. Every bite seemed to be an effort, and he periodically massaged his temples. Their headaches should be starting, and maybe the nausea would hit Spellman while he's speaking. But, that would be to much to hope for.

On the other side of the podium, Goldman, who was seated next toEdwards, looked flushed and wiped his brow with a handkerchief. Periodically, he looked down the table at Spellman, and in those looks were traces of fear. It was important that they suffer as Nicky had suffered. Relishing their dread, he prayed that they would be terrified in the end.

By the time Edwards had finished the compulsory witty commentary and introduced Spellman for his speech, Bell wasn't sure that the judge would be able to perform. When he stood, Spellman was shaky, and he looked pale and unsure of himself. However, once he got to the microphone, and started to talk, he suppressed his physical symptoms. By the time he finished, Spellman was in control of himself.

Edwards made the closing remarks and the dinner was over. Bell positioned himself close enough to the edge of the podium to overhear their conversation. "Are you okay?" Spellman asked.

"No, I feel awful. I'm chilling; I'm sweating; hot flashes, and my gut's on fire."

"Let's get out of here. Janell keeps a pharmacy in her purse, so God knows what she keeps at home. We'll get you something there."

"How's your headache?" The fear was in Goldman's voice this time.

"No better; no worse. This has nothing to do with Rosewood. Mine was nerves. Yours is likely some European flu bug. Let's go."

Bell began to clear the dishes from the head table. The annual stag dinner of The One Hundred Club had been a rousing success in ways the participants would not begin to appreciate until tomorrow. Bell yawned. In a couple of hours, he would be sleeping in his own bed.

CHAPTER
24

Nora's breakfast the next morning was scrambled eggs, pancakes and coffee from Burger King. "I don't wish to favor one fast food chain over another," Bell said as he opened bags of food. Her cooperative attitude elevated his already effusive mood. Maybe he could tell a joke. Jokes were something he wasn't very good at anymore.

"Nora, are you aware that Jesus was really Italian?" His blue eyes twinkled and a mischievous grin transformed his face.

"No, I wasn't," she said puzzled.

"Well, he was thirty before he left home. He spent all his spare time with a bunch of guys, and his mother thought he was God. He has to be Italian." Bell guffawed and slapped his thigh in merriment. When Nora realized that it was a joke, she laughed with him, but the laugh was strained.

"You're in excellent spirits this morning, Alex," she said.

"Yes, I am, and by the end of the day, all accounts will have come due: all debts will be paid. I am truly sorry to have put you through all this, but there was simply no other choice.

"When will you let me out? What are you going to do?"

Shaking his head sadly, he stopped to frame his words. It was important to him that she understand. "Society contains creatures far more lethal than anything in this containment facility. This organism has proliferated until there is one under every rock, waiting to destroy anyone who lifts the rock."

"They are without conscience, morals, ethics or principles. Right, wrong and justice are abstract concepts to them. They walk about on two legs in the guise of men and women, but beneath their camouflage they are carrion who tear at the fabric of society."

"We call these two-legged jackals lawyers, Nora. They will drag anyone into court as long as there is money to pay them, or a chance to profit at someone else's expense. They cripple our industries with product liability claims and personal injury suits. They get murderers and rapists off on technicalities, and they think they are above retribution as they hide behind the laws they themselves make. That stops today. None of these vermin will ever feel safe again!" he said, his voice rising as it had done that day in the lecture hall.

"A particular pack of these vultures ruined my life, and took away the dearest thing in the world to me. God has directed those responsible, plus selected others at the convention center to pay. I'm going to feed them my pets."

"My God!" Nora exclaimed, "You plan to kill all those people? Alex, you can't. In the name of God you can't."

"Nora why can't you understand? God brought them to me. God gave me the intellect to control the virus. This is my destiny. God has ordained it. Can't you see. These are not people, these are lawyers. I'm not killing people. I'm a divine exterminator, ridding the world of human cockroaches."

The expression on her face was one of shock mixed with fear. He had frightened her again. How he had done that? What was it that he said? "Enough unpleasantness. Let's enjoy breakfast. This will be the last opportunity we have to talk with each other."

"Why, Alex? I still don't understand why. It would help if I knew. You're a brilliant man with so much to offer" she said quietly.

Her patronizing annoyed him, and he answered her sharply. "Enough, Nora, please. Your young man will come back with what you need to know. I have no doubt about that. You should marry him, Nora. There are not many like him around. Now, let's eat."

After they had been eating quietly for a few minutes, Nora asked, "How did you work safely with the filo virus in this facility?"

"You may have noticed that there are three rooms like the one you have been confined in at this end of the facility. The one farthest from this one is not what it seems. It is a one room level-four containment facility. I've connected it into the air exchange system, then modified the system to be more effective. I installed special materials into the walls, an airlock door behind the wooden one and so on. Before I got interested in germs, I obtained a degree in mechanical engineering. I knew it would come in handy someday."

Pouring more coffee for her, he continued, "When you caught me in the Raycal suit, I knew my ploy could not go on. I kept the suit in a box marked "hazardous waste". The box has never been inspected."

"What about an accident? Weren't you afraid of a spill?"

"If you will recall, I told you my virus cannot reproduce. Even if there was a complete environmental failure, the damage would be acceptable."

"What would be acceptable damage, Alex?"

"Two, three hundred casualties in the ultimate worst-case scenario. In reality, it wouldn't be nearly that high."

"Three hundred dead, and you consider that acceptable?" Nora gasped, unable to hide her repugnance.

Three hundred was not so great a number for the advancement of science. Wasn't she a scientist? Why couldn't she see? Maybe his math professor in college was correct when he told him that he did think on a higher plane than other men.

Sensing his displeasure, Nora hastily changed the subject. "Tell me how you used the street people. If they ask me afterwards I need to know."

"In the beginning, I experimented with *E. Coli.* I found that by altering the amino acid sequencing, I could control the degree of gastrointestinal infection produced by the bacteria."

"That was the work that earned you your Nobel nomination, but I thought you never reached complete control of the organisms."

"You didn't read the correct periodicals. I never published *all* my data. Detective Cox will have found the proper periodicals, and he'll fill you in," Bell said cryptically. "I had more important plans than satisfying a sanctimonious band of hypocrites who need to give away blood money."

"Blood money? I don't understand, Alex,"

"The Nobel prize is awarded from the interest on a fund that was established by the man who invented dynamite. To quiet his conscience for the death and destruction his invention unleashed upon the world, he waxed philanthropic and tried to buy his way to a more pleasant afterlife, as he neared his own death."

"Anyhow, I learned all I could from the bacteria, but when I was ready to use a virus, I had to be more careful. I gained maximum benefit from each subject before they were sacrificed." He spoke as if he was talking about laboratory rats, because that's all they were to him, sophisticated experimental animals needed for his research.

"It took three days of incubation to create new subsets of virus with new properties. I infected winos by feeding them contaminated bottled water, and later wine. Every day I drew blood, observed physical changes."

"It took years to learn to control the destructive effects of my virus. Once I did, I began experimenting in Akron." Finishing a bite of pancake, he took a sip of coffee. "How many victims have been credited to your serial killer here in Akron?"

"Five. The three infected men and the last two uninfected ones."

Feeling the urge to brag, Bell said, "There were nine! Nine! Your boss, the incompetent Doctor Peters, ascribed the deaths of the first four to natural causes. I only resorted to my elaborate subterfuge when the external signs of the disease would have been apparent, even to an incompetent ass like him.

So, I gave him a serial killer to chew on. I'm afraid I didn't count on you, my dear."

"Me?"

"Yes, you. If the illustrious Doctor Peters had remained on the case, I would not have been discovered. Unfortunately, you came along and did your usual, thorough job. I sincerely respect you, Nora. You are a fine doctor."

"Thanks, I guess."

"It *was* a compliment. There you have it. I have been able to take a lethal germ, harness it, make it my tool. I have kept it from becoming a weapon of mass destruction. Instead, it will be the sword of my vengeance."

"One more thing. I can also render the filo virus totally harmless," Bell continued. "That's right. When the four proteins are arranged in the correct combination, and a magical step I discovered is added, the virus becomes inert. I tested it on myself. I drank a whole pint of altered virus. Not so much as a loose stool. And, I served it in the wine at a faculty tea. Not one symptom."

"That's the secret to controlling dangerous organisms. We *must* understand the amino acid sequencing. Once we do, we can control the destructive effects of these natural killers, and the armageddon I describe in my lectures will become a bogeyman."

"With control comes responsibility. I will show the world the potential danger that can occur from the misuse of this knowledge, and, at the same time, the means to control it."

Standing, he began to clear the remnants of their meal. A frown wrinkled his brow. "Nora, I do not wish to cause a generalized panic. When this is finished, C.D.C. will be here. Be my spokeswoman. Reassure them. There will be no epidemic; no plague. Only the target group will be effected. No one else will suffer. The virus cannot reproduce. Only the guilty will die." His tone was apologetic.

When he held out his arms to her, she reluctantly embraced him. When she did, he hugged her as a parent would a child. Feeling her stiffen at his touch, he pushed her to arms length. "I know that you don't understand, and I wish things could be different," he said, the weariness of the great responsibility he had undertaken threatening to crush him with its weight.

"So do I," she said, with regret in her voice.

"I'm not going to restrain you this time. I won't be back. My graduate students will return from their sabatical at noon. I have left instructions for your release on my desk. They should rescue you before tea time. Once again, I wish to apologize for your humiliation and discomfort. Please, don't hate me, Nora."

"I don't hate you, Alex. I want to help you."

"Thank you, my dear, but I'm afraid I'm beyond help," he said, and he knew that he was.

CHAPTER
25

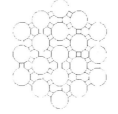

eaving the containment lab, Bell went to his car that was parked next to Nora's. He had been driving hers the past three days to avoid suspicion. His co-workers were accustomed to seeing his car sitting outside at all hours. Her's parked there might invite inquiry. To much had gone into this, and he could leave nothing to chance.

The Plymouth Laser was a good car for high-speed driving, and, with the back seat folded down, there was enough room for what he needed to take with him. It took him several minutes to transfer the contents of Nora's car to his, loading two suitcases and a shipping crate of books into the back of the sedan. A laptop computer and a briefcase filled with floppy disks took the last whisker of space.

As he looked around the campus for the last time, a pang of sadness tugged at him. This had been his life. After today, he would never be part of the academic community again. Shrugging off the feeling, he savored his revenge. Removing his lab coat, he folded it neatly and dropped it into the trash container at the curb.

Twenty minutes later, after a brief stop to arrange for a courier delivery to the *Beacon Journal,* he was in the employee's lot at the Knight Center. Retrieving the waiter's jacket from the back seat, he put in the brown contact lenses and checked the wig and mustache in the mirror. Removing the shopping bag from the car seat, he went inside.

Three people were setting the thirty round tables that would seat the diners. Skirting the breakfast room, he made his way down the stairs into the basement and stopped in front of a door marked, DANGER:HIGH

VOLTAGE. Setting to work on the door's lock, he opened it in seconds. Glancing quickly up and down the hall, he slipped inside.

The room was a maze of metal boxes and multi-colored wires, but he went directly to the box that controlled the public address system. From the shopping bag, he removed a pair of insulated, needle-nose pliers and stripped an inch of insulation from two different wires. To the bare wires, he attached alligator clips from two other wires connected to a tape recorder.

Next, he turned on the battery-powered timer, and the digital display winked on. Pulling a copy of the morning program from his pocket, he scanned it, checked his watch again and set the timer. Plugging the tape recorder into the outlet at the end of the timer, he set the recorder to play. Folding the empty bag neatly, he set it next to the timer, pocketed the pliers and left the room.

The breakfast area was now alive with activity. Uniformed staff scurried to complete the last-minute arrangements for the breakfast. Passing three of the conference participants sporting plastic, name badges, Bell smiled, bade them a cheery good morning, and went into the bustling food preparation area.

Hefting a circular tray holding half a dozen filled, water pitchers, Bell carried it into the main dining hall. From his pocket, he took a pint of clear liquid and added splash of it to each of the pitchers. Stirring each of them with his finger he set them on the six nearest tables. He repeated the process four more times until a pitcher of special water rested on each table. Perspiring profusely, he looked again at his watch. Damn! It had taken too long.

Returning to the kitchen, he approached the pitchers of orange and grapefruit juice. Two servers were already there, and each picked up a tray and went out through the swinging doors. Bell hurriedly added the solution to each remaining pitcher. That would have to do. Maybe they would all drink water today. Bell pocketed the bottle.

"You, there!" a voice boomed from behind him. Bell's heart felt as if were being squeezed by a giant fist. Holding his breath, he slowly turned around.

The head chef, a dumpy man with thick glasses, an exaggerated panniculus and a sour disposition glared at him. "Get your lazy ass moving. I want those trays out there now!"

Breathing a sigh of relief, he said, "Yes, sir. Right away, sir," and picked up a tray.

"Wait a minute," the chef commanded as he walked up to Bell. Taking a pitcher from the tray, he filled the cup in his hand with juice. "These rich bastards won't miss a little o.j.," he growled.

Squinting at the name tag on Bell's jacket he said, "Jose? You don't look like a greaser. You spicks are lazy shits. Get to work."

"Things aren't always as they seem to be, sir," Bell said politely. An urge to let the stupid son-of-a-bitch drink the tainted juice was so strong that Bell was almost unable to overcome it. But, he did. Turning abruptly, he swung the edge of the tray against the coffee cup, and it flew from the chef's hand onto the floor where it shattered.

"You clumsy bastard!" the man screamed, his face turning purple with rage.

"I'm terribly sorry, sir! I get so nervous when I try to hurry. I'll clean things up!" Bell added distress and panic to his voice.

"Get the fuck out of here, and get that God damned juice on the tables, you moron!" The chef screamed at him.

Hurrying from the room, Bell seethed. "Yes, massah. Right away, boss," The arrogance and bigotry of the man offended Bell. His retribution was aimed at those who had destroyed his life. When he met animals like the ignorant chef, It made him wonder if God was telling him that he still had not grasped his total missions.

From the noise level in the foyer, the breakfast crowd had nearly assembled, but he knew that attendance would be down. A third of them had been at the dinner the night before. He wanted to stay as long as he dared. It was a calculated risk. By the end of the day he would be the most hunted man in America. After he left, newspaper accounts of the subsequent events would have to suffice. In the end, he decided he had to see at least some of the show first-hand.

CHAPTER
26

Fever, cramps and diarrhea had left Aaron Spellman weak as a kitten. The last three bowel movements had contained significant amounts of blood. What if this was the infection that had killed Clara Johnstone? It couldn't be! He hadn't come this far in his charmed life for it to end this way.

What little sleep he had gotten was disturbed by dreams of Teddy Arborgast, leering at him. "See you soon, Aaron," he had repeated over and over again.

Teddie Arborgast's last day was frozen in his memory, to be thawed, replayed and frozen again at will. The sagging railroad bridge had been condemned for over a year. Metal signs displaying ominous skull-and-crossed-bones underscored every neighborhood parent's lecture on the dangers of the infamous railroad trestle.

It had taken him half the morning to shame ten year old Arborgast into the manly game of chicken. Eleven-year-old Aaron had played it a dozen times already, and he'd never lost.

There was fear in Arborgast's eyes as he crabbed under the sign and onto the creaking platform that held the first of the rotting, water barrels that were used to extinguish fires on the wooden structure. Every board cracked and snapped under their weight and the entire structure shuddered in the summer breeze.

A hundred feet below, clearly visible through cracks in the walkway where entire boards had succumbed to decay, torrents of water gnashed at the jagged rocks with a sound that added a suspenseful chorus to the dangerous game. Aaron could almost feel the rush of exhilaration that the fear in Arborgast's eyes had fanned.

"Come on, chicken-shit," he had urged as he darted nimbly to a position fifty feet out on the walkway that paralleled the rail bed. The handrail was splintered and sections of it were missing and, coupled with the dizzying height, added to his euphoria. Turning, he placed his hands defiantly on his hips. "Well . . . . " he challenged.

Teddy was a coward, but he wasn't stupid. He had watched Aaron's progress intently and hesitantly began to locate and step on exactly the same boards Aaron had used. Gaining confidence with each step, he had mustered enough courage to snarl at Aaron though clenched teeth, "I ain't no chicken-shit, you bastard!"

Two steps later, the entire section of walkway on which they both stood vibrated. A sharp crack, like the snap of a bull whip rang out. Teddy swayed as the dilapidated section of walkway moved.

"Aaron!" Teddy had shrieked in terror amidst a background chorus of groaning wood.

The wooden slats canted wildly outward, and Teddy was thrown against the rotting railing. It bowed and held, but only for a moment. The boy's arms had flailed in windmill fashion as he tried to reach the solid railroad ties beneath the rusty tracks. In Aaron's mind, the laws of physics were suspended, and the scene took on a slow-motion, surrealistic quality.

Large support beams beneath the sidewalk had cracked, splintered and given way. A shriek of tortured metal emanated from the rending cleats and nails as they were pulled free or were torn in two by the shifting mass of the structure. The detached segment hung suspended before collapsing into the chasm. With an agonizing scream, Arborgast plunged like a rag doll to his death. The destruction had stopped two boards away from the one on which Aaron stood.

Since that singular day on the trestle, Spellman had felt immortal. Death had been an abstract concept to him until this morning. Now, for the first time in his life, he was afraid. Death was real, and he felt it reaching for him. But, if he was still alive, he wasn't as sick as the others. Burning up with fever, he hoped that he was thinking clearly.

The walk to the bathroom was an adventure. Swaying, dizzy and disoriented, he held onto the wall to keep his balance. The floor undulated like a snake, reminding him of something from the *Twilight Zone*. By the time he reached his destination, his silk pajamas were drenched.

His reflection in the mirror was worse yet. The skin on his cheeks sagged, and he had huge, dark circles under his eyes. He must have bitten his lip during the nightmare, because his lower lip was swollen and bruised.

"Shit! Shit! Shit!" he moaned. He had to give the keynote remarks for the breakfast in less than an hour, and he looked awful and felt worse. Slowly, he began to wash his face when he was seized by violent abdominal cramps and collapsed onto the commode.

CHAPTER 27

ashing down the jetway at Cleveland Hopkins Airport, Marty weaved his way through the crowd like the old Hertz commercial, with the football star leaping over benches and running through the airport.

The Park and Fly bus was closing its doors to leave, but he made it in time to bang on the outside of the door before the driver could pull away. Opening it, she said, "Just made it. What's your row number?"

Ten minutes later speeding down I-71 toward Akron, he dialed the office number on the car phone.

"Homicide, Sergeant Dorsey speaking."

"E.L., it's Marty. I'm on my way in from the airport."

"I'm glad you finally learned the difference between east coast and west coast time. It was only midnight here when you called. I've run the check on our boy like you asked, Dorsey said. "Got to admit you picked a winner. I checked the F.B.I. and Justice Department tracking files and the I.R.S.. Found the usual stuff, but somethin' didn't seem kosher. On a hunch, I called a friend at the Pentagon this morning. She checked the C.I.A. files that we don't have access to. You owe her a bottle of scotch. If Joe citizen knew how much we keep on them in our data banks, they'd flip out. Your Doctor Bell is something."

"Born Alexander Bellangier fifty-five years ago in San Francisco, just minutes ahead of his twin brother Nicholas. Their father was a successful electrical engineer who made a fortune with a number of aerospace patents in the early 60's. Mother inherited several million when her industrialist father croaked. Both parents were only children of only children, and the twins were their only children. Both boys were brilliant, but aside from that they were as different as okra and soybeans."

"Is that an old southern analogy?" Marty asked. The question was accompanied by the first smile to cross his lips since he had left the library.

"Just making sure you were paying attention, what with jet lag and such. The boys struggled through a silver spoon childhood. Alexander was gregarious, athletic, adventurous, while his younger brother was introverted, sensitive and bookish. Alex was the all-state tailback, and Nicholas made the highest score ever recorded on the National Merit Scholarship Exam, with old Alex only a point or two behind."

Shaking his head, Marty found it difficult to fathom the Alexander Bell he knew in a football uniform. Bell's personality traits were more like those that Dorsey had ascribed to Bell's dead brother.

The revelation came like a jolt of electric current. That's what didn't fit! In the lecture room, he had been Alexander Bell, and in his office, he had been Nicholas. Marty wondered at the depth of the man's psychosis. Had Bell taken on the personality of his dead brother?

"They were joint valedictorians at the prestigious Bonita Valley Prep School with identical straight A averages," E.L. continued. "Stanford was next for Nicholas, where he obtained a degree in chemistry while Alexander followed daddy's footsteps to M.I.T. where he got a degree in mechanical engineering. Both were Phi Beta Kappa, Magna Cum Lauda and all that crap."

"Alex got caught up in the Viet Nam thing, and was off to Fort Benning, Georgia for Ranger training and later the Special Forces. After the first tour, he re-enlisted twice and went to Viet Nam five different times. Shitload of medals, including a silver star, three bronze stars and purple heart with cluster.

"The only fly in Alex's ointment concerned the deaths of several prostitutes in Saigon. A half dozen boom-boom girls were beaten to death over a six month period that coincided with his last tour in Nam. Bell fit the description of the perp that was last seen with the girls. They called him in for questioning twice, but couldn't get any hard evidence. The potential witnesses all got amnesia and couldn't I.D. him. When his tour was up, he skated."

"Meanwhile, little Nicky was busy graduating first in his class at Stanford Medical School, doing a five year, surgery residency and two years of vascular fellowship. He was opposed to the war and joined in a few peace marches. Despite that, the brothers were thick as thieves."

"After the war, Bell got a master's degree in Chemistry and a Ph.D. in molecular biology, both from Harvard." E.L. pronounced it Ha-vahd. Alex went into research while Nicholas started saving lives."

"I love this technologic age," E. L. said before continuing. "Computers are boss. While the good doctor was workin' on his masters and his Ph.D., he worked part time for the C.I.A.. Was one of their best infiltration spooks. This was all in his closed file, and remember, you owe Sharon a bottle of Scotland's finest. Alexander Bell is a very dangerous man."

"What about the financials?" Marty asked.

"Just when it looked as if they would live out the great American dream, their parents went down in the crash of their private jet. Since there were no other living relatives, the brothers Bellangier became very wealthy orphans."

"Just how wealthy?" Marty inquired.

"Each got about ten million. Neither of them married, so when Nicholas took his swan dive four years later, Alex got his dough too. His net worth is about twenty-five mill now."

"Wheee," Marty whistled. "Where does he keep the loot?"

"I ran a financial profile, but it ain't gonna make you happy. Six months ago, Bell liquidated all his assets.

Had the entire bundle transferred to a bank on Grand Cayman Island from whence it was immediately disbursed into dozens of accounts that get lost in a maze of untraceable wire transfers. 'Less I miss my guess, Doctor Bell is about to pull a Houdini and disappear."

"It all fits. This is about revenge on the law firm who prosecuted his brother. He's contemplating mass murder to get even for a dead brother. Get a warrant, and I'll swing by and pick you up."

Already got the warrant. You got gut feelin's, I got hunches. He was so good with disguises, that his operative name was Chameleon. Bell could change his appearance and identity quicker than a frog's tongue can flick a fly. If he slips us now, he's gone."

"Thing that made him so good was his ability to actually become the person he was disguised to be. If he was a truck driver, he could ten-four good buddy with the best of them. If he was the Duke of Earl, he'd sing your socks off."

"I'll be there in fifteen minutes." Pushing the end button on the telephone, Marty mashed down on the accelerator.

CHAPTER
28

ooking at his watch, Kevin Slaton, M.D., noted that Mickey's left hand was on twelve and his right hand was on eight. The first hour of his seven-to-seven tour as shift leader at Summa Health System's City Hospital emergency room was over, and it had dragged by. As he debated whether to go to the back and have a cup of coffee or check out the sore ankle that the orderly had ushered into the second cubicle, he stretched and yawned. The coffee won.

He was nearly to the duty lounge when the door to the squad bay burst open and a frantic team of paramedics wheeled in a cart on which lay a middle-aged, black man covered with blood.

Cursing under his breath, Slaton grabbed a waterproof gown from the wall and put it on. Pausing to add a cap, a mask with a plastic shield covering the upper portion of his face and a pair of rubber gloves, he walked to the trauma bay. The trauma team moved into action with the efficiency of a military drill team.

One nurse searched for access to an additional I.V. site to compliment the one the paramedics had started in the field; an anesthetist established an airway; another nurse attached monitoring devices, and the trauma resident arrived to direct the effort.

"Why the hell didn't you call? You're always supposed to call with a trauma so we can get ready," the resident grumbled at the paramedic.

"Sorry, Doc, we didn't get a chance to call. Besides, this isn't a trauma. This dude has blood coming out his eyes, nose, every place. He came out of his room at the Hilton and collapsed in the hallway, bleedin' all over the carpet. The room was a mess."

"Who is he? Anybody know?" Candy Timmons, the trauma team charge nurse shouted above the noise of the resuscitation.

"Folks at the hotel said his name is Roosevelt Edwards. He's an attorney from the convention at the Knight Center."

"I don't get a pressure. What's the EKG. show?" shouted the resident.

"Straight line," the tech answered.

"Do we have any blood yet? His veins are empty! Start CPR and hit the clock!" the resident ordered. Candy Timmons started the clock that recorded the length of time the cardio-pulmonary resuscitation lasted.

The automatic doors from the squad bay hissed open again, and a second team of paramedics wheeled in another middle-aged man. As they came through the door, the patient arched a spray of black vomitus across the gurney and onto the floor. The man looked like a carbon copy of the one in the trauma bay.

"Who the hell is this?", Slaton asked the paramedics with the second victim.

"His name is Everett Goldman," said a striking blond woman who came up the ambulance ramp and into the hallway. Her eyes had the vacant look of obvious shock, and her dressing gown was covered with blood. "Call Judge Spellman. Ev is a friend of his." Her knees buckled, and she pitched forward. The paramedic caught her and eased her to the ground.

Simultaneously, the radio behind him crackled, and a frantic voice said, "Squad twenty-two in transit from the Sheraton Suites Hotel in the Falls. Two middle-aged, white males. They're filling the back of the ambulance with blood. Lawyers here for the convention. Code red."

"My God," Slaton said grimly, a chill coursing through him.

CHAPTER
29

urning onto the campus at the medical school, Marty saw Nora's car, and he felt as if his heart had stopped beating. He had called her apartment and checked his recorder, but why was the car here?

"Pulling into the space next to her car, E.L. said, "Looks like the doc's back from Columbus. That's her little runabout isn't it?"

"I hope she didn't come to see Bell." Marty got out and felt the hood. "The engine had been on sometime this morning." That was a good sign, he hoped.

Running down the hall toward Bell's office, they found it empty. Through the upper, glass portion of the wall, they could see the entire room. There were two yellow post-it notes on the computer. Marty tried the door. It was open.

Walking to the computer, he read the notes. One was addressed to the graduate students relaying the new access code to the lab. The other was addressed to him. He read it to Dorsey.

Dear Sergeant Cox:

If I am correct, you will find this note before my graduate students arrive at noon. By now you will know the why, and Nora can tell you the how. You will have come to arrest me. I'm sorry to disappoint you, but I cannot permit that. I loved my brother more than my own life. Those who murdered him will be dead when you read this. If they are not dead, they soon will be. I had originally planned to punish only Goldman and Associates, until Mayor Johnstone helped me to realize that mine was a more global mission. I have a chance to purge society of a killing disease called lawyers. Only the guilty will suffer. I know that puts us at odds and I regret that. I hope we do not meet again, for that would spell disaster for one of us. From what you now know about my background, the disaster would most likely be yours. Take care of Nora. She's a fine woman and a wonderful physician. I deeply regret any discomfort I caused her, or anxiety I brought upon you. Best wishes to both of you. Be happy together.

Alexander Bell

Snatching the other note from the computer, he headed for the stairs. Calling over his shoulder to E.L. as he ran down the hall, he shouted, "Get out an APB on Bell and cover all the airports, bus and train stations from Chicago to Pittsburgh. Get his plate number to every uniform in the tristate area. If we miss him, he's gone for good."

Taking the stairs two at a time, Marty was breathing heavily when he reached the lab. Finding the keypad he tapped in the four digit number and turned the wheel. The door didn't open. In his haste, he had miskeyed the code. Taking a deep breath to calm himself, he deliberately punched in two, three, five, five. Ironically, Marty realized that the numbers spelled out Bell on a telephone keypad.

The door swung open, and Nora rushed out. Throwing herself into Marty's arms, she began to laugh and cry at the same time. She repeatedly apologized for the way she looked, and he repeatedly reassured her that she never looked better.

"Let's go," Marty said. "We think Bell's headed for the Knight Center. I think he's prepared to kill everyone there. E.L.'s getting out an APB, and here's the note he left for me."

They met E.L. running up the stairs. "Gee, Doc, tough night?."E. L. asked when he saw Nora's appearance.

"Get your butt in gear, partner. We got to get to the convention center. I'm not sure what he's going to do. With his explosive training, he might blow up the place, but I think it has to do with his viral research," Marty said to E.L.

"Oh, my Lord! I know what he's going to do," Nora cried. And, if he's wrong about any of his theories, it could be worse than an explosion!" Nora filled them in on what Bell had told her as they dashed for the car.

"Holy jumpin' Jesus," E.L. said. "He could turn those lawyers into walkin' plague factories." E.L.'s aversion to germs caused him to shudder at the thought. "That makes runnin' up these stairs and riskin' a heart attack justifiable."

The cellular phone in E.L.'s pocket rang. The look on his face told Marty things had gotten worse. "Yes . . .Sure . . . We're on our way to the convention center now," E. L. said, before snapping the folding bottom of the phone shut.

"Looks like our boy didn't wait for all the lawyers to get together at the convention center. We've got the E.R.s at City, General, St. Thomas and Cuyahoga Falls General filled with lawyers from some fancy dinner party last night. They're pukin' blood all over the place. Three confirmed deaths so far. The hospitals are goin' nuts. They've shut them all down except for more sick lawyers. They're talkin' plague."

"Drop me off at City. It's on your way to the convention center, and I can help. There's no danger of contagion. Bell engineered the virus so it can't reproduce."

E.L. slid behind the wheel. "This is the part I love," Dorsey said. "Sit down and buckle up, children."

Backing the car around, Dorsey screamed out of the lot onto the highway as if he were driving his Corvette instead of Marty's sedan. Reaching under the seat, he located the flashing, red light and clamped it on the dashboard, while Marty activated the siren. With a racing downshift, E. L. executed a four-wheel drift and turned onto the interstate. Burying her head in Marty's shoulder, she refused to look up until they came to a stop in front of the emergency room.

A dozen ambulances were lined up hood to trunk, and the ramp resembled a combat zone. Hospital security, reinforced by uniformed sheriff's deputies, patrolled the sidewalk. One of the deputies confronted Nora as she headed for the automatic door.

"Sorry, but you can't go in there. The Health Department has shut down the E.R. for the present time. It isn't safe for you to go inside."

"I'm Deputy Coroner Daniels, and I'm going inside." She kept moving and the officer stepped in front of her.

"Let me see some identification," he said politely.

Realizing that Nora didn't have any identification, Marty pulled his shield and showed it to the officer. "She left in a hurry. No I.D. on her. I'll vouch for her."

"Okay, Sarg," the officer shrugged and stepped aside.

Marty pulled her to him, and kissed her quickly on the lips. "I'll be at the Knight Center.

Be careful. You're the most important thing in the world to me. And remember what I said about wimpy old plagues."

"Don't worry." Nora hugged him fiercely. "I will. If Bell was really able to do what he told me he did, I'm in no real danger. You be careful, too. He's crazy." Moving past the ring of security, she went inside and found the tall man in blood-spattered trauma gear.

"Excuse me for not shaking hands," Slaton said sardonically, holding up his blood-stained, rubber gloves.

"Quite all right, Kevin. What's the damage?" Nora asked, as she started to put on the protective trauma uniform.

"Twenty-six, so far. General has twenty; St. Thomas fifteen and Falls General another ten. We're full up, and at least ten more have been diverted to Barberton. We have twelve more on ambulances headed God knows where."

"Are all of these still from the dinner party last night?" Nora asked. "Have any come in from the convention center?"

Slaton blanched. "All of the ones here, and as far as I know at the other hospitals, were at The One Hundred Club Dinner last night at the Quaker Hilton. What about the convention center? You mean there's going to be more of this . . . Jesus!"

"How many deaths?" Nora asked.

"Sixteen," Slaton said grimly. "Seven more will be dead in half an hour. No idea about the other hospitals. C.D.C. will be here any time. They've been tracking something similar in San Francisco. Four dead out there."

"It's a long story, Kevin, and I'll fill you in on it when we have more time, but it's the same source. This is a deliberate infection with an altered strain of Ebola virus. One that he engineered so it can't reproduce. There won't be an epidemic. None of the staff here is in immediate danger if they use precautions and avoid puncture wounds or direct blood to blood inoculation."

Looking at her skeptically, Slaton said, "That's more like science fiction than science. You expect me to swallow that?"

"When Star Trek debuted, they used hand-held devices called communicators. We thought that was science fiction. Now we call them cellular phones. Today's science fiction is tomorrow's reality. I believe Alex Bell did exactly what he said he could do."

The door crashed open, and four marines in chemical combat gear came through, rifles at the ready. Behind them was a man in his mid-forties, medium height with square shoulders and a trim, athletic build. Tonsured baldness capped an oversized head, and the remaining gray-streaked, black hair curled around his ears in unruly ringlets.

"Get away from the door," he shouted at an orderly who was standing by a cart near the door. When the orderly stood rooted in open-mouthed disbelief, the man gestured, and a marine aimed his rifle at the center of the frightened man's chest. "I said get away from the God damned door!" The orderly fled into the emergency treatment area.

"What the hell?" Slaton sputtered.

"I'm Doctor Welton Birney from the Center For Disease Control, and by authority of the United States Government, this facility is under complete quarantine."

Stunned, Nora and Slaton followed Birney into the emergency room. The Marines blustered along behind him, as Birney shouted orders. Slaton came up behind Birney and grabbed him by the shoulder with a bloody glove. Birney spun around in an agitated fashion.

"What the hell do you think you're doing?" Slaton demanded.

Looking with disdain at Slaton, Birney's voice was patronizing. "If you had been paying attention, you would already know. I told you when

I came in. I'm Doctor Welton Birney. I'm from the Center for Disease Control in Atlanta, and I am in charge of this situation. I expect the full cooperation of everyone here." His smile was oily. "And, who the hell are you?"

"I'm Kevin Slaton, and I'm the senior, emergency medicine specialist on duty." Kevin's face flushed, and his jaw tightened defiantly.

Keeping her voice even, Nora said, "And, I'm Nora Daniels. I'm the deputy coroner and . . . "

Cutting her off before she could finish, Birney said, "Thank you, Doctor Daniels, but we won't be needing any local help. We can manage the situation quite nicely ourselves." The intonation was that of an exasperated parent explaining the obvious to a child.

Nora tried a different tack. "Doctor Birney, I have some information about the situation that may be of assistance. By the way," she said, extending her hand, "my friends call me Nora."

Ignoring her outstretched hand, he looked back at her coolly and said, "My friends call me, Doctor Birney."

The relationship deteriorated after this subterranean beginning. Birney proved to be as arrogant and obstinate as the first impression implied. As he listened to Nora's story, the expression on his face made her wonder if she should offer him a laxative. Birney then grilled her about the details of Bell's revelation without hearing any of her answers, asking the same things over and over as he barked orders to his uniformed henchmen.

Finally, Birney said impatiently, "If you will excuse me, Doctor, that's the biggest pile of crap I have ever heard. I'm not about to allow some cockamamie yarn spun by a researcher at a second rate medical school dictate the handling of a major, infectious event. We'll know in a couple of hours what we're dealing with. Our lab people are quite competent."

"I already know what it is. It's a genetically altered strains of Ebola filovirus." Nora's face was a mask of controlled exasperation.

"I have shut down all the hospitals who treated patients and quarantined everyone who had any contact with them. The National Guard will be here to relieve the local law enforcement people and insure order. We'll handle things," Birney assured her.

"Damn it!" Nora flared. I *told* you these organisms have been genetically engineered not to reproduce. None of this is necessary."

"If anyone could really do that with a virus, they would be making millions of dollars in industry and winning Nobel prizes, not trying to kill a bunch of lawyers. Just toddle on back to your lab."

"He's worth twenty-five million, and he has been nominated for a Nobel award." She stomped off in a huff, leaving Birney standing open-mouthed in the hall.

Slaton smiled at the befuddled Birney and said. "Sure has a way with words, doesn't she? By the way, when you're finished with your Napoleon imitation, I'll be in the back drinking coffee. If you need any of us local-yocals, you just call. By the way, the gurneys are starting to pile up at the doors."

CHAPTER 30

Treasurer Annette Judy, the only officer of the Trial Lawyers Association present at the breakfast, looked nervously around the room. Spellman was due to speak in five minutes. Where was he? It wasn't like him to be late, and the turn out was poor as well. The room was only half full. This was not a good way to start the convention.

Watching the waiters clear the tables, Annette realized that everyone had finished eating and sat sipping after-breakfast coffee. Something would have to be done soon. Annette spied a past officer, Sam Hinton, at the front table and was about to ask him what she should do when the public address system whistled.

"Ladies and gentlemen, may I have your attention please?"

Annette looked toward the empty podium. Who was talking? Where was the voice coming from?

"Don't bother to look for me. You won't find me. Since your speaker is unable to be with you this morning, I have graciously agreed to take his place. In case anyone is thinking about leaving, I'd suggest you remain to hear me out. Your lives may depend on it."

"William Shakespeare is one of the most quoted authors in history. William did have a way with words. There's an obscure quote of his that I'd like to share with you. It has never been a favorite of those in your profession. It's from "Henry VI", Part II, Act IV, Scene II, Line eighty-six. Impressive documentation don't you think? Attorneys quote chapter and verse as they twist the law to their own purpose. It is only fitting that I do likewise."

"In the Bard's tale, the conspirators Dick and Cade are plotting traitorous deeds. It is Dick who makes the suggestion, "First thing we do, let's kill all the lawyers. To which Cade replies, "Nay, that I mean to do."

"There you have it. Poor Cade never got to be king and didn't live long enough to implement the plan. If he had, what I do today would not be necessary, and I dare say the world would be a better place. No one has ever tried it, even though this sound philosophy was given to us over three hundred years ago. Since William died in 1616, the world has been waiting for someone with the imagination and ingenuity to accomplish the task."

"I must humbly admit that I am that man. The empty chairs at your breakfast are mute testimony of my ability to do what I say. I visited the One Hundred Club dinner last evening and spiked the punch so to speak. This morning they're all *dying* to get to the hospital. And, most them will die soon after they get there." A gallows humor chuckle filled the hall.

The microphone shrieked feed back, and a string of questions exploded from the audience.

"Whose voice is that? Is he crazy?"

"What's he talking about?"

"What does he mean kill all the lawyers?"

Annette held up her hand for silence. "Be quiet! Listen!"

The microphone hummed for another few seconds. The voice returned. "Enough display of bad manners and outcries of protest. It is time to begin the trial. The legal profession is on trial today for murder, and I am judge, jury and executioner."

"I would like to call my brother as the first witness, but alas I cannot. You see, my brother is dead. He was guilty of trying to save the life of a worthless piece of human debris. When the man lived, and lost his leg to infection, he called in an eater of carrion, a lawyer."

"Your disingenuous guest of honor, Everett Goldman, had no respect for the heroic effort to save a leg that was doomed to be lost. All he saw was a chance to destroy my brother and make a substantial amount of money in the process. He toyed with my brother, as a cat would a mouse under its paw, and Judge Aaron Spellman held Goldman's coat while he did it."

"If this was a unique circumstance, I might be tempted to let it pass, but it is not. You are all the same. Your profession has no honor. You only wish to win the point, regardless of the costs, or the consequences. If someone has a valid point that would destroy the lies you create, and you can get it disregarded on a technicality, you gloat. Today, that immunity is canceled. From this day forward, you are accountable for your sins. I shall see to it personally."

Two men near the door stood to leave. They froze as the voice on the speaker said, "I would not leave yet if I were you. If anyone stepped out while I was talking, you may wish to find them and tell them that they are dying. But, why would you? You don't care any more about each other than you do the people you sue, the society you disrupt or the laws you manipulate to the advantage of the moment."

"If you think I jest, let me tell you that anyone who has had a sip of water, or a drink of juice has been exposed to a disease that should kill nine out of ten of you. There is no antidote. There is no treatment. If you are infected, you will die. Since you are all guilty that is your sentence, death. Divine providence will determine which of you is the lucky one in each ten."

"In keeping with strict jurisprudence, you may appeal the sentence. I know more about the virus you have ingested than any man alive. To be politically correct, I should say person alive, shouldn't I? There is one thing about this virus that I don't know. I don't know how long it takes the virus to be absorbed from the gut. If you empty the content of your gut before the virus is absorbed, you may have a chance. Then again, you may not. I don't really know."

"I will leave you now. Those of you who have not already thrown up from sheer terror, will need to induce vomiting. If any of you are fortunate enough to survive, remember that the Death Angel will be watching you. Your sins will no longer go unpunished. Have a nice day."

With a shriek of electronic feedback, the voice on the speaker cut off. "Annette, what the hell is going on?" cried Aubrey Hinton, who had made his way to her side.

"I don't know, Aubrey. We had nothing to do with this."

"You'd better get up there and say something. From the looks on their faces, we're about to have a major panic."

Moving to the microphone, Annette tapped it with her finger to be sure it still worked. Impromptu speeches were not her forte, but Hinton was right, she had to say something. "Ladies and gentleman, I wish to assure you that this was not a practical joke. I have no idea who the voice belonged too, or where it was coming from."

"Where *are* the rest of the people who were supposed to be here? Where's Spellman? Where's Goldman?" shouted a beefy man two tables away. "Is there any truth to what that voice said?"

"I don't know. I'm going to call Judge Spellman now." Hinton handed her a cellular telephone.

In her purse, she found the private number Spellman had given her.

When she had completed the call, she stumbled to the microphone, pale and shaken.

"Judge Spellman is in an ambulance on his way to the hospital."

A man in the back of the room broke for the door in a dead run. His action triggered universal panic, and everyone in the room stampeded for the exit doors. Tables were overturned. A waiter with a tray of dishes was bowled over. Two men leaped on the stunned man and pummeled him with their fists, demanding that he explain the mystery voice. An elderly barrister in a wheelchair was thrown to the floor and trampled.

In minutes the room was empty, save for the casualties. Annette helped the fallen man back to his wheelchair and comforted the worker whose tormentors had given up and fled. Trance-like, she walked to the foyer.

The entrances to the rest rooms were jammed with pushing, shoving humanity. Three separate fist fights had broken out as everyone tried to get through the doors at the same time.

Security forces waded into the melees by the restrooms and were no match for the mob, who routed them in minutes. Annette heard sirens.

The police were coming. My God, what a disaster.

Looking toward the side of the room, Annette saw one of the waiters standing against the wall near the kitchen. His arms were folded, and he had a smile that matched the smug look on his face. Didn't he know what the hell was going on? Why didn't he try to help? She'd decided to get his name, so she could report him.

Crossing the room she thought, *Aaron is really going to be pissed.* They had given him a lot of grief from the board when he appointed a woman chair of the local arrangements committee. Now they'd blame the whole thing on her. Shit! And, she had to screw Spellman twice to get the damned job. Now this! Tears of frustration filled her eyes.

Spellman! Spellman was on the way to the hospital. Forgetting all about the grinning waiter, the enormity of the mysterious voice's warning struck home. Sticking her finger down her throat, she started to retch.

CHAPTER 31

he total chaos in the foyer of the convention center made Bell feel elated. It was the classic example of humanity driven to the lowest common denominator. Survival was the only thing on their minds, and they didn't care how much they debased themselves. He had faced possible death a dozen times in the jungles of Viet Nam, and he never reduced himself to the animal level.

Two men burst through the front doors of the center. On their heels were a number of uniformed officers. One of the two men was Detective Cox, the other likely his partner. Perhaps he had stayed long enough. It was time to go.

Moving calmly to avoid undo attention, Bell moved toward the door at the left of the foyer that connected with the service tunnel. When he was almost to the door, he looked back over his shoulder. Annette Judy was talking to Cox and pointing frantically in Bell's direction. Ambling through the door, he broke into a run as soon as he was on the other side.

Bolting down the stairs two at a time, Bell was at the second-level landing and turning down the final set of stairs to the basement when the door at the top crashed open, and the two detectives came onto the upper landing.

The thin detective leaned over the railing. "Stop, police!" he shouted, his voice echoing in the stair well. When Bell kept plunging downward, the policeman fired a round in his direction. The sound of the gunshot reverberated in the confined space, and the bullet ricocheted off the brick wall to the right of Bell's head and imbedded itself in the door frame.

Before the detective could get off another round, Bell was into the service corridor running hard. Passing the room that he had been in earlier to rig the sound system, Bell turned the knob and opened the door a crack. There was a service door at the end of the corridor that opened onto the rear loading dock, and he sprinted towards it.

Twenty yards farther, the corridor curved sharply to the left toward the loading dock and the side of the building that faced Mill Street. Pausing in the shadows, Bell could see down the corridor in the direction he had just come. Moving silently, and very cautiously, the two detectives were working their way down the corridor. They were breathing heavily from the race down the stairs. He was not.

When they reached the door Bell had left open, they stopped. Cox nodded to his partner, who went into a crouch. When Cox nodded a second time, his partner went into the room low and fast, his weapon extended in front of him. Cox followed high and dove to the left as he went through the door. It was a classic hostile room entry, and Bell nodded his approval at their professionalism. He wouldn't underestimate them if they got close.

Moving swiftly to the end of the hall, Bell turned the handle to the loading dock door. It was locked! Damn! He wouldn't have time to get it open before they would be on him. There was a second door to his right, and when he tried it, it was open. Darting through the door he switched on the light, a naked 100 watt bulb, and found himself in the room used to store building materials for scenery and the exhibition booths A quick inspection of the perimeter told him there was only one door. Frowning, he sighed, got into position and settled down to wait.

The wait was short. They came through the door in the same fashion they had entered the other room, only this time, Cox came in low, and his partner came in high. Bell clenched his jaw in anticipation. Their division of labor and alternating of risk marked them as professionals who worked well as a team. He must be careful.

Holding his hand in the air, Cox made a circular motion with his extended index finger and the partner began to circle the room clockwise. A second sweep of the finger indicated Cox would search in the opposite direction. That's what Bell had expected them to do, and he tensed.

Moving into the gloom, the partner inched carefully along the aisle around the outer perimeter of the room, pausing at each of the right-angled branching isles that accessed the storage bins. At the third aisle, the man crouched and peered tentatively around the corner. Finding it empty, he stood and turned to continue searching.

As he turned, Bell uncoiled from his hiding place behind a sheet of masonite. Planting his left foot, Bell stepped forward with his right foot and slammed the extended rigid fingers of his right hand into the surprised man's solar plexus. Bell felt the fingers make contact with the tiny cartilage at the bottom of the man's sternum, and it cracked under the impact.

With a soft grunt the man sank to his knees. The blow was perfectly delivered, and the resultant loss of breath coupled with the intense pain that burrowed through his chest kept the man from making a sound. Slipping his hands around the man's throat, Bell applied firm pressure over both carotid arteries. The detective made a feeble attempt to struggle, but lapsed into unconsciousness as his brain was deprived of oxygen. Easing the man to the floor, Bell moved toward the door.

As he reached for the door handle, Bell heard the click behind him. "Don't move, Doctor Bell. I don't want to have to shoot you, but I will. Turn around slowly," said Cox.

Doing as he was told, Bell rapidly assessed the situation. Cox was moving towards him with a revolver pointed at the middle of his abdomen. Another professional move, Bell thought. A man could be shot in the chest, and still keep coming, even if the bullet struck his heart. Gut shots were so painful that they usually incapacitated the victim. If the detective would come just a little closer.

Cox stopped three feet away. "Well, well, well, if it isn't the efficient waiter from the Spring Hill Country Club. Excellent disguise, Doctor Bell. I see now why you were an effective operative."

"Yes, I was, Sergeant Cox. And, I knew that you were a fine detective and would come back from San Francisco with all the information you needed. That's all right now. I've accomplished what I set out to accomplish."

"E. L., by the door," Cox called out. "I've got him."

"I'm afraid your associate can't hear you," Bell said, taunting in an attempt to make Cox angry. An angry opponent was easier to handle than a calculating one.

"What did you do to him, you bastard?" Cox cried angrily.

"See for yourself," Bell said sarcastically, inclining his head in the direction of the outer aisle.

Tensing to strike, Bell never took his eyes off Cox's face. When the Sergeant's eyes flicked in the direction of the nod, Bell stepped forward and karate kicked the weapon from Cox's hand before he could look back. The pistol slid across the tile floor and disappeared under one of the bins. Recovering more quickly than Bell expected, Cox lunged at him with a football tackle.

Crashing onto the floor, Bell knew that he had to regain the momentum. Cox's skills were rudimentary, but he was strong. Hand-to-hand combat was something that Bell was very good at. The willingness to use whatever force was required to win, without hesitation even if he had to cripple or kill his opponent was what made him good.

The detective was on top of him with his right shoulder buried in Bell's midsection. When he got his breath back from the fall, Bell slammed both his cupped hands against the detectives ears with enough force to break the man's eardrums. That seldom happened. The eardrums only perforated twenty percent of the time, but the pain produced by the blow was exquisite and disorienting.

To his credit, Cox cried out in pain, and although his grip slackened, he still hung on. Arching his arms outward, Bell struck Cox simultaneously in each temple with closed fists. With a grunt, Cox went slack, and Bell rolled to his right.

With considerable effort, Bell extracted himself from beneath Cox and was nearly to his feet when the detective grabbed him by the legs. Staggering, Bell nearly lost his balance. Wrenching his leg free, Bell fought the urge to kick the persistent Sergeant in the face, and drive his nasal bone into the center of his brain, killing him instantly. Instead, Bell struck Cox smartly across the throat with the knuckles of his extended fingers. The blow didn't break Cox's windpipe, which also would have killed him, but he would have trouble breathing for awhile.

All the fight went out of Cox, and he lay gasping for air and clutching at his throat. Stirring from the aisle to his left warned Bell that the partner was rousing from his anoxic slumber. Turning out the light to slow the partner's progress, Bell went into the hall.

It would be risky to stop and pick the lock on the loading dock door, so Bell ran back down the service corridor the way he had come. Taking the stairs two at a time, he paused on the top landing to straighted his disheveled uniform, calm his breathing, and wait for his pulse to normalize. He was in splendid physical condition, but the last few minutes had been taxing. Opening the door, he stepped back into the foyer.

Order had been restored, and uniformed police were everywhere. Through the windows, he could see other officers on the street outside. Retreating into the kitchen, Bell found it empty. The chef whose life he had spared had obviously left before the brawling started. An apron was draped over the back of a chair, and a chef's hat sat on the counter. Removing the false mustache, Bell took off the waiter's jacket and put on a pair of black, plastic glasses that he carried in his shirt pocket. Tossing the wig into the trash barrel, he pinned his name tag to the apron. Slipping the apron over his white shirt, he added the chef's cap, picked up a folder that lay on the counter top and went into the foyer.

At the door, the uniformed patrol man stopped him. "Where do you think you're going?" he asked gruffly.

In a most offended tone, Bell answered, "Chef Ardon just called from the City Club. He went back over there after the breakfast here. There's a dinner for the mayor at the club at seven. Chef forgot the recipe for Mayor Albertson's favorite salad dressing. I'm taking this over to him."

"You got I.D.?" the officer asked suspiciously.

Bell pointed to the City Club name tag pinned to the apron.

"I guess you can go. The guy we're looking for has black hair and a womb broom. Sign here."

Taking the pen from the officer bell scribbled W. Shakespeare on the proffered clipboard. Tipping his cap to the officers on the sidewalk, Bell walked to his car, got in, and drove away.

Thirty-five minutes later, Bell drove the car into the long-term parking garage at the Cleveland Hopkins International Airport. A uniformed officer checked each vehicle at the garage entrance.

Anticipating the airport surveillance, Bell had made a brief stop at a rest area on I-71 south of the airport to change into a gray pin-striped business suit from the trunk of his car. Plastic glasses and a gray wig changed his appearance to conform with the picture on the driver's license he showed the guard. Looking briefly at the photo on the license, he looked at Bell, and waved him through.

He transferred the contents of the car into Ezra Troyer's truck that he had parked there last night before catching the last airport shuttle back to Akron. Three hours later, he arrived at the Detroit International Airport.

Abandoning the truck in short-term parking, Bell went to the Northwest Airline counter and picked up the ticket he had ordered on the computer the day before. "Have a nice flight, Mr. Bronson," the attractive clerk said, handing him the ticket and checking his baggage. "You may wish to go to your gate immediately. The plane will be boarding in a few moments. Don't worry, your bags will make it."

When Bell got off the plane at Stapleton Airport in Denver, he claimed his bags and proceeded to the men's room, entering an empty stall. Closing the door, Bell took off the suit jacket he was wearing. Opening the gym bag he was carrying, he changed the pin-striped suit for a white golf shirt, tan slacks and a windbreaker. Extracting a pair of low-cut Nike's from the bag, he replaced the tasseled loafers he was wearing. Removing a red, shaggy-cut wig and a pair of dark glasses from the bag, he put them on and changed the baggage tags for the third time.

Alexander Bell, The Chameleon, deposited the gym bag in the trash, left the stall and walked to the Continental Airlines counter where the computerized ticket ordered under the name of Thomas Callihagn was waiting. Flashing a hundred watt smile, Bell showed his Irish passport to the agent, and the man gave him the ticket. Thanking the agent in a Irish brogue that would have made the mayor of Dublin proud, Bell went to the international gate to await his flight to Shannon Airport.

CHAPTER
32

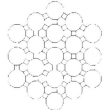

arty and E. L. sat quietly in the squad room. In the twenty-four hours following the meeting of the One Hundred Club, one-hundred ten of the one-hundred-twenty lawyers who were at the dinner were admitted to the hospital. Fifteen others escaped with varying degrees of gastrointestinal, flu-like symptoms. Five men drank nothing but coffee and were not exposed. The infection rate of those exposed was an astounding eighty-eight percent. Of the those hospitalized, one- hundred-three died within twelve hours of admission, for a kill ratio of ninety-four percent.

Since the onset of the outbreak, Marty had developed a new admiration for the medical community. They had responded to the disaster in the finest tradition of the profession. Regardless of their area of expertise, they joined the fray. Doctors, nurses, orderlies, technicians, cafeteria personnel, and the support services at the hospitals worked around the clock until it was over.

The melee at the Trial Lawyers Breakfast resulted in seven admissions for injuries suffered in the riot. Only one was listed as critical, and he was expected to survive.

Nearly all the attorneys at the breakfast had diarrhea for most of the day. Scores of them choked the city's already overburdened emergency desks, threatening law suits if they were not immediately admitted for treatment of their fatal disease that supposedly had no cure. Dozens more demanded to have their stomachs pumped. Officers were dispatched to keep order.

When none of the lawyers died in the next twelve hours, the crisis eased somewhat. Then, the special edition of the *Beacon Journal* hit the street.

The first section of the newspaper documented the tragedy of the One Hundred Club. It was dubbed the "Deadly Dinner," by the columnist. The second section contained a letter that had arrived at the editor's desk by courier. It was from Doctor Alexander Bell.

To The Citizens Of The Civilized World: I know that many of you who read about the deaths of the lawyers in Akron, Ohio will be appalled by what you will consider barbaric behavior. I had reasons for such drastic action. Detective Martin Cox, of the Akron Police department knows those reasons and will supply the details. But, I assure you, my conscience is clear. The legal profession has long twisted the laws to their own ends and perverted justice to the point that they deserved this purging.

My little practical joke at the convention center should be ample proof of their subhuman status. A harmless dose of catharsis, applied with a suggestion that there was someone in their midst who cared as little for the misery of their fellow human beings as the legal profession does, drove them to fits of deplorable behavior and public conduct that would not become the lowest of our primate relatives.

I hope my exploits in Ohio have given lawyers everywhere food for thought. Your Death Angel is watching you. The next time you corrupt the system, trod on your fellow man simply for gain, I may be sitting in your courtroom. If I am, will the constitutional symptoms you feel the following day be simply the flu, or will it be my handy-work? Think about it.

An interview by Marty followed the letter, cataloging the tragedy of the Bellangier brothers, and the events leading up to the One Hundred Club dinner. There were multiple photographs of Bell, both current, and from his days in college and the military. There were interviews with people from Bell's past and extensive speculative psychological profiles concerning Bell's mental health. Descriptions of the massive manhunt that was in progress finished the special edition. Nora's discussion of the medical implications closed the edition.

"It's been over forty-eight hours and there's no trace of him," Marty said in a voice that was still hoarse from the blow Bell had delivered to his throat. "I don't think we missed any bases. We did everything we could. The Feds had plenty of time to cover the airports, international departures, things like that. There should have been at least a nibble, but there was nothing." Marty shook his head sadly.

"I know. There's no proof that he ever left the country, but I'd bet next month's pay that he did. It's like he dropped off the end of the earth. I guess he earned that Chameleon handle," E.L. said glumly.

"How's your headache?" Marty asked.

"Headache's all gone, but I can't take a full deep breath yet. The lower part of my rib cage feels like I done been kicked by a mule," E. L. answered. "That Bell's one tough mother. Why didn't he kill us Marty? He could have."

"He could have, but he didn't. He had already murdered a hundred people, so two more would have made no difference. Why?"

Marty turned his hands palms up. "He seemed to have some twisted sense of right and wrong, and we weren't the enemy. In that note he left, he even wished Nora and me happiness."

"I'm gonna get some coffee. Want a cup?" E. L. asked.

Declining the offer, Marty turned to the summary of the pursuit of Bell as E. L. left the office.

This morning, the Cleveland Police had found Bell's car at the Cleveland Hopkins Airport long-term parking area. Despite being dead tired, Marty was set to drive up there, but E. L. talked him out of it.

"It's a waste of time," he told Marty. "Glove box, bed, seats, even the ashtrays were clean. Nobody will remember seeing anyone fitting Bell's description, or any of the disguises we know about. He's too good."

Reluctantly, Marty had agreed. He was still having trouble hearing out of his left ear, and the bruises over his temples throbbed. Then, there was the sore throat and rasping voice. The only thing that sounded like a good idea was a shower and eight good hours of sleep.

CHAPTER
33

t had taken another two weeks for things to return to normal, and Marty still felt tired as he and Nora stood waiting for the elevator on the ground floor at City Hospital. The frustration of being trapped inside the hospital under quarantine had drained Nora emotionally, and left her edgy.

Working side-by-side with the hospital staff, Nora had spent seventy-two straight hours in the emergency department with only an occasional catnap. She didn't mind the work. The hardest part had been dealing with Birney.

His arrogant attitude had nearly precipitated a riot. The quarantined volunteers conceived a plan for a massive breakout. Many of them were on the verge of exhaustion, and their tempers were short. They had heard what Nora told Birney about the possibilities of further infection, and when it was obvious that the outbreak was over, Birney's insolence was more than they could stand. It had taken a Herculean effort by Nora to lobby them into aborting the attempt. The lunacy had continued for five more days before Birney was forced to relent when no new cases had occurred outside the originals.

The elevator door opened, and they stepped into the hallway. Nora took the chart from the holder by the door of room six-thirty-one. "Samuel Allison went home yesterday, so that makes him the last survivor to be discharged. Cal McCray, our infectious disease chief, is managing the case," Nora said, as she paused to flip through several pages in the chart.

"All values normal," she announced replacing the chart, and they entered the room.

"Good morning, Judge Spellman. You're looking better today."

Nora, my darling, you're not a very good liar, Marty thought. Pale and wana, Spellman had lost fifty pounds. The charcoal sport coat hung loosely from his shoulders. Some of his hair had fallen out, and there was considerably more gray in his sideburns. The only thing unchanged was his arrogance, as he confirmed Marty's impression of Nora's ability to lie effectively.

"You are a liar, Doctor. I look like a piece of shit, and you know it. There's a gaggle of reporters waiting in the lobby, and I have to face a bank of TV cameras looking like Dracula's latest meal."

"Even if you don't look good, the important question is how do you feel?" Marty asked.

"A hell of a lot better than Goldman," he said sarcastically.

"I'm sorry about him. I understand you were friends. He was already dead when your secretary brought him in," Nora interjected.

"I know, there was nothing you could do for him," he cut her off rudely. "That's the line you use when they don't understand the problem and don't know what to do, isn't it? And, we were never friends. I just worked with him for a little while. Being in the hospital kept me from having to go to his funeral and pretend to be grieving. The only thing I want to be sure of is that I'm over this thing. I've thrown up enough to last me for the rest of my life."

"You are safe, Your Honor. And, you're not contagious either," she assured him. He acknowledged the information with a grunt.

The nurse came in with his discharge papers and a wheel chair. Scribbling his signature on the bottom of the page, he opened the manila envelope containing his personal possessions. "There damn well better not be anything missing," he barked at the nurse, who reassured him that it was all there. Rubbing the Rolex briskly on his sleeve, he put it on his wrist.

"Judge Spellman, I have to push you down to the backdoor in the wheelchair," the nurse said, flashing him a cheery smile. "Legal requirement, you know."

"I'm not going anywhere in that damned thing. If I fall, I'll sue your ass off anyway." With Shelia trailing him like an obedient hound, he barged past Marty into the hall.

CHAPTER
34

Breakfast is ready, Mr. Johnson," said a lilting Caribbean voice from the hall.

"Be right there, Emmanuel," replied Alexander Bell.

Finishing the last two paragraphs of the *Newsweek* cover article about the most diabolic killer since the Holocaust, Bell threw the magazine across the desk, his face reddening in anger. The article called him a butcher who had slaughtered innocent people in a twisted plan for revenge. The fools didn't understand anything! Even though he had explained it all to them, they still didn't understand. And, despite being dosed twice, Aaron Spellman was still alive. That would have to be remedied.

Pushing back the chair in agitation, Bell walked to the window and gazed out at the Atlantic Ocean as it lapped serenely against his private Jamaican beach. With his ability to access the C.I.A. computer files, he had maintained several identities, complete with passports, service records, social security numbers and work histories. They were useful when he worked at Langley, and it was easy to keep them updated. The identities would not be impossible to find, and Detective Cox would eventually trace them to The Chameleon, as he had planned.

It had been his good fortune to help program the first megacomputer that they had installed at the agency. He had written the files that stored germ warfare and poison research data. That also gave him an opportunity to insert a backdoor. This special file allowed him access to the main data banks regardless of the number of times that they changed the passwords and entry codes.

He planned to leave several of his old identities to be found by his pursuers, since he had recently used this backdoor to create new ones that would be impossible to trace to him. One new one was for Daniel Johnson, a semi-retired stockbroker. Two weeks ago, Alexander Bell had ceased to exist, and he was now permanently Mr. Johnson.

At the cheery table on the patio was a native dish of curried goat, prepared by his chef. Since he began his periodic stays at the beach house three years before, Bell had become partial to the local delicacy. Next to the goat was a dish of tropical fruit, black coffee and a copy of the "New York Times."

The paper showed no more understanding than the magazine, and by the time he was finished with the article about the maniac in Akron, breakfast was spoiled. They were as bad as the despicable lawyers! All they did was twist the truth so they could sell their yellow rags. Walking through the tropical garden on his way to the building behind the fence, he felt the rage growing.

Reaching the electrified fence that was topped with razor wire, he removed two unique keys from the chain around his neck. On the base of one key was a miniaturized transmitter that was half the size of a postage stamp. Using the tip of a ballpoint pen, Bell depressed the switch in the center of the device that he had invented. The electric fence deactivated. The key unlocked the door in the fence. Opening the heavy steel door, Bell went inside. The door locked automatically when it shut. When he depressed the transmitter twice, the power in the fence came back on. The anger inside Bell was a living thing, and the security procedures that he had installed to keep curiosity seekers at bay only served to irritate him.

Using the second key, Bell unlocked the cinder block building covered with a heavy coat of stucco. Three feet beyond the wooden outer door was a metal airlock. Tapping in the security code, he entered the holding room of the containment facility.

Stripping naked, he put on the surgical scrub suit, white athletic socks and cotton gloves. As he taped the ankles and wrists of the suit, he pictured the authors of the articles. They were just like the lawyers who had driven him to use the extreme measures they now called insanity. Someone had to teach them a lesson. Opening the locker, Bell removed the Raycal space suit and began to put it on.

CHAPTER
35

pellman's entourage filed onto the loading dock by the emergency entrance to the hospital where discharged patients were delivered to their families. The nurse who followed helplessly with the empty wheel chair breathed a sigh of relief when they were safely at the departure door. "Good luck, Judge Spellman," she said, and he ignored her.

"Does your moronic driver have things straight?" Spellman snapped over his shoulder to Shelia, who walked the obligatory two paces behind him. The tone of his voice was cruel and condescending.

"I told him to wait till you signaled before he brought up the car," she said, her voice an imploring whine.

A crowd of reporters and cameras clustered around the loading dock. Anchor people from every TV station in the area stood preening for their moment on camera. Many Marty didn't recognize, and were most likely from national networks or syndicated publications. What an opportunity for Spellman to launch his political career, and his emaciated appearance would help. The rumor around the hospital said he would announce his plans today. By the smug expression on his face, it was obvious that Spellman was ready.

The Channel Five anchor woman, a leggy blond with a cover-girl face held out a microphone.

The triumphant look on Spellman's face was evident despite his ravaged appearance.

"Judge Spellman, how does it feel to be a survivor?"

Before he could answer, the crowd surged in on him. They shouted his name repeatedly and fired simultaneous questions. It reminded Marty of a Presidential press conference when the reporters rudely shout, Mr. President! . . . Mr. President!

As they rushed toward Spellman, the Cox gut grumbled, and Marty looked anxiously around the crowd. Something was wrong. What was it? All he could see was the feeding frenzy of reporters. Security had been beefed up by half the plain clothed force in Akron.

Holding up his hands, Spellman waited until they had quieted down. "If you'll back off and give me a little space, I'll answer all your questions one at a time," Spellman said. To Marty's amazement, the reporters did just that. Looking around the circle of reporters, the judge smiled and launched into the impromptu speech he had been rehearsing for weeks.

They questioned him for half-an-hour. Finally, he said, "I'm still a bit weak, and I'm going to have to stop now. But, I *am* a blessed individual. I owe my life to the doctors and nurses at Summa Health Systems. I feel fine. My darling wife is going to take me home and feed me some chicken soup." He put his arm around Shelia, who beamed at being asked to share the limelight.

Marty nervously scanned the crowd. Nothing.

"One last question, Judge. Are you afraid Bell will try again?"asked the Channel Five blond.

"I'm not afraid of Alexander Bell." He signaled to the driver and the white limo crept forward. "I haven't been afraid of anything since I was ten years old," he said in a confident tone.

The limo came to a stop, and Spellman walked toward it. Instinctively, Marty moved forward with him. Something at the rear of the vehicle caught Marty's attention. A withered, black man dressed in a worn army uniform walked around the car. A bank of medals including the silver star glittered from his chest.

The soldier lifted the nickel plated service issue Colt forty-five and pointed it at Spellman's chest. "This is for my son, *murderer!*"

With a collective shriek, the assembly of reporters dove for cover. Marty shoved Spellman aside as the man pulled the trigger five times in rapid succession. One of the metal-jacketed missiles hit the nurse with the wheelchair and slammed her against the loading dock wall. The other four shots ripped harmlessly into concrete or bricks. Leaping to his feet, Marty tackled Cedric Willis, Senior and tore the weapon from his hand.

The old man offered no resistance. "It's okay, officer. I ain't gonna' give ya no trouble," Willis said quietly, as tears rained down his weathered cheeks. Cuffing the man's hands behind him, Marty pulled him to his feet. Willis glared at Spellman through red-rimmed eyes.

"Ever since I come home from the war, I can't do nothin' right. I was in Ko-rea," Willis said. "I shot lots of men. That's why they gave me these medals. I killed men who was just doing their job like I was. They didn't do nothin' to deserve it, except they was tryin' to kill me. You deserved to die for what you done to my baby! Why couldn't I kill you? Why? Does the Devil protect his own? He was all I had, and you took him cause I got mixed up and parked in your parkin' place," Willis concluded as the press swarmed in to catch every word."

" Who's gonna give my boy justice? Do what you want with me now. I stopped livin' the day that man killed my boy," Willis concluded and hung his head dejectedly.

Marty turned Willis over to the uniformed officer who had been directing traffic and went to Nora who was holding a compression dressing over the nurse's chest while the trauma unit assembled from the emergency department.

"I don't think the bullet hit anything vital. Did some damage to her lung. I think she's going to be okay," Nora said. "I'll be inside with her."

Spellman sought refuge in the back of his limousine, and the driver was inching his way through the mob of reporters toward the exit gate. *Go ahead and run,* Marty thought. *They'll still find you.*

CHAPTER
36

wo months later, Marty sat with Nora and the Rileys at The Carnelian Room in San Francisco watching the lights of the city wink on from a window table. Patrick raised his Jamison's and said, "To new, old friends. All the happiness in the world to the two of you. May your love last as long as the Irish."

They clinked glasses and drank. Nora looked self-consciously at the glittering diamond on the second finger of her left hand. "Getting used to the weight yet?" Corin asked.

"Yes, I think so. I get teased about it back home, too. Some of our friends think we're rushing into things, but after what we went through in the first three weeks of our relationship, it's like we've know each other forever. Besides, I found a good man, and I don't want to let him go."

"Take it easy, Nora. Next thing ya know, he's gonna have a head so big he'll have to get a new uniform hat." Patrick said, his eyes twinkling with mischief.

"We don't wear uniforms in homicide as you well know." Marty said, glaring playfully at Patrick.

"You're gonna need one, because you're gonna be moonlighting doing traffic control at shopping centers to pay for that rock." Patrick burst out laughing.

"I don't think so." Marty retorted when order was restored. "I'll still have enough left to fly you back to be my best man. You promised, and I'm going to hold you to it."

"And, if he doesn't, I'll break one of his appendages, and you don't have to ask which one," Corin chimed in sweetly.

The spur-of-the-moment decision to fly to San Francisco and have a long weekend with the Riley's had been a good one , and Marty was glad he had made it. The evening had been perfect, until they were seated in the Riley's family room, sipping coffee and Bailey's Irish Cream. That was when the conversation inevitably turned to Bell. "What do you think they'll do with Willis?" Patrick asked.

"Wouldn't surprise me if he was acquitted." Marty said. "The nurse that he shot has recovered fully, and she has asked publicly that they go easy on Willis. She's really a classy gal. My bet is a conviction with a suspended sentence and probation."

"When the whole story got out, a group in the community started a petition drive for Spellman's impeachment. He's done as a politician. Won't be able to get elected dog catcher. That may be worse for Spellman than dying."

"A couple of the TV camera's got Willis' little speech on tape. It'll be on Twenty-Twenty, Hard Copy and the evening news for weeks. It's as spectacular as the housewife who waxed the perp who raped her daughter," Marty concluded.

"I read about that," Corin said. "They let the man off on a technicality, even though he confessed to the rape. The girl's mother shot him right there in the courtroom."

"I did the post on the Willis boy," Nora said, "It was brutal. If I were on the jury, I couldn't convict the father."

"What about Bell?" Patrick asked. "Anything new?"

"Not a thing. He's vanished. There's nothing . . . except some circumstantial evidence that's been in the papers."

"I want to hear your version," Riley coaxed.

"He drove to the Cleveland airport and parked in the lot. We recovered an abandoned Plymouth Laser registered to someone who doesn't exist with his prints all over it. He never rented a car, because the only out-of-town one way rental that day went to Columbus. That proved to be legit. Guy was a business man making a swing though the center of the state before going back to Phillie."

Marty accepted Corin's offer of more Bailey's.

"A truck that was abandoned at the Detroit International Airport. was registered to an Amish Farmer from Sugar Creek named Ira Troyer. Troyer has a tax history, social security number, work history, but the address is a corn field. Even in Amish country, where there are a gazillion Troyers, nobody knows Ira. I spotted Troyer shadowing Spellman the day of the Willis boy's trial. Even ran his plates because he looked suspicious, but didn't roust him because I had no good reason. Now, I'm positive it was Bell.

"That's where the facts stop and the speculations start. Bell left Detroit, probably under yet another name. He either flew directly out of the country from there, or he flew to another airport and left the country from that one. If I were him, I would have done the latter. He's out there somewhere, behind an airtight new identity."

Clenching his teeth Marty renewed his silent vow to never stop looking for Bell. "With his background of covert operations, his ability to change identities at will, and his monetary resources, anything is possible."

"Do you think you'll ever find him?" Corin asked.

"The F.B.I., Interpol, and the police agencies of most of the civilized world are looking for him. Iran offered him asylum, but I doubt Bell would take them up on it."

"Unless he gets pissed at the Shiits," Patrick said, then howled at his own macabre joke.

"Do I think we'll ever find him?" Marty said, turning his outstretched hands alternately palms up then down. "I don't really expect too. He's brilliant, and he's The Chameleon."

"At least what he told me about the virus was true. There were no more deaths in San Francisco after the mayor and the other three lawyers. Same in Akron after the original outbreak."

"Isn't it odd that two members of Goldman's firm turned out to have natural immunity?" asked Corin. "What do you suppose the odds of that are?"

"Incalculable," Nora replied. "We have no idea what part of the genetic makeup controls naturally immunity. Spellman, Worthy, and fifteen of the lawyers in Akron have natural immunity, which is unusual. There seems to be a higher instance of natural immunity with the altered virus. That could lead to a potential vaccine, if we could ever figure out the biochemistry."

There was silence for a few moments and Nora spoke again. "I feel sorry that medicine has lost Bell's genius. His work has such positive implications for solving the riddles of viral infection. The things that he has discovered could be mankind's salvation, if a real Ebola pandemic ever occurred. I'm going to use the notoriety of this case to raise some funds and start a research effort to see if I can figure out exactly how he did it. He told me, in general terms what he did, so I should have a good starting point."

"That's very admirable, Nora," Corin said, "But, I know one thing for sure." Corin paused and the others looked at her expectantly. "I won't rest easy until we find him."

"Neither will I," Marty added grimly. They all nodded in agreement.

EPILOGUE

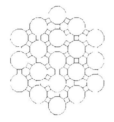

inety days from the morning he cut his finger in the prosection lab, Clarence Mackey awoke with a headache and a feverish feeling. He had the headache when he came home from work the night before, and it was worse this morning. Clarence wasn't quite sure what to make of the headache. It made him feel uneasy, but he had something like that before, but he couldn't remember when it was. Today was Saturday, and he didn't have to go to work. Turning over, he tried to go back to sleep.

By noon, the headache was so intense that the slightest movement nauseated him, and his joints ached so badly that tears trickled down his slack cheeks. Picking up the phone, he dialed Doctor Nora's phone number. When he got her answering machine, he left a message. Since he felt so rotten, he decided to go back to bed.

Then the cramps started. At three that afternoon, he dialed nine- one-one as Doctor Nora had taught him to do. He hoped he wouldn't get in trouble if he wasn't as sick as he felt like he was.

The ride in the ambulance was a blare of loud noises and flashing lights that made his head hurt worse. As they rolled him up the ramp into the emergency room, he felt a searing pain in his belly accompanied by a sound that reminded him of the time his mother tore an old bed sheet in half. With a moan of anguish, Clarence began to vomit fluid that looked like fuel oil mixed with bright red clots of blood.